CATCHING THE SUNLIGHT

Harriet Hudson titles available from
Severn House Large Print

Tomorrow's Garden
To My Own Desire

CATCHING THE SUNLIGHT

Harriet Hudson

Severn House Large Print
London & New York

This first large print edition published in Great Britain 2006 by
SEVERN HOUSE LARGE PRINT BOOKS LTD of
9-15 High Street, Sutton, Surrey, SM1 1DF.
First world regular print edition published 2003 by
Severn House Publishers, London and New York.
This first large print edition published in the USA 2006 by
SEVERN HOUSE PUBLISHERS INC., of
595 Madison Avenue, New York, NY 10022.

British Library Cataloguing in Publication Data

Hudson, Harriet, 1938 -
    Catching the sunlight. - Large print ed.
    1. Women biographers - Fiction
    2. Sculptors - United States - Fiction
    3. Fountains - Hungary - Budapest - History - Fiction
    4. Large type books
    I. Title
    823.9'14 [F]

    ISBN-10: 0-7278-7488-8

Printed and bound in Great Britain by
MPG Books Ltd, Bodmin, Cornwall.

Remembering Pam with love

Acknowledgements

Some moments in one's life remain in the sunlight of memory for ever, and the wedding of Alistair and Zsófi Binks in Hungary was one of these. It was at that happy time that I saw the Mathias fountain, which gave me the idea for this novel – not immediately, but over the months as I looked at the photographs and relived the weekend. So my great thanks to Alistair and Zsófi for inviting my husband Jim and myself to their wedding, and to them and Zsófi's family for their generous help afterwards in answering the questions with which I bombarded them. My thanks also to our friends Marion and Ned Binks who asked us to join their family party at their son's wedding, and who took time on their future visits to Budapest to answer my questions and endlessly photograph the Mathias fountain for me. That the weekend was such a memorable time was also due to Pamela Houghton, Clifford Long, Christopher Binks and Julie Metcalfe, who dubbed us honorary members of their family during the wedding celebrations. My thanks to them all.

My thanks are also due to my agent Dorothy Lumley of the Dorian Literary

Agency, and the Severn House team: to Anna Telfer, who so carefully copy-edited the script, to Piers Tilbury, who distilled its spirit into the splendid jacket design, and above all to Amanda Stewart, my editor, who first liked the idea of this novel, and has transformed it into book form with all Severn House's usual expertise and efficiency.

One

What am I doing here? I asked myself crossly.

I'd taken a whole day off just because Tony Loring had said, 'You might find it interesting, Lucia.'

He had had that careless, knowing smile on his face that made me instantly convinced that interesting was precisely what I wouldn't find it. Then my usual perverse nature made me decide to look for the crock of gold at the end of the rainbow yet once more. Besides, it would be a day out for my mother.

'I said it would rain,' the lady murmured happily from the passenger seat. 'You know what Tony's like. It's bound to end in disaster.'

The rain bucketed down the windscreen, all pubs had long since vanished from the roadside, together with our hopes of lunch, and even my usual optimism deserted me.

'I'm hungry,' Mum pointed out.

So was I, but I wasn't going to admit it. I nosed down the single track lane, wet branches arching over in a green jungle above the car. I wasn't even sure it was the right lane, since Mum had the map and it didn't show every tiny byway. The Kentish skies

9

lowered above us, and there was a rumble from my stomach. If there's going to be a happy ending to this day, I told myself viciously, please let it make its appearance soon,

As if by magic, a faint sunbeam smiled at us through the windscreen, and the rain hesitated, then stopped. An encouraging, if battered, brown sign at a fork in the road spurred me on. The lane wound on down into the valley, red-tiled cottages and white-cowled oast houses peeped through the trees. I turned a corner and found what we were looking for: the entrance to Edenshaw, or as it is popularly known round here, Carr's Folly.

Shangri-La it was not, or at least not if judged by the entrance. The white gates were invitingly open, but in need of paint. The board with admission times looked business-like enough, however. Ahead of us, the gravel drive disappeared round a corner into wood-land, lined with thick rhododendron bushes. I was hooked immediately. This is the kind of path I like, the kind with a question mark at the end of it. Will it lead to the wicked witch, or to the prince's castle?

I am always convinced I'm heading for the latter, my mother the opposite, which probably explains everything. The optimist and the pessimist, raising the perennial question of who gets most out of life: the one who hopes and is disappointed, or the one who expects nothing. Ah, but what if one is

10

not disappointed? The stakes are high then. Unfortunately, in my love life at least, I'd never quite found the answer, though at 32 I'd had plenty of time to prance down cul-de-sacs.

My last dead end had been with Robin Holman with whom I had been convinced I might find my happy ending for life. Robin had been on the production side at the firm that publishes my books. He understands how machinery works, combined with a miraculous grasp of what looks pleasing to the eye. We had split up twelve months earlier after three years together. Three *good* years; we both agreed on that. Everyone who wasn't Robin or me had thought we were headed for connubial bliss, and was slightly puzzled because we still lived in our separate flats, Robin in Fulham, while I, keeping the Thames between us, remained in Putney.

I suppose the Thames must have been significant, a barrier to be crossed by a bridge. Our bridge was never fully built. Robin was all for moving in together, but I held out. What for? I couldn't explain it to anyone, not him, nor to myself. I loved him, Robin is kind, madcap, and a terrific lover, and so far as I could tell we lived in the same way, comfortably and casually. He would wistfully ask me to commit myself to co-habitation, with marriage or without, he didn't care which. Commit was something I couldn't do. I kept *meaning* to do it.

He'd said sadly, when I tried to back out of

a half-given promise a year ago, 'You won't take a leap, will you? Call yourself an optimist? You couldn't cook an egg sunny side up.'

I'd been so wounded, I committed there and then. I'd move in with him next week, I told him.

It had loomed over me. And what did Cinderella do when the magic hour of midnight struck? She gathered up her glass slipper from where she'd dropped it and ran for her life.

After that, Robin went to work in Paris. I hadn't seen him since.

'I bet there won't be anything to eat,' Mum remarked gloomily, as the drive threatened to continue for ever.

I drew a deep breath, but just as I was about to reply, the Peugeot turned a corner, and there before us was Carr's Folly.

It was just a very large rambling Victorian red-brick house, with a few mock gables and ugly turrets, the kind of house we tend to laugh about from the standpoint of our superior twenty-first-century architecture. But there was something about it that caught my interest.

'Looks promising,' I remarked hopefully, as I locked up the car.

'You'd find Wormwood Scrubs promising,' Mum snorted.

'So it is, to a man in Alcatraz.'

'I bet you a pub dinner tonight there's no food here.'

'Done.' I knew I'd have to pay up, I wasn't going to lose face. My mum is all of five foot four inches, her Italian descent gives her pent-up energy and determination, and it's a hard job keeping up with her. I seem perpetually to be in some kind of Alice in Wonderland Caucus Race, always landing up the same distance behind her – though always ready for the next round. She has the dark hair of her Italian mother, but otherwise all we have to show for our ancestry are our names (hers is Giuletta, anglicized to Julia), and a passion for cooking large pots of pasta. I'm light brown in hair colour, inherited from Dad, who is definitely British in looks. I get my height from him too, so I tower four inches above Mum.

I pushed open the door of Edenshaw House cautiously, though why I expected dragons behind it, I can't imagine. It seemed a wise step at the time.

Dragons there were not. Instead, a plump young woman at the reception desk gave us a friendly smile. I paid up and bought one of the glossy guide books to the pictures and sculptures in the house and garden.

'Next year I'll be a concession,' Mum dropped in casually, hoping for an exclamation of surprise. It didn't come and I tried not to laugh.

'You start here,' the woman said brightly, pointing to a room leading off this entrance hall. 'There's quiche today,' she added.

Quiche? Did I hear aright? I did.

'In the restaurant,' she explained, slightly surprised at our obtuseness. 'It's quiche every day in fact, but it has salad with it, and it's good.'

'Restaurant?' I repeated, looking round hopefully.

'In the coachhouse – go outside and turn left.'

'Afterwards,' I said firmly to Mum, as she showed signs of marching straight off there. 'Before.'

I'm glad I caved in. We needed fortification for what was to come – especially me.

Twentieth-century art was only a half-open book to me, and thus the name of Charles Carr rang merely a distant bell, when Tony had mentioned it. He was an American businessman, a very, very rich one, partly through inheritance and partly through his own efforts. He worked in New York, which is where the new waves of young American artists of the 1930s had gathered, and to which the even newer waves of post-war European artists flocked. Paris, thanks to the disruption of the war, was no longer the hub of international artistic life. Charles, so Tony explained, had been deeply interested in the Social Realism movement of the 1930s, and continued his interest in every new movement that came along. Owing to his business activities, however, he was necessarily on the fringe and what little work of his remained from these days seemed to be reaching after a

14

style of his own, rather than rushing off to follow Abstract Expressionism or any of the new groups then forming in the US and Europe.

In the mid-1950s, however, having made his pile, he moved to England. He buried himself in this Kentish valley and devoted himself to painting and sculpture as hectically as he had conducted his business life. He never married, or at least gave no indication that there had ever been a wife, and he had died in 1994 aged eighty. Since then, the collection in his house and garden – he rarely sold his work – has become part of the Edenshaw Foundation, which not only runs the museum but operates a scholarship system for artists to study abroad.

An interesting tale, but nothing remarkable, I had thought. After all, this sort of thing had been done before. There was the Henry Clews museum near Cannes, a fascinating tale in itself, for example, and so there was nothing in Charles Carr's story to explain that knowing grin on Tony's face.

'I think you'll find it interesting,' he had repeated. 'After all, why did he do it?'

The use of that magic word 'why' always gets me going, and Tony knows it. Why had Carr settled in Kent to devote himself to art without any apparent need to share his message – if message there was – with the outside world until after his death? Then another 'why' popped up. Why, if Carr had such a personal mission to paint and sculpt,

15

hadn't he devoted his whole life to it right from the beginning? Why go into business? From Tony's account, he was extremely well-heeled from his family's fortune, and so could have afforded to follow his own course without starving in a garret. Did he have two passions, one pulling him towards business, the other to art? Probably it was as dull as that. My interest waned, but not sufficiently to resist when Tony urged me for the third time to visit this place.

Anthony, I should explain, collaborates on my books for children. He illustrates them, I write them, and he's a friend, not lover. He's seventy this year and likes to sit back and mix up a cauldron of mischief now and then. He is a superb illustrator, so I suffer the side effects patiently. There is nothing old-fashioned about his quirky sense of humour; he keeps a sharp eye on life too, and both are reflected in his work. Nevertheless, he likes to stir that cauldron now and then, and it's all too easy for me to jump in up to my neck. I decided I was going to go easy on Carr's Folly – just in case that quirky sense of humour was directed straight at me this time. After all, Tony, as he casually and belatedly mentioned to me, is a trustee of the Edenshaw Foundation.

The quiche was good, and even Mum was restored to good humour.

'What is it we're going to see?' she asked me. With no clues from Tony, I'd been able to

16

tell her little on the way here, so I picked up the guide book.

'The major part of the collection,' I read out, 'is *The Happening*, and–' I turned over the pages '–I gather that's found in the gardens and in the old ballroom in the house.'

Mum looked interested. 'In my young day,' she observed, 'a happening was a pop event, music, poetry, everyone doing their own thing on stage and the audience pretending to participate.'

'It can't have the same meaning here.' Live music and poetry in an art collection? All the same, it whetted my appetite a little.

Since the sun was showing every sign of vanishing again, we opted to make for the gardens first. Fate, however, intervened – or that's how I like to think of it now.

There were only a few other visitors there that day, and we had the house almost to ourselves. The recommended tour obviously kept the best till last, which was natural enough since the gardens were all part of *The Happening*, and should follow the ballroom collection. The first room was interesting, however. These were early thirties work, Depression scenes, a Ford motor car in a desolate landscape, a cinema audience, all – so the guide book informed me – influenced by the Mexican Diego Rivera, but there was nothing here painted after 1938. The following room displayed experiments in the vastly different styles of Surrealism and of Grant Wood's *American Gothic*, and the remaining

17

four rooms showed his later work after *The Happening*. As *The Happening* was dated 1955–65, this meant he had nearly thirty years of artistic life after that, and yet there seemed nothing to indicate a major theme in this work. It was fun, almost light-hearted, compared with his early stuff, experiments in pop art, portraits, post-modernism, etc. I particularly liked a portrait entitled *The Butcher*. The butcher was a jolly man, I felt I'd like to have known him, for there was a touch of *The Laughing Cavalier* about him. Or was it Charles Carr who laughed?

The last room was filled with fun sketches, paintings and sculptures in terracotta and wood, of trees, animals and birds. Each of them, however, bore a human side. A knowing face peered from the trunk of an oak, a serpent bore a human face, a bird donned human legs. Only one bore a serious theme. A rain forest wept, its trees hanging down in sorrow as their own grim reaper arrived.

'They're meant,' I told Mum, 'to indicate that nature is keeping an appalled eye on the doings of mankind.'

'I don't think much of them,' was all Mum replied.

'Some of it's OK.'

'What,' she announced crossly, 'was Tony thinking of?'

'Perhaps just a nice day in the country.' It sounded weak even to me, and I knew Tony must have had more in mind than that. This unstartling beginning made me all the more

18

unprepared for our entrance into *The Happening.*

Colour, light, paint, movement hit us from every direction. There was no light from the outside for the great ballroom windows had obviously been shuttered to provide wall space. The room was perhaps 100 feet long and 35 feet wide – and it was high; the Victorians did nothing by halves. Every wall was covered in a mural and the ceiling was painted, presenting at first sight a jangle of colour so strong that it did indeed seem to have the quality of an audible shout of – of what? Of rage? Of delight? Of pleasure? Then I realized there was sound as well, as compelling as the visual image, music I identified eventually, first as the 'Carmen Suite' and later blaring out the Venus music from *Tannhäuser*. It was overpowering, a battering upon the senses. I wanted to flee, but I seemed rooted to the spot. Mum too was momentarily silenced.

Then I realized we were not alone, for there was a man studying the west wall mural, so still he might almost have been part of it.

'What's it all about?' My mother broke her silence with a vengeance.

I had no answer for her, for I was still too dazed, but I did my best.

'A happening is what you make it, isn't it?' I said at last.

We had disturbed the man's concentration, for he glanced round curiously. I was totally unprepared for what happened next.

19

I fell in love.

This isn't a trite statement made from hindsight, it was true. In all my 32 years, it had never happened to me like this before, even with Robin. I recognized it for what it was, however. I tried to dismiss it, telling myself it was the effect of these pictures making me so dizzy that I had to put out an arm to my mother to support myself. Even then I knew it wasn't the pictures, it was him.

I'm tall, and he looked slightly taller; he was in his early to mid-thirties, I supposed. Objectively, though I wasn't capable of rational thoughts at the time, there was nothing very striking about him. Well-cut casual trousers, open-necked shirt, a mop of light-coloured hair, and a face that owed nothing to classical Greece, and everything to English open good looks. Well, looks anyway. I couldn't have decided then whether he was handsome or not. I didn't care anyway. He was now part of my life.

I wanted to talk to him, know about him, and most of all I wanted to hurl myself into his arms and feel them around me here, any-where, and most certainly in bed. Ridiculous, my heart cried. He must be married, said my brain. You're just sex-starved, proclaimed my body. I'm in love, the whole of me replied. Even if he vanished right now, nothing could change that.

'But what are they *about*, Lucia?' came my mother's aggrieved demand. She takes it as a personal affront if she can't get to grips with something.

I half-hoped the man, *my* man, would stroll up to enlighten us, but, after his initial look, he seemed oblivious to us, engrossed once more in some detail of the mural.

I managed to choke out a few words. 'The guidebook suggests we look at the east wall first.'

That was the inner wall, not the one under investigation by the focus of my thoughts. Reluctantly, I dragged myself over to the mural, and even with such competition my attention suddenly concentrated on it. It was a night scene, but not dark and not sinister. Far from it. It was lit everywhere by lights in the buildings, and an invisible light that shot its beams across the whole canvas, all ninety foot or so of it. It was Impressionistic, but somewhat after the style of Arshile Gorky. It was a city scene, of restaurants, clubs, lights, and people. In one corner was a walled city perched on a hilltop like a Provençal village, at its side the form of a Toulouse-Lautrec type Jane Avril dancing, head thrown back sensuously. The central image of the mural was a woman, however, swathed in a white evening dress, dark-haired, splendid in her beauty, triumphant in her sexual power; the fluid lines of her body moved above and away from the evening-suited adorers who would capture her. She was a flame flickering in the night round which the moths danced. There was a giddy hedonism about the scene that compelled me to watch it, even though my

21

heart was prancing around on the other side of the room.

'Where is it?' asked my mother. She had confiscated the guidebook. 'It just says "The City".'

'It can't be New York,' I said flatly. Did it matter? It was, it existed and that was what moved me. I tried though. 'It looks flamboyant enough for eastern Europe. Vienna, perhaps?'

'Budapest.'

It was the man who had spoken. Of course he had. It was inevitable.

'And the other murals too?' My voice seemed to belong to someone else.

'Yes.' His eyes briefly held mine as if he were curious about what he saw, then he turned away as if he regretted speaking. I wanted to cry, 'How do you know it's Budapest?' but the words stuck in my throat. I'd never been so sure of anything in my life than that I was in love with this man, whom I didn't even know. So how, *why* did he not feel the same?

I blurted out the first thing I thought of. 'Had Carr been on a business trip there?' How banal can one get?

He turned back to us. 'I don't know. The murals explain themselves, don't they?' He said it politely enough. He couldn't know my stomach was churning over with tension.

'Yes.' I lied. I couldn't tell whether they did or not.

'He was a diplomat there for a time,' the

22

man offered.

Funny. Tony hadn't said anything about that, only that Carr was a businessman.

'I'm sorry,' I said. 'We're interrupting you.' Somewhere in my racing mind I could hear Mum telling him – me? – about her weekend in Budapest.

He smiled, and my world ignited. Contact at last. 'The audience and its reactions are part of the experience,' he said. '*We* are *The Happening*, you two and me. That would have pleased Charles.' A pause, then: 'I'll leave you to go on "Happening" then.' And he strolled through the entrance.

I couldn't race after him, and in any case Mum was still talking avidly about the glories of gypsy violin music. I consoled myself that if fate intended us for each other, we would most certainly meet again. This wasn't an entirely satisfactory conclusion, however, since fate was dependent on what I decided to do. My decision – taken reluctantly – was to be sensible.

That was relatively easy in this astounding Hall of the Happening. The west wall, opposite the night scene of the city, was entirely different. This was the sinister one, though it was not, so far as I could tell, a night scene. Instead, it was alight with the flames of hell in vivid reds and oranges. What had seemed a city given over to pleasure, now appeared a sinister prison. Hands were held up in appeal to an unresponsive heaven, and the central figure, the woman, now turned in upon her followers, as though the prize once they captured it was found to be fool's gold. There was a cynicism and despair about this mural that had been lacking in the reckless whirl of its companion piece.

'Lucia,' Mum remarked sternly, as though there was to be no argument, 'this must be the uprising in '56. I remember it, of course.'

Naturally I'd heard of it. The students, spurred on by the intellectuals, had marched for independence and freedom against the Soviet regime, and a general rebellion followed, which was brutally and treacherously put down by the Soviets. Was this mural of the uprising? It could have been, but surely its companion piece could not have been of any post-war era?

The other panels bore a simpler message. The far wall was an almost lyrical portrayal of a woman and a man, symbolized by flowing forms, nude bodies which arched with each other, not touching, but on the point of doing so. Everything was light. No darkness here. The woman's face was covered by a lock of her fair hair caught by the sunlight that radiated through the whole painting. The man was poised above her, both figures so yearning towards each other that one felt swept into their desire. I felt my own body stir, wondering whether *my* man had walked out of my life for ever.

The wall with the entrance doorway bore two panels, one depicting the woman, the other the man. The woman was turned away, the man's head was thrown back in despair. The figures of both panels were impressionistic, but I had little doubt that this represented the pain of love, whereas the wall at the far end bore its glory. I turned to look at it again, the two figures oblivious to all else around, in a surreal landscape of idyllic skies and meadows, where the barely visible shapes of what might be butterflies shimmered against the sun.

When I had recaptured my breath, I said to Mum, 'Charles Carr must have had one hell of a love affair in Budapest.' Perhaps I was personalizing it too much, however. Perhaps they were merely symbols of love, the light and the dark, and therefore represented an amalgam of the total experience of love rather than his own memories.

'Humph,' Mum observed. 'How unlike your dear father. Cup of tea?'

'No,' I replied, partly as punishment for putting me down, partly since I was eager to continue the trail, now and not later. Perhaps the gardens might provide enlightenment on the murals, and I admit I had a sneaking hope that we might run into the man again. I refused to face the probability that even if we did, we would merely exchange polite nods, and pass each other, like ships in the night. Something, I told myself Micawber-like, would turn up. And I was right.

We emerged from the house and strolled across the grass lawn towards the start of *The Happening*'s garden walk. Charles Carr and the now absent man strove for dominance in my mind. It struck me he had spoken of Charles as if he knew him, which was interesting. When we reached the entrance of the enchanted woodland in which Charles Carr had created Part 2 of his *Happening*, I was even more certain that I was going to enjoy this. The garden hung on a hillside, and the guidebook warned us that it was not for the elderly or disabled. Paths criss-crossed each other, some rose steeply from a central terrace, others descended equally steeply. It was, we were informed, called the *Garden of Man and Woman* by Charles Carr, but in our present enlightened age it should be looked on as a 'Garden of Love'.

Promising. I was all for that.

'Do we wander?' Mum asked. 'Or does Mr Carr have a recommended route?'

'Apparently not. Let's wander.'

I had said the right thing. I had donned the glass slipper again and my prince duly appeared. Just by the entrance, there was the man studying a rocky outcrop in the hillside from which a two-sided Janus head had been carved. The face towards us was smiling and welcoming – the sculpture I hasten to say, not the man's.

Just as I prepared some bright comment about following him around, he too exuded welcome.

'Love,' he said.

I gazed at him, wondering what miracle was this? Then he blushed – yes, really – as Mum merrily announced, 'I'm all for it on the whole.'

He smiled at her. 'This statue, I meant. It represents the two faces of love. That's what the garden is all about.'

'Doesn't a Happening tell you that by itself?' Damn, I groaned to myself. Why do I have to whip back an automatic put-down *now* of all times?

'Not,' Mum said hollowly, 'from what I remember of those events. One stood there desperately trying to find the inner meaning that everyone around you had obviously grasped long since.'

'I'd hate you to feel that way here,' the man replied gravely.

'You could come with us, and give us some clues,' Mum suggested.

Fervently I forgave her all her sins of omission and commission over my entire life-time and opened my mouth to speak. Then I quickly shut it again in case I put my foot in it, for everything was going quite nicely without me.

The man looked questioningly at me. A warm happy glow spread throughout my body. 'What a good idea,' I answered simply.

Obviously he felt this might be sarcasm on my part, for he felt the need to introduce himself.

'I'm one of the trustees. David Fraser.'

Mum grew quite excited. 'It was Tony Loring suggested we come here,' she almost purred. She's fond of Tony and since

27

presumably David Fraser was a chum of his, I couldn't have backed out of this threesome even if I'd wanted to – but, believe me, I didn't.

'Great. Then I'll have to come with you, or he'll never let me hear the end of it.' His grin was just for Mum, but I told myself I was included.

And so we set off along our long trail, David and I, and it never occurred to me once to look at the other face of the Janus carving or to wish I'd brought the traditional ball of twine to find my way back to Robin and safety.

Two

I don't know what I'd imagined lay behind Charles Carr's creation in this garden. I suppose, having seen *The Happening* in the ballroom, I thought we'd be passing through another symbolic re-enactment of his personal experience in one way or another. We weren't. It was more as if we were passing through the kind of enchanted land that I conjure up in my children's stories. Right and wrong battle it out on a flat playing field, whether that be the old-fashioned fairyland or its more modern face, represented by other galaxies, prehistoric monsterlands or alternative world backgrounds. This one, I decided,

28

looked as if it might fall somewhere between the two, a crazy looking-glass world where light looked through the mirror and saw dark reflected back.

Monsters, carved in wood or stone, snarled out from bushes, hobgoblins pranced among the trees, rabbits nestled contentedly together, man and woman, sculpted from one block, sat hand in hand or entwined in love, content in each other's company.

'The idea,' David told us cheerfully, 'is that you go up, you go down, on whichever path you like. I won't be doing any pointing. You make your own mistakes in a garden devoted to love.'

'That I can do all too well,' I quipped. He obediently laughed, as I had intended, but if I'd hoped for a personal glimmer in exchange, I was disappointed. 'In that case, you can consider this garden one long love affair, warts and all.'

'I'll have to take the warts side,' Mum put her spoke in. 'Lucia would fall flat on her face. She has too many stars in her eyes to see them.'

Everyone laughed at that, even me.

'So that's why you named her Lucia – the light,' David joked.

'And then she stuffed me full of pasta so I wouldn't be.' Trust me to bring the tone down when inside I was singing like a bird. This preliminary banter seemed like taking our seats in preparation for the curtain to go up on the entertainment.

And entertainment it was. There seemed no other visitors in this garden today, or if there were, the dense greenery and maze of paths hid them from us. It was like stepping forth into a lost world where one didn't know whether to expect Shangri-La or Dante's Inferno. I suppose that's love too, and it was fitting therefore that David and I should be side by side. I felt I'd known him a million years, with no need to talk unless I wished, no need to search for clues to his life. No need to wonder if he felt as I did. There was no doubt in my mind that it would work out. Our path, I told myself, was heading upwards.

At present, the main path was on level ground, though it twisted and turned with many smaller side routes, each of which promised to share its secrets. Mum lagged behind exclaiming over *viola riviniana* and the *blechnum tabulare*. I know the Latin names since I'd been used to Mum's enthusiasms all my life, but my heart was always with my father's quiet 'See this Flower of Love, Lucia?', or 'See that Witch Grass, darling?' Which brings a garden alive for a child: antirrhinum or snapdragon? And Charles Carr's garden cried aloud in favour of life. Despite all his avowed intentions, David took us along one side path, which led to a small pond fed by a trickle of water from higher up. The rocks that surrounded it were covered in green moss, and at its side a small marble woman bent over to admire her own reflection. It was beautifully done.

30

'Mirror, mirror, on the wall, who is the fairest of them all?' I murmured. 'I wonder if Charles Carr ever found his fairest of them all?'

David glanced sharply at me, and I wondered why. It seemed a legitimate idle comment. Anyway, he didn't reply. 'Look up there,' was all he said, as we returned to the main path. He was pointing upwards, and through the trees I could see a cottage of some sort on the top of the hill.

'Is that where we're heading?'

'Everything is up for grabs here,' David naturally replied, but he peeled off his sweater and tied it round his shoulders as if in preparation for the climb. 'Up first or down?'

'Up,' I said valiantly, just as Mum cried:

'Down!'

We decided to split up. Mum's eye had been caught by the sight of some pink hebes further down, and David and I went upwards. It was peaceful in this green woodland, the occasional sunbeam dappling leaves still wet from the rain. There were gentle rustles and birdsong, there were nettles and mud, but Charles Carr's sculptures lived amiably with them all. Or perhaps amiably was not quite the word. It was more an acceptance that love brought its darknesses, that the double-sided Janus figure that had greeted us at the entrance was entire of itself.

We turned a corner and I stopped in sheer delight. Before us in a glade in the woods was a stone sculpture of a man and woman embracing, which had all the tenderness of Rodin's *The Kiss*. Or was tenderness the word? As I drew closer there seemed more a sense of desperation about it, of clinging desire and possession. Perhaps I was wrong, however, for a moment later I saw it differently again as I stepped back to rejoin David. The glade was encircled by bushes and trees all, it seemed to me, arching towards the couple, as if the whole of nature were looking down approvingly, not disapprovingly as in the house collection. I felt suddenly shy, as though even watching this with David was a statement of how I felt about him. The breeze was stirring chimes in the trees, and that with the birdsong was a happening in itself. David's and my happening.

I stumbled over a tree root as we left the glade and David steadied me. The touch of his hand on my arm made me want to cry out, 'Do you feel like this too?' Of course I didn't, but only because I couldn't.

'Are you an artist?' I blurted out with great originality.

'No. I'm a historian. Art history, though.'

'And you knew Charles Carr.' I made it a statement not a query, and David was obviously taken aback, though goodness knows why. It was hardly an intrusive question. All the same, I felt I'd put a metaphorical foot wrong, as well as my physical one just now. I had nothing to lose, though, so I ploughed on.

'Back there in the house, you called him

Charles.'

'Did I?' he muttered.

'Yes. And you said he'd been a diplomat. I assumed you knew his whole story.'

'It doesn't follow. Anyway, you can ask Tony if you're interested. He'd be the one to tell you. He worked with Charles Carr.'

I had an odd sense of thorns suddenly appearing from nowhere to block my path. It was puzzling that Tony had been holding back on us, but for the moment more important considerations took precedence. 'I will,' I said defiantly. 'It's all part of the upward path.'

'You still want to take it?'

Stymied, I didn't know whether he referred to the path before us leading up to the cottage, or to a yet untrodden path between us. In any case, I had only one answer to both: 'Yes.'

I didn't quite punch the air, but my hands must have been moving expressively because suddenly I found one of them clasped in his – probably, I told myself with rare caution, because the path was rather sticky at this point even though there were rough wooden steps hewn out of the wet earth.

All around us were sculptures of small animals, some in trees, some under bushes, some looming out quite scarily. More interestingly, human faces were carved into tree trunks, eyeing the unwary traveller with sardonic or benign looks. At the bottom of the final flight of steps a dragon about to take off in flight confronted us unexpectedly. Its bulging eyes and claws would be a fearsome sight to any prince hoping to find his true love at the top, and it certainly gave me pause for thought. But of course we continued.

It was July so the wild roses were still in bloom where the woodland was thinning out, and when at last we reached the building, it proved to be a true fairytale cottage, with roses round the door and sprawling over the roof. A sculpted cat sunned itself on the peg tiles, blithely indifferent to the blackbird on the chimney. The pink whitewashed building was quite small, however, and semi-circular in shape, which was unusual.

David let me go in alone. How could he have done so, I wonder now, knowing what lies inside? Was he just playing fair? Perhaps, but he might have given me a hint.

It was terrifying, and I heard myself crying out. Instead of a bower of love, or of cosy domestic bliss, these walls too were covered with murals. The largest, facing me, was almost entirely filled with the huge face of what might otherwise have been a beautiful woman, but it was distorted in a snarl of hatred. Huge teeth seemed to leap out of the canvas as if to devour all entrants. The two side panels represented the woman's enormous bulging arms, which curved round the walls as if holding the viewer in a terrible embrace.

I came right out, feeling, and no doubt looking, decidedly queasy.

'I'm sorry,' David said. 'I couldn't warn you, could I?' I think he was sincere, and his expression was anxious, as though the mere thought of those murals affected him too, though he must see them frequently. I couldn't forgive him though.

'Was that Charles Carr's idea of love?' I asked shakily.

'Only half.'

'Half is too much.'

'I shouldn't have come through this garden with you.'

'Why did you?' It slipped out like an accusation.

'I think...' He hesitated, then plunged on: 'I liked your chin.'

I was stupefied. 'Is that your speciality? The chin in Chinese painting of the Ming Dynasty maybe?'

'I like the way you stick it out, just as you're doing now, and as you did back in the house.'

As compliments go, it didn't rate highly, and his expression was hardly one of fervent admiration but I was ridiculously pleased. 'Thank you. Do I have any other warts you'd like to point out?'

He came close to me, inspecting my face mock seriously. 'None that I can see.' He leaned slightly closer, his brown eyes looking full at me. 'Any on mine?'

His expression was still deadpan, and I didn't want to break the spell. One move and I might be in his arms; a wrong move and we would be walking decorously downhill. There are make or break points even this early in a relationship and I was all for the former in this case.

'Not one,' I said.

'Good.' But it was the latter result all the same. He turned away, with an offhand: 'Your mother will be wondering where we are.'

What a great line to nip the early seed of romance in the bud. And with this topsy-turvy thought in mind, I followed him downhill – though by another route than that by which we'd come. I was so entranced by the new delights we met along the way, that I almost managed to convince myself that the monster up above and the setback that followed had no relevance to David and me. This enchantment was scheduled by fate to go on for ever, so far as I was concerned. The stars in my eyes were firmly back in place.

The lower part of the garden was, unsurprisingly by now, a surprise. It led round the side of the hill, with sunny slopes among the greenery, and then bent round into the dark again. It seemed completely divorced from the deceptively attractive first part of the garden, as though we were indeed headed for the inferno that lay at the end of the primrose path.

We came upon another pool. This one was larger, and set against the hillside; the rocks of the hillside formed a grotto for a stone-sculpted centrepiece of five figures. It was half hidden by screening bushes, and I nearly missed it. Indeed, I would have done so had

David not broken the rules again and nudged me to it. The top figure was a knight or king in hunting outfit, Robin Hood gear rather than a Jorrocks. Below him were three dogs and two retainers, one standing holding a curving horn, the other bearded and sitting with his back to the viewer, looking up at the knight or king. Below those, on the one side was a monk-type figure, judging by his cowled head, although his jauntily displayed leg seemed far from monklike. He sat proudly with a falcon on his wrist and a dog by his side. On the other side, balancing the pyramid, was a woman, no, a girl, fondling a deer and looking towards the bearded retainer. The bare ankle and foot below the full skirt suggested that she was hardly a princess.

The sculpture wasn't remarkable in itself, only in that its style was straightforwardly representational, gothic in its flamboyance and ill-fitting with Charles Carr's symbolism. I realized in fact it was a fountain, for a small stream of water came from underneath the rock on which King Robin Hood, or whoever, was standing.

'What is this all about?' I asked David.

'I don't know. None of us does. It's always been a puzzle. I even wonder if it was already here when Charles began the garden. It's a completely different stone, let alone style, to anything else he did.'

'That's possible, I suppose. Who lived here before?'

David didn't know, and so I decided this

must be the explanation. I thought it would go from my mind, but oddly it didn't – probably because it was so very ordinary. Or was it because David spoke with such a studied indifference?

At last we arrived at the focal point of the lower gardens, the inferno. There was no sign of Mum, who must be deep in the bushes with her notebook or reviving herself with tea. And she would need some revival after this. This was no cottage. This was a brilliant red hellhole, with jagged wooden painted flames emerging from it, so realistic they seemed to be licking the entrance, waiting to close around and devour the first victim to enter.

'You're coming in with me this time,' I said firmly.

David agreed amiably. 'It's a fair cop.'

I had half a suspicion forming in my mind as to what I might find, and I was not disappointed. Within the mouth of hell was a painted paradise which was in stark comparison with the cottage so apparently welcoming at the top of the hill.

Here the room was even smaller, so small there was barely space for the two of us. It was odd standing there in the dark, feeling and hearing David beside me. I could not tell what his thoughts might be, but I hoped he was sharing mine.

Here were the lightness and joy so lacking elsewhere. A symbolic woman in white was holding a man to her breast in love. Perhaps it was not love alone, but compassion or forgiveness, but nevertheless it was peace, it was happiness, and its simplicity brought tears to my eyes. Sentimental tears? No, for in some strange way it was the end of the story, as presented by the garden.

'Are you glad or sorry you chose the upper one first?' David asked me quietly, as we made our way back to the garden entrance.

'Glad. It just shows it pays to be optimistic. See what reward we received at the end.'

'I wonder if your mother went up the hill afterwards.'

'I hope not. I'd never hear the end of it.' I hesitated but I had to ask it. 'David, what is this all about?'

He looked at me, as he held a branch back so that I could get by. 'I don't know.'

'You must. You're a trustee and an art historian,' I said indignantly. Yet when I looked at him, I could have sworn he was telling the truth.

'Certainly I'm a trustee. I see that the money is spent properly, and that the trust is being managed well. That doesn't mean I'm an authority on Charles Carr's work.'

He was prevaricating. That was quite clear. 'I can understand that,' I said quietly, 'but you must get asked questions about this place, both from the people who come here as tourists and by academics and critics. You must know *how* he came to do this work, even if you don't understand its message.' I took a deep breath. 'For instance,' I continued casually, 'he must have had either some affair of his own in mind for *The Happening* or he used a particular model at the time, or probably both.'

I had scored a bull's-eye. The look he gave me was definitely hostile, and he turned away from me as surely as the man on top of the fountain was ignoring those below him. 'Ask Tony,' was all he said. 'He was his assistant in the late 1950s.'

'And suppose he doesn't know? Are you going to let future generations just go on wondering?'

'Why is it important, Lucia?' He sounded very detached. 'After all, it's clear Carr wanted to convey the meaning of love; personal experience is irrelevant.'

He'd got me. Zap. I honestly tried to think out a truthful answer. 'I suppose,' I said at last, 'it's what I do.'

'Do?'

'It's my job,' I amplified. 'I write children's stories. They're based on the quest. The quest for the Sleeping Beauty; the quest to find Cinderella; Dick Whittington's quest, the quest for the Holy Grail, and any other tale you care to name. But mine are recast in modern terms.'

I suddenly wondered if that was what had drawn me to the fountain we'd just seen: it had all the elements of a quest in it. I tried to dismiss this thought, as a puzzle solved, but the fountain still refused to go. Odd.

'Fairy stories are just that, Lucia. They

40

aren't real life.'

I was disappointed in him.

'Now that,' I replied sadly, 'I really do dispute.'

He held his hands up in mock surrender. Or was he lightening the tone deliberately as a defence? 'I yield.'

'No, you won't. You'll fight. What evidence do you have that fairy stories aren't part of real life?'

'The world today. I rest my case, m'lud.' He was laughing now.

I wasn't. 'It's not a very good one. Fairy stories are the basis of every story there ever was and what we all try to live. We try to fight our way through obstacles towards the happy ending. The battle of life.'

'There aren't any automatic happy endings in that.'

'Now there's pessimism for you. It might be true, but the quest says we must seek it. It's the prince that wins through who gets the princess's hand.'

'But are there any princesses?' He was grinning his head off, but I had a sense he was taking this seriously now. Good, because so was I. 'Fairy tales are out of fashion. How do you keep your readership?'

He was trying to turn the conversation away from Charles Carr. OK, I'd humour him.

'It's the basic theme that interests me, whether it's in *Star Wars*, *Lord of the Rings*, King Arthur, or Harry Potter. They're different guises of the same thing. And so,' I

41

prepared to punch hard, 'is my interest in Charles Carr. I'd like to know more. In fact, I'd like to know everything.'

No doubt now. His face had frozen over.

'Has there ever been a biography of him?' I continued.

'No.'

'You said that fairly abruptly. Do you plan to write one yourself?'

This time the 'No' came out even more vehemently.

'Has anyone ever wanted to write one?'

He glanced at me. 'No entry' was written all over his face. 'The possibility has been mooted.'

'But never got anywhere. Why? Because the trustees are against it?' I asked sweetly.

'Lack of material.' He didn't exactly snap back, but it was a very firm answer.

'There must be material if one digs hard.'

'No purpose would be served. His work is the record he would have wanted.'

'It sounds as though there are deep dark secrets in his life. Are there?'

'I don't know.'

I was getting exasperated. Somewhere deep in there was a man I could love, did love, but would he please stand up and be counted?

'What about his family? Is there anyone who might be hurt by a biography? Maybe they would want to help with it. Tell me honestly, David, what the problem is. I can understand the word no, and drop it if there's a good enough reason.'

42

'Drop what?' His voice was dripping icicles now.

'I'd like to write Charles Carr's biography.' I suddenly realized that's exactly why I was so interested. I'd never written a biography, only odd bits of journalism, but there was no reason why I shouldn't. I knew how to write books, I knew how to research. I'd had some art training, and with a little help from David and Tony I'd be splendidly placed. I admit the latter idea was uppermost in my mind, but the biography was fast becoming a reality there too. It would be a great idea.

'I believe Carr had family in the States,' David said, after a pause, 'but I doubt if they know about his life after he left. There's no way you could write a biography even with their help.'

'Why? Just give me a good reason.'

David was clearly furious, but at bay. 'I don't need to.'

I'm ashamed to say I was on the point of blackmailing him, by saying I'd give it publicity in the press with the hint of a big dark naughty secret, but stopped in time. I wasn't actually sure Carr was a big enough name to attract attention. Anyway, that wasn't a road I would normally go down, and I wouldn't do so now.

'You give me a reason for wanting to do it instead,' David said. He wasn't exactly cold now. Just detached, as though he had been through this in his mind many times. Any rapport we had established in the garden had been well and truly dispersed.

'To make the work more widely known.'

'Not good enough, Lucia. There's no story to tell, and if there was it would have gone with Charles to his grave. The work must stand alone, as he always said.'

I pounced. 'Did he? I didn't think you knew him well enough for that.'

He had the grace to blush. 'Believe me, it was his wish. He might even have put it in his will. I can't remember. You can ask Tony if you like. He'll support me on that.'

On that? Not on everything, was the implication. Or was I reading too much into it. 'Did he expressly say no biographies?'

'I think his words when he spoke to me were: "no snoopers".'

I felt I'd been hit in the face. I said nothing more, but just walked away. I heard him start to say something but I ignored him, intent on exiting from the infinitesimal part of his life I'd shared with him. Fortunately Mum reappeared, waving furiously from the other side of the lawn. It seemed the parting knell had been rung. The house was closing for the day. I walked into the car park with Mum, only half listening as she talked of gardens and plants, but little of Charles Carr. Not a word of *The Happening*. Not a word of David Fraser. Today might never have happened.

I swallowed back my anger, frustration and loss as we drove out of those once elegant white painted gates. He was probably married anyway.

Three

Unfortunately, I woke up the following morning still in love with David. There was only one problem, I told my muesli crossly, I could see no way of bridging the gap that had arisen between us yesterday, or even of providing a convenient excuse for seeing him again. After all, he'd been deliberately rude to me. Gloomily I wondered whether I was fixated on him. Would I, for instance, qualify as a stalker if I contacted him again? More to the point, what on earth would I say if I did? He was a trustee of the Edenshaw Foundation, and he had made it quite clear there was no way that he or anyone else was ever going to be empowered to write a biography. Yet the more I thought about it, the more I failed to see why. A biography, even if limited in circulation, would raise funds for the foundation, and visitors to the gallery would be increased in number and improved in understanding if more were known about the artist.

I stared at my computer screen. Somehow, chapter five of *Four Dogs and a Dinosaur* was failing to grip me. Instead, I was forced to face the fact that it might not be biographers in general whom David disliked, but me in particular. He didn't think I was up to the job.

So? I rallied and rang my agent.

'Ah,' said Sue. 'I'd been wondering what had happened to you. What happened to the first six chapters I was promised?'

'On their way tomorrow,' I answered gaily, exaggerating the truth. 'Now, I've got something else to throw at you.'

I could sense her immediate interest. I am not exactly a household name, but I represent that thing beloved of my agent's heart, a nice little earner.

'What is it?' Sue quite rightly always inclines to the cautious approach.

'I'm thinking of a biography.'

Silence the other end of the phone. Then: 'Whose?'

I explained with every bit of enthusiasm that I could muster, which was quite a lot. 'It's got a sure market,' I finished weakly, when the response was all too obvious.

'But you have to have *heard* of Charles Carr to go to this place Edenshaw,' she pointed out. 'It has to be a mega book, or nothing, to get noticed nowadays.' She clearly thought I was losing the plot.

I tried everything I could think of. The answer was still: 'It's not mega, darling. It's specialist. Stick to the fairytales.'

I refused to be put off. There were other avenues, I told myself. Sue's understandable opposition sharpened my thoughts. This was

46

something I wanted to do, even if it had to be tucked into my 'spare' time. Quite why I wanted to do it I wasn't sure. I have to admit that getting in touch with David again was certainly a factor, but there was more. I sensed there was a story there, and more to the point, a story that would interest me because it was a quest. I hadn't been on a personal quest for many a long year. If there was no commercial market for such a book, then a specialist publisher would surely be interested, despite the lack of big bucks. Failing that, I could self publish; or the foundation could publish it. Now there was a thought.

But it all came back to David. Who had said no. And who was a trustee.

But only one trustee, I reminded myself. There was at least one other, and probably more. My trump card was that I knew that trustee and I was already dialling his number.

'You've been holding out on me, Tony.'

I wiped my sandals on the mat, threw off my jacket, and sank into a shabby leather armchair. Tony lives in a world of his own. I love it. His flat is at the top of a Notting Hill Victorian terrace house. All life hums in the street below him, and he has his own kingdom up here. It is packed. It is an Aladdin's cave, in which pictures, newspapers, and books, live happily in piles on chairs, tables and floor. His studio is much the same, covered with sketchbooks, crayons, reference

47

books, and half-finished or failed drawings. I feel rather like an elf myself when I go there, crawling amid paper mountains.

'How is that, light of my life?'

This kind of remark might make one assume Tony is gay, but he isn't. At least, not to my knowledge. He was married once, but his wife died yonks ago. Since then, he has taken to his craft in a big way. Before that, it was a sideline and he worked on a Fleet Street newspaper, the *Globe*, I think. He is a superb cook, so he has no problems on that score, and, apart from the need I mentioned earlier to stir a cauldron from time to time, seems to have got his life organized well – even if such a word seems not to apply to this flat.

The problem was that this present cauldron seemed to involve me, and I needed to be clear about the part I was playing for him. He brought me some coffee, and some rather nice Florentines he had 'just whipped up', so he informed me. He has a nice face, does Tony, a kindly uncle sort of face. It's only when one notes the sharp eyes, and the smile that isn't *always* aimed at you, preferring its own inner knowledge, that the kind uncle changes into Merlin.

'Not our usual day for getting together, Lucia,' he remarked. We normally meet on Mondays to make our joint decisions for the week ahead.

'This is about Charles Carr, as you must know full well.'

48

'Didn't you enjoy it? Julia said you'd had a most interesting day.'

So Mum had put her spoke in first. That's the trouble with triangular relationships and as he was Mum's contact first, I can hardly complain. Well, I could, but it wouldn't do me any good.

'It was,' I agreed. 'Now tell me why you wanted me to go there.'

'Charles Carr deserves to be more widely known, and I knew you were interested in art.' Tony was wearing the puzzled expression he puts on sometimes when we disagree about the suitability of some of his more outrageous illustrations. Unfortunately the answer came just too quickly to convince me.

'He does and I am,' I agreed, giving him my best smile. 'Tell me, Tony, did you send me there in the cause of Charles Carr or to meet David Fraser?'

'I wondered if you might run into him.'

'That's no answer.'

'Are you accusing me of matchmaking, Lucia? I'd never stoop to such bad taste.'

'Accusing wouldn't be my way of expressing it. Faulty judgement maybe.'

'You didn't like him? Now that surprises me. Most people do like David.'

'I did like him. He doesn't return the compliment however.'

'And that surprises me even more.' He waited.

'We disagreed strongly over Charles Carr.' It could do no harm to tell him.

49

He did not comment, but watched me carefully as I drank my coffee. I knew I was on the right track. It wasn't simple matchmaking, it was something deeper than that. Something he didn't want to, or couldn't, tackle himself.

'I too think Charles Carr should be more widely appreciated,' I continued. 'I want to write his biography, but David doesn't want it done.'

'Ah.'

'Why are you looking smug, Tony?'

'A biography,' he repeated, as though such a thing was an entirely new concept to him.

'My agent says it wouldn't be commercial. There are other ways of publishing it, of course, but I wouldn't do it without the help of the trustees. How many are there?'

'Five. David, myself, Sir Rupert Packard (for show), Norman Fellows, who was Charles's solicitor, and Myrtle Jenkins.'

'Who on earth is she?' I knew of Sir Rupert of course. He was the head or ex-head of countless art societies and galleries, and Charles's solicitor was understandable too.

'Charles's housekeeper.'

'You're joking.'

'No. And Charles wasn't joking either. He said he wanted the voice of common sense on the board, and that was Myrtle's.'

'What's she like?'

'Fiftyish now. Down to earth. Married.'

'Was she just the housekeeper?'

'Hanky-panky in the broom closet? I've no idea and that's the truth. Charles was sixty-

50

odd when she came to work for him, so maybe he settled for common sense. It's a rare enough gift. He left her a tidy sum in his will, but I think she still does the school dinners.'

'And plays an active role as trustee?'

'Yes. David is the most active, though, partly since he lives nearby, and partly because our Myrtle isn't too hot on maths and art.'

'Would it be any use my going to see David again...?' It was good to know he lived near Edenshaw House.

'I doubt it if he's said no once. That doesn't surprise me though.'

'Why's that?'

'Perhaps he hopes to write one himself one day.'

'He says not.'

'Pity. David tends to mean what he says. I doubt if there'd be any talking him round, even by you, sweet Lucia.'

'Especially not by me,' I agreed ruefully. 'How about your own views, Tony?'

'Have you ever been a trustee, Lucia?'

'No.' I was suspicious. Tony was clearly trying to wriggle out of something.

'A trustee's role is not to initiate, but to observe, to check that the trust is being run properly, that its finances are in order and that its officers are behaving properly as regards the law.'

'You're telling me that even if you have a view on the biography it isn't relevant?'

51

'I'm telling you all I can do as a trustee is to check that such a project is in the overall interests of the trust.'

'And why shouldn't it be?'

'That, my dear Lucia, I can't tell until I can judge all sides of the project.'

'Have you ever,' I asked sweetly, 'fallen down a rabbit hole into Wonderland, or strolled through a wardrobe, or climbed though a mirror? Sometimes I think you got stuck on the wrong side.'

'Sweetie, in this world of ours that may be no bad thing.'

I was getting nowhere, and decided to start at another point.

'David told me you worked with Charles Carr once. I always thought you were a journalist.'

His amiable smile never wavered, but I know Tony well. I know when I can go no further and this was just such a moment.

'I was a journalist. I also had art training. It isn't given to all of us to change the world with our talents, however, and I decided if I couldn't be Michelangelo, I might as well earn money. End of story.'

I backstepped. 'If I went ahead with this biography, with or without the trust's consent – though I think it has to be with, if I want to publish it – would you be prepared to talk to me?'

'These are deep waters, Lucia.' He didn't seem perturbed, merely warning me.

'But you pushed me in, Tony.'

'I did. Something had to be done.'

'For Charles Carr?' Now I was getting somewhere at last.

'Perhaps.'

'Then would you talk to me about him?'

'Do you still want to continue?'

I leapt forward in one enormous bound. 'Yes.'

'Then you'll have to talk to Magda.'

I closed my eyes, half in despair at this new joker thrown on to the table, half in relief that at last I was making progress. 'And who is Magda?'

'Mrs Magda Harding is the CEO of the Edenshaw Foundation.'

'The what?'

'Chief executive officer. She's not a trustee. She's appointed by the board to run the museum and foundation administration.'

'Then she's subordinate to you.'

'No. Magda initiates, the trustees sit back and judge. Much easier,' he added with relish.

'Sounds a cinch. What's she like?'

'Very efficient. She's part Hungarian, married to Michael Harding, filthy rich local businessman down there in Kent. Nice chap though.'

'Hungarian? Is this something I should pick up on, Tony?'

'Yes. She's also Charles Carr's granddaughter.'

'And a pain in the neck?' Excitement was suddenly tempered with wariness. I was beginning to see where I was being led. There were troubles in the smooth running of Edenshaw House, but at the same time I was being offered the chance of meeting Carr's granddaughter. Where there were granddaughters there was a family chain, much closer than ancient siblings in the States. There must be archives, memories, and photographs. Obviously this was why David had been so reticent. He thought she would refuse. All right, all it might need was for me to persuade her that I was a goodie, not a baddie.

Tony didn't answer my question. Enough said – or not said. 'Will you send me there with your blessing, Tony?'

'You may need more than that, ducky.'

Halloway House near Tunbridge Wells was a far different cry to Edenshaw. The paint was fresh here, the drive was open as if to display the grandeur of the old Wealden house set back beyond the green lawns. A triple garage adjoined the house, and a Mercedes sunned itself on the gravel forecourt. Half of me thought it was splendid that such old houses should be preserved with the money of the rich, the other half thought it strange that one generation's hovel should be a later one's palace. I already knew what I would find when I went in. Antiques, not necessarily priceless, but carefully chosen, in exquisite taste combined with comfort. Was I envious? Not a whit. I would be scuttling back to

Putney with great relief. The responsibility of running something like this would terrify me.

I had expected to go to Edenshaw House again, so I had been surprised when Mrs Harding suggested I come to her home. She had an eight-year-old son, she explained, and this was school holiday time. Although there was an au pair, she liked to be at home when she could.

In a way, I found it easier to be away from Edenshaw House, so that I could put that encounter with David right out of my mind. I wanted to concentrate on getting the main issue resolved before I met him again – if indeed I ever did.

The door was opened by the au pair – at least, I presumed she was. She was a tall blonde girl who could have been American or Swedish, but when I heard her accent the question was answered. The latter.

'Mrs Harding comes soon.' I received a charmingly casual grin and a request to stay please in the large drawing room with a conservatory at the far end. I could see huge hothouse plants peering at me. This was a room such as I had pictured, elegant and spacious, and I imagined Magda Harding would match it in poise, style and general affluence.

After Tony's reticence, I certainly didn't expect the Magda I met. She came flying in, full of apologies for keeping me waiting. True, she was slim, she was elegant, crying Versace, Gucci, and gold bracelets all over her, but she was also warm and charming. That wasn't what struck me first, however. I was struck dumb with amazement.

She was quite the most beautiful woman I had ever seen. I'm not hot on beautiful women, since most of it comes from self-assurance and money rather than nature, but this was something else. She was stunning and the effect owed little to her clothes since she was dressed in a cream cashmere sweater and jeans. Her long dark hair, her expressive brown eyes and her complexion, combined with her genuine warmth, left me blinking, and wondering why I'd bothered to dab lipstick on or even comb my hair this morning.

'I'm so sorry, Miss Cooper – oh how stupid. Lucia, do you mind? I'm Magda. Tony tells me–' she poured Earl Grey tea with expertise '–you are keen on Charles Carr's work.' She had a slight accent that betrayed her origins but only enhanced her charm.

'Now I've seen it, I am. I want to know more about it – and about him.'

She smiled at me, a smile that embraced the world in its warmth. Perhaps I'm overdoing it here, but I couldn't take my eyes off her – she had a hypnotic quality. 'Did Tony tell you Charles was my grandfather?'

'On your mother's side or your father's?'

'Mother's. My grandmother was Charles's model.'

'Here in Kent?' I really grew excited now.

'No. In Budapest. Charles painted her from

memory, from photos and, as you saw, often symbolically.'

This was wonderful. I was making strides ahead in my knowledge with a few brief sentences. Why on earth hadn't Tony told me this? Or David? There had been no mention of a model. 'So Charles Carr married his model,' I said.

'No, but today, what does that matter? Perhaps then. Not now.' Magda became businesslike. 'Lucia, Tony says you want to write Charles's biography. Tell me, why do you wish this?' She leaned forward earnestly, inviting me to share everything I felt about it. And I did. I only left out one factor: David.

'I feel his pictures need explaining,' I concluded.

'The guide book provides that.'

'Not sufficiently. It explains them in art jargon, but it doesn't...' I hesitated, reluctant to go too far and alienate her. 'It doesn't explain the man behind the artist. Did you know him?' Magda must be in her early thirties, I supposed, though age was not the first thing one thought of when looking at her.

'Yes. I came here in 1992 from Hungary and he did not die for two more years. So I knew him and I too fell in love with his work.'

Belatedly, it occurred to me that she might have written the guide book herself, and I asked her.

She grinned. 'No. David Fraser did it. Have you met him?'

'Yes.' Well, I should have expected it. It certainly explained his antagonism to a biography.

'If you write this biography, we would work closely together. Yes?'

'Of course,' I replied blithely, then remembered what I'd heard about good biographies and living descendants. They don't always mix. Living descendants have their own ideas about their ancestor, and can sometimes be reluctant to let the warts emerge as well as the good side. While I don't believe in warts for warts' sake, I do believe in the truth – so far as any one person can claim to have reached it.

How simple it sounded, but I was already sure that I could work with Magda, and what little she had told me so far, convinced me that it might after all be possible to gather the necessary material to recreate Charles Carr's background.

Magda questioned me closely on my credentials, on my plans so far as I had them, and my motives. I answered her as far as it was possible, and she seemed satisfied.

'It is not my decision alone, you understand. I have to discuss it with...' A slight pause. 'The trustees. They would want to see sample material, whether we publish it ourselves or if you find an outside publisher.'

I agreed that was fair. My children's work was hardly an automatic passport to being able to write a specialist biography. Then I asked her: 'Are there family records?'

'There are some. Mine, for instance. And the trustees all knew him, even if in his later life.'

'Tony would be in favour,' I told her honestly, 'but I don't think David would be.'

She laughed, to my surprise. 'David is no problem, believe me, Lucia. David keeps everything inside his head, he will not willingly share it with others. Charles belongs to him, and to him alone. I think perhaps,' she considered carefully, 'that is because he is not an artist himself. Charles is his other half, Charles's work is his work. Does that make sense?'

'Yes. It would certainly explain a lot.'

Her only other question is whether I would do the sample material without payment, and this too seemed reasonable. I agreed to do a couple of specimen chapters provided I was given enough meat to produce them in the way of archive material and, for example, her and Tony's recollections.

Towards the end of our discussion, her husband joined us. Michael did indeed seem pleasant – and clearly idolized the ground upon which Magda trod. He was one of those amiable indolent-looking Englishmen whose appearance often blinded one to the sharp eyes of a man who was far from indolent within. Obviously so in this case, judging from Tony's description of him as a prominent businessman.

I was introduced to eight-year-old Toby, to whom I took an instant liking, and the afternoon ended happily. I drove back to Putney exhilarated and undampened even by the A21. At least, I was excited about Charles Carr. About David I wasn't so sure. I even wondered whether my instinct had let me down, and whether love at first sight had betrayed me. No, I decided. It hadn't. There might be some problem there, but nothing that couldn't be worked out.

1938

Charles strolled along the Ferenc József quay in love with the world and especially with Hungary. This was his first overseas posting, the first time he had ever left the States and it was an eye-opener. New York sent his pulse racing, but it hadn't got the charm of this city. Whatever you could say about the Horthy regime, the people looked flamboyantly content. A two-sided city was Budapest: the old part Buda, with its palaces and quiet residential streets; and Pest, the other side of the Danube, where the US Legation was, and the hub of the city, with the opera, museums, the grand hotels, and restaurants. There were two sides to everything in life, Charles thought. He liked both sides of Budapest; he'd climbed the steps to the old citadel and the Royal Palace, and roamed the hills where the great Hungarian aristocracy still ruled the roost – now that wouldn't happen in the

States. He loved – who wouldn't? – the Danube itself, that great wide sweep of water with its wonderful bridges, that seemed not to separate the two halves of the city but to be their natural heart. And he loved Pest, too, where the real life went on, its streets full of cafés, milk bars, shops, markets, and most of all people, from the jostling, loud and cheerful crowds about their daily life, to those strolling in the late afternoon by the Danube or taking cocktails on the Carlton terrace. There was music everywhere, from gypsy violins to opera, giving a hum to life in Pest that kept him smiling all day long.

He was glad now that he'd followed Dad's advice and gone into the foreign service. What use was painting, he asked himself, if you knew nothing of the world to paint about. Sure, he could paint what he saw before him, but he wanted more than that; he didn't know what it was he sought, but it had to give him a reason to put paint on canvas. There was a lot going on in the art world in New York just now. These last few years had brought European ideas into the New York art world. They didn't all turn into Dadaists overnight, but it opened up the field, made them confident in what they were doing, and some great work was being achieved. Not by him, though. He wasn't going to give up painting, but he just needed to live a little first. Things were looking threatening in Europe right now, with this Hitler on the rampage, and though Britain was doing its best to calm him down by letting him have what he wanted, that wasn't going to satisfy him for long. The only thing necessary for the triumph of evil is for good men to do nothing. That's what Edmund Burke had said a couple of hundred years ago, and it was still as true today.

Charles had liked the idea of coming to Hungary, poised as it was between eastern and western Europe. It had its political links with Austria and Germany, born of the past, but its heart was pro-British and the West. Now he was here, he liked the country even more.

'Hello, American.'

László Gáli, a young Hungarian he'd met at a party last night, was shouting at him from a table on the Carlton terrace. He'd been intrigued to meet Charles, they were of the same age, and the same level in their respective jobs – László was in the Hungarian foreign ministry. They'd taken to each other at once.

'You join us, yes?'

Charles willingly agreed. There were four more in the group, all introduced one by one; they were all from the Hungarian ministry save one, who was French. They were a jovial crowd and, though Charles's Hungarian wasn't that good yet, he managed to follow most of what was going on. The Frenchman, bored with coffee, called for wine and several bottles of Tokay went down well with the group. The evening was beginning to pass splendidly.

'Heh, American,' László cried after a while, 'we eat, yes?'

Huge plates of something he didn't recognize suddenly appeared before them. In the legation they had an American cook who did his best to recreate home delights, so Hungarian food was unknown to Charles, save for the occasional ghastly sandwiches at a milk bar or café which looked so good and tasted so foul. This looked altogether different though.

'We make you honorary Hungarian, if you eat all that,' László laughed.

'What is it?' Charles looked dubiously at the large pile of vegetables and meat, of which he recognized nothing.

A consultation produced the answer of goose legs, potatoes, cabbage and onions. Charles did his best, helped by more wine, and won himself a round of applause. He was pleasantly drunk by the time he was finished. He wanted to sleep, he wanted to dance, he wanted to see the town, he wanted to collapse right there. His companions decided for him, and as there was nothing in his small room to attract him back to his lodgings, he let them. He was propelled out of the restaurant, made to walk some way, and then miraculously managed to pile into a large car. Perhaps it was a taxi, but he didn't know or care.

The city was dark now, but there was light streaming from everywhere. If only he'd been sober, he would have liked to paint it. Inside the cafés were scenes of frenzied merriment; it seemed like another world, which he couldn't enter as they flashed by. They seemed to be crossing a bridge, but it wasn't to Buda. He worked out that they were on an island, which must be the one he'd heard was a popular resort by day and by night with gardens, swimming pools and restaurants.

'Margit Island, American,' László shouted. 'We pay here. We pay for you, Charles. You like girls?'

'Yes, yes,' he mumbled.

'Then we go to nightclub by Grand Hotel, American Charles. More drinks, yes?'

'More drinks, no,' he groaned.

They had to leave the car and walk along a moonlit path to the club, although Charles's walk was more a stagger, supported by his companions. There seemed to be a stiff entrance charge if the amount of money being flung at the entry desk was any guide, but he decided he felt too ill to protest. There were, he realized when they entered the club, some very odd things in Hungary. Gathered in the entrance hall were men dressed as women, women as men, and beyond on the dance floor were some men dancing with men. What his parents, back home, with their traditional, almost Quaker values, would make of this he decided not to contemplate. Instead he prepared to throw himself into the party.

Just as he handed over his coat, a new group came in. A special one, judging by the doorman rushing to hold the door for it. It was mostly men, but there was one woman. The most arresting, eye-catching – no, beautiful – woman Charles had ever seen. Or if not beautiful then the most mesmerizing. She was swathed in furs up to her chin, and the face, framed by short dark hair, compelled all eyes to fix on it. It was not vivacious, as those of other women here, it was the face of a woman sure of herself, of her sensuous attraction and her power to enchant. He watched her fascinated as she swept along on her triumphal path. She divested herself of her furs, revealing a long white satin dress beneath, closely hugging her slender figure, and with one huge diamond at her breast.

He watched, completely sober now, until suddenly for just a moment she turned and her eyes fastened on him. He was lost, spellbound, as the power in those eyes seemed to draw him to her, to speak of a bond between the two of them that they and they alone shared in the huge crowd. Her mouth seemed to hover on the edge of acknowledgement of this bond, but then she turned away, laughing and joking with her entourage as they went to their table.

Four

The sound of the telephone made me jump. I'd been miles away – in Budapest, of course. I'd been wondering when Charles Carr had been there, and how he had met Magda's grandmother, his all-important model. It was from there, obviously, that the story of his love affair stemmed. When was it though? During the 1956 Uprising, as Mum had assumed? The US Embassy, or Legation as it was at that time, had a high profile as it was there that the head of the Roman Catholic church in Hungary, Cardinal Mindszenty, fled for asylum, an asylum that lasted fifteen years. No, that wouldn't fit, I realized, for in the mid-fifties Charles Carr must long since have ceased to be a diplomat. It had to be earlier, so it was probably during the Second World War. But as the US was at war with the Nazi-occupied states they wouldn't have had even a legation then. Or was Hungary neutral? Perhaps Charles had been there immediately post-war when the Russians had taken control.

Still musing, I picked up the receiver prepared to snarl at the invasion of my privacy by call centres on a working day. Well, I was supposed to be working. I'd arranged to go down to Edenshaw House on the morrow to talk to Magda again at her request. She'd now had a chance to discuss the biography with the trustees and didn't want to talk about it over the phone. It sounded ominous, but as usual I hoped for the best.

'Lucia?' The voice was male, and somewhat hesitant.

'Speaking. Who—'

'David Fraser. Does that ring a bell?'

Believe me, it rang all the bells of my heart. Somehow two or three weeks had slipped by while I was waiting to hear from Magda, and I had mentally put my love affair – or lack of it – on hold while I was waiting to hear from her. On the other hand, David had been remarkably and unnecessarily rude to me when we last met. Oh heck, so what, I thought. Life is too short to play games.

'Hello, David.'

'I wanted to apologize. It's a bit late I know' – (Never too late, David) – 'but I mean it. I had to ask Tony for your number. I hope you don't mind. You can slam the receiver down if you like.'

'I'm still here,' I told him cheerfully. 'Listening.'

'I shouldn't have spoken to you the way I did.'

'Forgiven. You obviously felt deeply about the question. Do you still?'

A silence. 'Do you mind if I don't answer that question over the phone? I'd like to talk

67

to you about it face to face, if you can bear it.'

'I think I could just about stomach that, David.'

'I'm glad you mentioned stomach. Can I take you to dinner?'

I thought about this. A candlelit dinner sounded a marvellous basis for romance, but there was a snag. There was the question of this biography between us. I genuinely wanted to do it, and David might still be a stumbling block. I needed to see things clearly, not through the bottom of a wine glass, wonderful though that might be.

'How about lunch?' I suggested brightly.

'Fine.' A pause. 'Do you know Dulwich Picture Gallery?'

It was then I knew I was still in love with him. The very place. Some of the greatest art in the world in the romantic setting of Dulwich. And I'd read about their terrific café. I'd been to the gallery years ago, and remembered it well. In the interests of not upsetting applecarts I decided not to mention that I was going to Edenshaw House tomorrow. Either he knew, in which case he would have mentioned it, since we could obviously have met in Kent. Or he didn't, and what he didn't know couldn't hurt us. Why was I being careful? Because I wasn't sure what quicksands might lie around. I needed to talk to Magda first.

I thought about ringing Tony to find out what had happened at the trustees' meeting to discuss the project, but decided not to. If

Tony was still stirring cauldrons he wasn't going to pre-warn me, and I didn't want to play into his wizard's hands by giving him a running commentary on what was going on. After all, side by side with my suddenly surging hopes for my love quest for David, was a growing determination to follow up my other quest – to know more about Charles Carr. Or were they part of the same story?

There was a great difference in my approach to Edenshaw House on this occasion. Now I had a real purpose, I could look on everything with a fresh eye. And, I reminded myself, a careful one. For that reason, I decided to let Magda make the running.

She was in business mode this morning, in a light blue trouser suit, which looked amazing with her dark hair. She was just as welcoming. She had the innate ability to smile at you as if you were the only person in the world needed to make her life complete. It's a gift that seems to come naturally to some people.

Her office was in one of the towers. I imagine in Victorian times it would have been a guest bedroom, ideally placed for those naughty weekends we hear so much about, when plates of sandwiches were left outside doors to indicate the coast was clear for lovers. Edenshaw House had seen many changes since then, at least in style. This room remained pleasantly unofficy, however.

'This tower is for archives,' Magda told me.

'I just cleared a space for a desk.'

It must have taken a little more than that, for the room next door was occupied by her assistant Pamela Taylor, a woman in her early forties, small and bustling in contrast to Magda's swanlike grace. 'Our Venerable Keeper of the Archives,' Magda announced in mock solemn voice.

Pamela laughed, although she seemed more formal than Magda. Perhaps it was necessary, for it was clear that archives here were no matter of bulging wardrobes that disgorged their contents all over the floor when their doors were opened. It struck me that everything would be carefully catalogued and computerized. I suppose it had to be to run the trust efficiently and indeed legally.

'Pam looks after the admin of the scholarships too,' Magda explained.

'How do you decide about the scholarships? Do the trustees do that?'

'No. They know the general plans, of course, but we have an advisory board which does the judging and makes the decisions. I have a casting vote just in case, but as there are nine on the board, it shouldn't in theory ever be needed, unless someone falls under a bus.'

It sounded very efficient, which was a good thing if I was to put my head and heart into this biography.

'We have quite a lot of scholars, who come to look at the archives,' Magda continued, 'usually the more specialist sort. Charles Carr has quite a following in the States – his family sees to that.'

'Who are?'

'Currently, William Carr, Charles's nephew who's on the point of retiring as head of the family firm. His sister is still alive, but she's ninety-odd and never got on with Charles anyway. There's an ancient cousin too.'

'Didn't Charles's father want Charles to go into the business?'

'No, the elder brother, Samuel junior, did that. The father wanted Charles to raise the family profile, so Charles went into the diplomatic service. When he came back from the war he built up his own china business though, a side line of china with his own paintings on it; he worked it up like crazy and then sold out to his brother, and came here with the proceeds.'

'And during the war?' So that cleared up my first query. Charles had been in Budapest during at least part of the Second World War.

'I'll tell you. I expect you'd like some coffee to recover before we plunge too deeply in. Or would a stiff whisky help?'

'Coffee will do, thanks.' We went down to the coachhouse restaurant, where I insisted on paying for the coffee and chocolate croissants. Though how Magda managed to look as slim as she did when chocolate croissants were on offer every day, I don't know. I'd be waddling like a very fat goose.

'Do I take it the biography is still on the cards?' I asked when I deemed the moment right.

'Of course.' Magda grinned at me. 'You don't think I'd have dragged you all this way if it wasn't, do you?'

'No.' I was much relieved. 'I couldn't assume it though – especially as I know one of the trustees at least opposed it.'

'I told you not to worry about David. The other four were in favour – with reservations, of course. And David's opposition might not be so strong as you think.'

Perhaps she was right. I thought of David's call, and that I'd be seeing him very soon. Surely what he had to suggest must represent some kind of compromise on his part? He wouldn't have bothered otherwise. I couldn't flatter myself that I'd scored a knock-out hit with my charms at our first meeting, merely that there had been a mutual attraction that might or might not be rekindled.

'Anyway,' Magda continued, 'legally the only role the trustees have with new projects is to be convinced that they are truly in line with the charitable purposes of the trust, and of course that it wouldn't be out of pro-portion with the resources available. I con-vinced them that it was bang in line with the trust's aims. Knowledge of Charles Carr's life would add to his reputation, and his work could then be seen in context. Also, it would raise revenue to further the scholarship funds. Its publication would be a major step in the publicity drive and publicity equals money.'

I realized that Magda must be a very good chief executive officer. Surprising she would want to do it with a young child and rich husband, but I was the last person to be sexist. It must be a challenge for her, for clearly she took her role seriously.

'So where do we go next?' I asked her, eager to get going. 'It seems to me the next question would be whether I or we look for a specialist publisher, or whether we downsize the scope of the book so that the foundation can economically publish it here.'

'I want to exhaust the possibilities of the first option,' Magda said promptly. 'Then we still have a fallback, although marketing is the problem. We can sell it here, or by mail order, but we haven't the resources or time to put it over on a wider scale and I doubt if you have.'

'No,' I was forced to admit. I couldn't see myself hassling and humping books round to booksellers. We then got down to the nitty-gritty.

The major condition the trustees had made, Tony included, was the sensible one that the foundation should see sample chapters. I agreed, because this was reasonable – save for one aspect.

'What if it's the content you don't like,' I asked, 'rather than my presentation? Suppose I produce something from my research that you don't approve of?' Quite why this occurred to me, I'm not sure, but it certainly seemed a point worth making.

Magda thought for a moment. 'We discuss

it with you, and if we're not convinced we bow out, and you're on your own.'

Again I agreed – with another 'but'. 'And if the latter part of the book doesn't please you? We'd be under contract by then.' This could be a stumbling block and I knew from Sue that it happened from time to time.

Magda frowned. 'Deep water, Lucia. We'd have to take that as it comes. The trustees would probably have to bring in an independent panel. Is that enough to go ahead on?'

It was, and I told her so. To tell the truth, I was determined to get those sample chapters done, come hell or high water.

'Good.' She bit energetically into the chocolate croissant.

'One last problem. I need material to kick off with.'

'That, Lucia, is no problem at all. We have enough archive material here on his family business and early life to start you off.'

I thought about this, but my heart sank. Archive material is invaluable but I knew I needed to know the man as well. And one central chunk of him was missing. Miserably I told Magda so. To my surprise she replied, 'Good, I'd feel the same way. My grandmother can't travel, of course.'

For a moment I didn't take this in. 'Your grandmother?' I repeated stupidly. 'You mean she's *alive*?'

'Oh yes. She's ninety, but very much kicking, believe me.'

'And she was really Charles Carr's model?'

74

'She was.' Magda was laughing at me now, for I was clearly displaying all the signs of a biographer overwhelmed by an unexpected treasure trove of information.

'I suppose you're going to tell me she lives next door to me in Putney?'

'Not quite. Budapest, actually.'

'And she's in good health?' Of course, she was in Budapest. That was the city on which David said Carr had based *The Happening*.

'She has more than a twinge of arthritis now, but she has perfect recall.'

It sounded too good to be true.

I was still reeling from this pleasant surprise the next day, when I was due to meet David. I rang Sue to say yet another couple of days would pass before she had the benefit of my chapters. I still had plenty of time to make the final overall deadline, so I couldn't see why she was fussing. I wasn't. Right now I had possibly the most important meeting of my life to think about: seeing David again.

I dithered over what to wear, littering my bed with discarded choices. In the end, I decided that fate, not me, was going to settle my future with David, so I put on a skirt and blouse, with a light jacket, and sandals. It was a warm day in early August, and casual was going to be my mood and my dress.

I began to panic as I left the car in Dulwich Park and walked back across the road to the gallery, where we'd arranged to meet. What did David look like? I only recalled how I had felt. Wasn't that a bad sign? A sign that my emotions were yet again running away with me? I had to remind myself that I was an optimist and believed in happy endings. And then I reminded myself that happy endings had to be earned.

'Lucia!'

David meanly stole an advantage on me by coming up behind me as I reached the entrance. I stopped and greeted him, and optimism kicked into play now I saw him again. It was a sunny day, God was in His heaven and all was right with the world. Nothing could go wrong, I thought. After all, I reminded myself, I had the upper hand. *He* was apologizing to me. *I* had won the battle over the biography. Actually the biography promptly fled from my mind as I looked at him. I forgot everything that Magda and Tony had gently warned me about in David's attitude to it. I stopped wondering just why he needed to see me so coincidentally with my visit to Magda. I just enjoyed the day.

I think he did too. We talked about everything under the sun at lunch and quite a few things above it. I was in the clouds and maybe he was enjoying it too for he showed no inclination to talk about controversial matters. The café is a relaxed place, and sitting by the window overlooking the gallery's pleasant grounds, London seemed a million miles away. We talked of what we would see in the gallery, of the Rembrandts, the Rubens, and other old masters, we agreed what a magnificent collection it was, and then gently moved on. We discovered we both liked pasta and both liked crime novels. We argued amiably over Christie versus Rankin and over P.D. James versus Ruth Rendell. We agreed they each had their place, and in the charm of this unity felt a mutual bond. We decided to walk round the park first and then tour the gallery. It would give us longer in the sunshine.

David didn't raise the question of the biography until we were nearly back at the gallery. August isn't the best month for peaceful walks, but it was most certainly fun. There were children, there were friends, there were families, there were business people. Their chatter, together with the birdsong, made a gentle soundtrack to our silent drawing together. I really felt I was getting closer to him, even though he had told me nothing of his personal life. There was no point at which I could have dropped in that casual question: Are you married? And so I hadn't.

Then he said experimentally, 'This biography...'

'Yes. I'm sorry you don't like the idea.'

'I don't. I think the collection should rest in peace.'

'Charles Carr himself recorded his story in paint and stone. It's as if he wanted it to be discovered.'

'Did he record it for himself alone though, or for the world to pore over? I hate the current mania for digging up dirt and prettying it up with a few odd compliments.'

'How do you know it's dirt in Charles's case, David?'

'I don't. And in case you're wondering, I'm sure you wouldn't dig dirt for dirt's sake.'

'His art shows there are two sides to the story. If whatever I find out confirms two sides, it seems reasonable to record it.'

'Does it?' He sounded so bitter, I was taken aback.

'Look, it may come to nothing. You must know what Magda has told me.' I quickly ran through it. 'So you see, the foundation,' I concluded, 'can back out if they don't like what I write.'

'But then you would have the material and be free to go and publish it anyway.'

I stood stock still. 'What is all this about, David? Certainly I would. But you can't know much about the publishing world if you think I'd get past first base with that. For a start, Charles Carr is not a household name, and merely having an interesting story would not be enough to hook a major publisher. No bucks in it. And a specialist publisher would need the approval of the foundation, or to be more specific, need their marketing support to sell copies at the museum, in order to have some hope of getting their money back.'

David's chin moved a few millimetres towards relaxation. Then he sighed. 'It seems I owe you another apology, Lucia.'

'Think nothing of it.' I was furious, however. This was the man I was committed to (though he might not know it), and he seemed to think I was lower than the low.

'How will you go about these sample chapters?'

'I've decided I shan't write a word, until I've been to Budapest.'

'Budapest?' He was genuinely startled, even shocked.

'To see Gréta Öszödy, Magda's grandmother. As his model and lover, she's the key to everything and an understanding of a person's achievement starts with the key, not with how he or she found the key. Charles's family comes later. Magda's arranging a meeting. I don't see why you're so surprised,' I added. 'I was thrilled when I heard she was alive. I couldn't understand why there was nothing about her in the guide, but it's all the better for me.'

Too late, I remembered David had written the guide.

He was standing at my side, but we were miles apart. He was lost in a world the nature of which I couldn't even guess.

'You must think me half-witted,' he said at last. 'Of course that's where you'll have to go. I see that.'

I relaxed. Everything was going to be all right. Or was it?

'I don't have any right to ask you this, Lucia.'

'Ask away,' I urged him. Better get this out on the table one way or another.

'Could I come with you to Budapest?'

He took in my stupefied expression and did his best to backtrack. 'It's quite all right. I wouldn't want to muscle in. I wouldn't aim to influence you. Nor do I want to keep an eye on what you're doing. I wouldn't be coming as a trustee, just a private individual. You must believe me.'

'So why do you want to come?' I asked, trying to keep a clear head while I was doing a mental jig of joy. 'Have you never met Gréta yourself. Is that it? Haven't you ever been to Budapest?'

It would have been so easy for him to lie, to give the easy answer. But he didn't. 'Yes, I know the countess. I met her once. And I've been to Budapest.'

There was something very odd here, *and* I noted the 'countess', but I was so overcome with the opportunities this might hold, a joyous leap forward for David and myself, that I ignored it. If I agreed, there was hope for us. I'd be a fool not to say yes. And I was, though it seems hard to believe now, no fool.

So Cinderella put on her glass slippers, grinned at him, and set out for the ball: 'I don't see why not.'

He was clearly pleased. As we went into the gallery, however, he made one last strange request. 'Do you mind not telling Magda I'm going to Budapest with you, at least for the moment?'

I was surprised, but I would have granted him anything at that moment. 'No problem,' I told him. After all, I convinced myself, his

80

reason was probably that of any man: he wouldn't want to indicate any climbdown to someone like Magda, and his getting interested in the biography might seem to him just that.

April 1941

'Who,' Charles had asked when she had passed on her way, 'is that?'

'That, American,' László told him, is the Grófné Gréta Öszödy, the *grófné* because she is a countess by marriage, lucky fellow. And before you start lusting after her, let me tell you most of the Hungarian aristocracy and half of that of the rest of Europe are before you in the queue. She will look at you when the Danube flows backwards, my friend.'

That had been over two and a half years ago. Charles hadn't forgotten Gréta, but they hardly moved in the same circles. Once or twice he had glimpsed her at legation receptions, at clubs or in restaurants, which was sufficient to remind him of that one startling gaze, that sense that they would meet again. They never had, or, if so, they had been divided by crowds and a social gulf as wide as the Danube.

In any case Charles had other things to think about than unattainable women. There were many pretty girls in Budapest with whom to while away an evening or even a night. For the day, there were far too many serious matters on the political front. The war preoccupied all thinking minds, positioned as Hungary was in the middle of Europe. Officially, Hungary was neutral thanks to the caution of the regent, Admiral Horthy, and the determination of Premier Teleki. Unfortunately they were so far indebted to the Nazis that they were their stooges in Charles's opinion. Always a mistake to take a bribe. But, Charles supposed, it was easy enough for him to take that view when he wasn't Hungarian. To the Hungarians, getting back chunks of Magyar territory, which they'd lost after the Great War, hadn't been a bribe, it was natural justice. Hitler was a cunning politician all right. Munich had enabled Hitler to turn a blind eye when Hungary occupied part of Czechoslovakia and in August last year part of Transylvania was given back to Hungarian rule. Then the regent had appalled them all, including his own prime minister, by going back on his undertaking of 'eternal friendship' and joining Hitler in attacking Yugoslavia. Yesterday, as a result, Teleki had committed suicide in the Sandor palace, and news had just come that his successor was pro-Nazi. Things were not looking good.

Superficially Budapest had hardly changed from the city Charles first knew. German influence was growing, and would obviously now increase. No one knew whose side anyone was *really* on. Many of the aristocracy were pro-British and now having to show false colours in favouring the Nazis. The social life seemed not to have changed, but to Charles it now seemed to have a vicious edge. There were many dark stories going round, and the regent, Admiral Horthy, was growing old. Foreign legation workers, such as himself, moved with care. Don't get compromised, was the rule. America, like Hungary, had kept out of the war, but like Hungary it showed its preferences. Unlike Hungary, however, it did not have to bow to Germany or to Britain because of proximity. Britain was fighting for its survival now, but few here dared display sympathy for its predicament. The terrible Margit prison was full of those who had made such unwise decisions.

Spring was here now, but this year brought none of its usual optimism. Dispirited, Charles decided to take a walk to the Károlyi Gardens, and for some reason took his sketchbook with him. The gardens fascinated him. It had once been the private garden of the great Károlyi family, in particular the popular Count Michael Károlyi, briefly head of the Republic after the revolution of 1918. His great yellow-painted Empire palace had been confiscated, and where the princes of Hungary used to walk was now open to all as an art gallery.

He sat on a bench under a lime tree and watched the people strolling by. The children, women walking their dogs, the aristocrats, the workers, the outsiders like himself. His attention was caught by an old man on a bench opposite, who was watching a child playing with a top. Idly Charles began to sketch the scene, intrigued by the look in the old man's eyes and wondering whether he could catch that.

'It is good.'

Absorbed in his task, he had been unaware that someone had joined him on the bench. Startled, he looked round, and immediately recognized her.

It was the woman from the nightclub. The woman whom László had said he would never get near. Well, a park bench was near enough for him, he thought with amusement. Her dog, a Pekinese, was at her feet and this time she was not muffled up in furs. She wore a lemon-coloured costume and scarf to match, but flecked with black. Black like her hair. This time the look she gave him was not a fleeting one across a restaurant, but only a foot or so away from him, and was only for him.

For a moment, he was dazed. 'Thank you, Countess,' was all he could think of to say.

'You are an artist, *méltósá gos uram*?' She seemed unsurprised that he knew who she was.

'Part-time.' Charles was amused at being thus addressed as a person of distinction himself.

'You are not Hungarian.' They spoke in Hungarian naturally, but Charles was well aware of his limitations in her language.

84

'American.'

'So. A part-time American artist.' Her eyes contemplated him for a moment, then fell to his work. 'That old man, he is good. You draw women, too?'

'Of course. I draw life.' How stupidly pompous that sounded, Charles could have kicked himself. The Countess Öszödy must have thought so too, for she laughed. 'Am I life, Mr American artist?'

What a question. He looked deep into the strange secrets of her eyes, the promise there, and the sparkling gaiety that challenged him to advance. 'Oh yes, you are life indeed.'

'You paint in oils, too?'

'I do.' He explained about his job at the US Legation.

'Good,' she said briskly. 'Then you come to my home and instead of old men, you draw me. Would you like that, *méltóságos uram*?'

'Carr. I'm Charles Carr,' he almost stuttered, then remembered that in Hungarian it should be the other way round. 'I'm Carr Charles.' How odd that sounded here, before her, yet he should be used to it by now. 'Yes, I'd like to very much.' Already he could see it, how he would pose her, stretching sensuously out towards life itself, taking it – absorbing it and giving it. He would paint her as all that man could desire.

Five

The long lazy days of summer ticked by – and without my meeting David. I noted each day come and go, partly content that Budapest was still to come, but partly agonizing in childish impatience, as if I were waiting for Christmas, and its treats from Santa Claus.

Magda had explained that Budapest was so hot during August that she wouldn't recommend my going immediately, and especially since her grandmother spent these months in the cooler air of her country house, and not in the city.

The country house sounded fine to me, but I agreed with David afterwards – oh what a distance a telephone line puts between you – that since Charles must have worked in Budapest, that's where we should go at least part of the time. It made sense to wait till September, or so I struggled to convince myself, even though I would have hopped on the first plane, provided David were on it too.

I tried once to ring him in late August, but there was no reply. I imagined him sporting under a foreign sky with bimbos attending to his every need – and I especially fumed about the 'every'. Finally, I could stand it no longer, and joined my parents on a trip to France where they'd taken a cottage in Brittany for two weeks.

'Just right for you, darling,' Mum said happily. 'You can dream about Celtic myths to your heart's content.'

For once it wasn't myths I wanted to dream about, or if so, I wanted to be dreaming about them with David. Since we fixed up the practicalities of our trip for September on the telephone, I only saw him once in six weeks, and that wasn't intentional. Not his intention anyway. I spent several days at Edenshaw House, since it made sense that the more I felt I knew Charles Carr in my bones the more I should get out of my meeting with Countess Gréta Öszödy. I pored over the archives, getting facts and figures into my head as well as on to my laptop computer. I studied *The Happening* murals as intently as David had when we first met, though I doubt if it was to the same effect. I ambled through the gardens trying to understand their full meaning. I decided that the woman represented in *The Happening*, the light and the dark of Carr's love, must be Gréta, and their love affair had so affected Charles's life that – I deduced – he had never married but devoted the rest of his life to recording it for posterity in his own way. The acquiring of the fortune that enabled him to do so and to establish the foundation, was all part of his post-war life plan.

Questions still shouted for answers, but

after a few weeks a framework of his life was beginning to emerge from what I read. I studied what little I could find about the history of Hungary in the Second World War, and tried to fit the picture of the Charles that I had built up in my mind into the maelstrom of intrigue, betrayal and atrocity that had been Budapest, especially after the Germans occupied the country in March 1944. There had followed a year of horror as first the Germans, then the Arrow Cross Hungarian Fascists, and then the Russians, took bloody control of the city.

One major question cropped up immediately about Charles. He was a diplomat, but because Hungary declared war on the United States after the Japanese attack at Pearl Harbor in December 1941, no diplomats from the American Legation could have remained in Budapest. Presumably his love affair with Gréta ended when they were forced to part, even though they either had a child together by then or one was on the way. After the end of the war, the Iron Curtain or other considerations must have kept them apart for ever. Gréta, after all, had been married, so Magda told me, and her husband was Gróf Miklós Öszödy, one of Regent Horthy's advisers. After the war, with Horthy in exile, and the Soviet Union in control, his position would have been precarious and visitors from the West would be suspect.

And what of Magda's mother, Charles's daughter? I plucked up courage to ask Magda

88

herself, hoping I wasn't opening up any wounds.

'She died in 1988, Lucia,' replied Magda. I could see the thought still greatly upset her, however, for she could only have been in her teens then.

'And that made you decide to come to Britain?'

'My grandmother had told me about Charles Carr. My parents had divorced and I no longer saw my father, so I came here to meet Charles in 1992. I was a Hungarian citizen, but when I married that meant I could stay here.'

A marriage of convenience? I wondered, but I doubted it. Magda looked too passionate a woman not to have married for love, and it was her good fortune that Michael Harding was rich too.

After returning from Brittany, at the beginning of September, I went down to Edenshaw for two more days. I had decided to book myself in at a local B and B so that I could get the most out of my stay. I had discovered where David lived, and the temptation to drop in was great as I drove by his house – quite innocently, since the B and B was in the next village. David lived in a hamlet called Wakeham Forstal, a mere cluster of houses and a farm or two. His home looked like the others, red brick and terraced, but to me it shrieked aloud of him. Proud of myself for my discipline, I drove on by. I'd be seeing him soon, I told myself firmly.

I hadn't seen Magda or Edenshaw for three weeks, and with Budapest to come I had felt relaxed and enthusiastic as I drove down to Kent. Not only did I expect Magda to be there, but there was another treat stored up for me. At last, since it was still during the school holiday period, when she was free of her dinner-ladying, I could meet Myrtle Jenkins. She of the common sense. She would, Magda had promised me, be at Edenshaw since she helped out at the restaurant during busy periods. I was getting quite used to quiche now, though to be fair, they varied the ingredients of the salads sufficiently to make it seem like a new meal each time.

Magda had provided me with a desk in one of the archive rooms, which was nice, and Pamela, being next door, popped in from time to time. I availed myself of their kettle, providing the odd jar of instant coffee and biscuits in the spirit of co-operation, and was made to feel part of the family. I continued my long plough through stacks of letters from Charles's family in the US, coming across the occasional nugget. His family business was in Buffalo, in New York State, and Charles had been born not far from Niagara Falls. In the second half of the nineteenth century and early in the twentieth, Buffalo had been a great industrial centre, and it was clear from the letters – all post-war – that the business was still doing well. Charles's father, son of the Carr who founded the family china business in 1880, was obviously still a prominent citizen, as was Charles's elder brother Samuel who took it over in 1952. I sketched myself a family tree according to the information I was gathering both from the archives and from Magda. Born to parents Samuel and Edith, Charles had three siblings, Samuel (now dead), the younger sister Mary, and Walter, who had died young. As Mary was no longer in touch, that left me with the 'ancient cousin' whom Magda had mentioned, so far as the older generation was concerned. There were nephews and nieces, of course, one of whom, Samuel junior's son William, was the one still running the business, but their knowledge of Charles would be hearsay. None of them, rather to my relief, had any direct responsibility to the foundation, so there would not be family problems attached to the biography in the form of vetoes.

Except, possibly, from the 'ancient cousin' about whom I now knew more. He was a bad egg in the form of Cousin Luke, son of Edith's younger brother, Charles's Uncle Matthew. Matthew had been in the military and seen service in the First World War; Luke Casey had 'gone wild' as the family termed it, in rebellion against discipline. Luke had roved first the States, and then the world, living by charm, theft and good luck. He was known to turn up, claiming he was 'applying for a scholarship', but his scholarship was merely to study booze. He was about eighty now, and came less often, Pamela had told me. Magda always dealt with him and I could

91

understand why. One look at Magda, and anyone would be putty in her hands, even hardened bad eggs.

'I've got some good news, Lucia.'

I looked up to see Magda, looking stunning in a cream trouser suit, which immediately made me feel like Cinderella in my working clothes again, though I was sure she did not mean to.

'I'm ready for it.' I'd found nothing of interest so far this morning. The drawback was, of course, that it was hard to tell at this early stage what might be interesting, and what was definitely not, so I took care to read everything.

'I've found a publisher while you were away.'

'Oh, well done.' This was indeed good news and I hadn't, to be honest, expected it.

'It's a specialist one, as you predicted. Wilkins Jenner. Heard of them?'

'Only vaguely.' That wasn't surprising since art wasn't primarily my thing.

'They work from Canterbury, but they market all over the country. They do rather splendid art books, and quite scholarly. Very well produced.'

'Will *Charles Carr and The Happening*' – this was our working title – 'fit their list? Biographies are rather different from art monographs and the like.'

'Yes, they're excited about it. It could be the forerunner of a new list for them.'

'Although biographies do need a different

production approach, since the text has to carry equal weight if not more than the art reproductions.' I was still dubious.

'They can see that problem,' Magda explained, 'but they've recently taken on a wonderful freelance who leaps on problems like this with relish.'

'Are they happy with me as writer?'

'Yes, in principle though again it depends on the specimen chapters.' Magda continued to explain the financial arrangements which although they keenly interested me, since I have to live, I shall omit since they are boring to anyone else.

It all sounded too wonderful to be true. There had to be a catch, I thought, but the more she talked, I couldn't see where it lay. I worked well with Magda, I got on well with at least one of the trustees (Tony) and had a truce with another. The material for the biography seemed either available or within my reach. Now the business arrangements were falling into place. So where lay the catch? Maybe Cinderella was asking herself that as the pumpkin coach drew up outside the palace and she alighted for the ball.

I didn't have to wait even as long as Cinderella. The snag arrived right away. In fact, it must have been parking outside Eden-shaw House at that very moment. Magda left, only to come back a few minutes later with the aforementioned freelance whizz kid.

Wouldn't you just know?

It was Robin.

'Good God,' he said, as he walked through the door. I know Robin well, and I could see it was as much of a shock to him as it was to me.

'What are you doing here?' I asked. It was not very original but it got us through those vital seconds of assessment as what the hell to say next.

'Do you two know each other?' Magda asked, again not very originally, especially as it was all too clear that we did, and that on my part at least it was hardly welcome.

'We're old friends,' I said lightly. It was true enough, if not the entire truth.

Robin gave the lopsided grin that I remembered so well. 'So we are. How are you, Lucia? So you're the dynamic new writer they've found. I didn't know you were going in for biography?'

The coincidence of this unfortunate meeting was not so great as it might seem, save that I had thought Robin safely in Paris for ever. Robin's flair, after all, is producing books where text and illustrations have to dovetail perfectly in all respects, style, size, appearance, one complementing the other. There aren't many experts as good as Robin around, and if he had decided to return from Paris, he might naturally have taken up a freelance life. He would obviously steer clear of my usual publishers, but he could hardly have expected to find me here.

'I'm still doing my children's stuff,' I explained, 'but I thought I'd have a go at something new.' We were still filling in time, both wondering, I'm sure, how – and if – this would work out.

Magda sized up the situation perfectly, deciding that we would neither of us faint nor physically attack the other. 'Shall I leave you to chat about the book?'

Robin and I continued mentally prowling round each other, while I made him a cup of instant and fished a biscuit out of the tin.

'I can see you bought these,' he said. 'Short-bread is one of your trademarks.'

Robin tends to the casual. He stripped off his sweater, and leaned back in the chair. My chair actually – typical of Robin. He then eyed me thoughtfully. 'I wasn't intending ever to speak to you again, Lucia.'

'I'm not surprised,' I said honestly. 'What do we do now?'

'Go on working together?' he suggested. 'I can't afford to throw up jobs just because I've got a broken heart.'

'Do you still have one?' I was disconcerted, as I'm sure he intended.

'Of course. Are you still with him?'

'Who?'

'The prince you left me for.'

Quandary. Was it worse or better to tell him I didn't leave him for anyone else. I decided on the truth. 'You know me, Robin. The same old commitment problem.'

'In somebody with whom I'm proposing to work with over the next year or so, that might indeed be a problem.'

'No, it won't,' I said firmly. 'I'm committed at last.'

'Congratulations.' He looked rather bleak though.

'To Charles Carr,' I amplified. It was the truth, even if not the whole truth.

He cheered up. 'Your trouble, Lucia, is that you see endings, not people. You make facts fit the result you want, and it doesn't happen. Don't do the same with Charles Carr, will you?'

Is that what I did? Was my happy endings theory always going to end in disappointment for this reason? Would it happen again with David, if I looked only at where I wanted to go and not at him? But that was what being in love was, surely? I dispensed with question marks and struggled back to firm ground.

'This is too deep for me, Robin. Shall we talk about the book?'

'Let's,' he agreed.

It was odd being back working with Robin, and far from unpleasant, once the initial tension subsided. Had we met first and *then* worked together it might not have succeeded, but we had been working colleagues before we were lovers, and so it might, just might, be possible to slip back together in that respect. At the back of my mind was also, I admit, the craven thought that working with Robin would certainly be ballast against David, if he continued to hover just out of reach. On the other hand, I didn't want to fertilize any lingering seeds of love Robin might still have for me. Robin is not one to wear his heart on his sleeve. He is interesting to look at; he has a languorous grace as he moves – or a convoluted India rubber elasticity, whichever way one sees it – that sits well with the impression he likes to put over that life sits easily upon him. I wondered whether he had moved on emotionally as he had in physical distance in the last year.

He told me he had visited Edenshaw House to see Magda once before and had studied *The Happening*, both house and gardens, with her.

'What did you think?' I asked.

'I couldn't get a feeling for them, to be honest. It's all there, but somehow it didn't work for me. I'll have to get to grips with it, though, if I'm to work on it.'

I told him how I saw the double-sided love affair and about my going to Budapest, and to do him justice, Robin refrained from any personal remarks about the light and dark of love. For that I was very grateful and offered him quiche and salad lunch on me. He accepted graciously and too late I realized he would be there while Myrtle and I chatted. Oh well, it didn't matter, I thought, then realized how strange this was. We seemed to be getting back on to a work footing, at least, almost too quickly. We chatted over lunch about Paris, and about my latest books, carefully skirting round the personal. Then suddenly, as can happen, conversation dried up, and we caught each other's eye with a quick awareness that there was something still alive, something that still needed to be said.

We didn't say it. I knew this meant that it was merely postponed, but perhaps, I thought hopefully, whatever the 'it' was, I would then be able to cope with it. I couldn't now and nor obviously could Robin, for he rather too consciously glanced at his watch and said he had to be going.

After he'd left, I had no time even to reflect on what might lie ahead, for I was taken right back to Charles Carr, as Myrtle Jenkins came to join me, bearing two cups of coffee.

I took to Myrtle immediately. She was small and dark, with intelligent darting eyes. She was a sparrow of a woman, and I could quite see why Charles Carr had valued her. Nevertheless she was guarded, as if, quite rightly, she was summing me up. I suppose I would do the same if I were in any sense an executor of someone's reputation, and someone of my age came strolling along to write a biography which might or might not correctly reflect the person I knew.

I took notes by hand on this occasion. I sensed I had to feel my way with Myrtle, and in any case I could talk to her again – unlike Gréta Öszödy.

'Sixteen years,' she answered in response to my obvious initial question. I asked her if she could describe the kind of man Charles was, but she either couldn't or wouldn't, and continued to play the humble housekeeper. 'A fair master he was. Always considerate.'

'Did you live in?' I had to get through this barrier.

'No. At the lodge where I do now. My husband's a gardener here. Anyway, the master liked painting all hours, and sculpting. He wouldn't want anyone else wandering round the house. I said to him once he needed better light, seeing him working away long after the light had gone on winter days, let alone the evenings, but he said no, it was all inside his head, and it was that that painted the light.'

I made a note of that. 'Interesting,' I said. 'Did he have visitors?'

'Of course he did.' She looked at me as if I were half-witted. 'He went up to London, he had folks here. Not often to stay, though.'

This wasn't the reclusive Charles Carr I had built up in my mind. 'Would that be his family from America, as well as his social life? Cousin Luke Casey, for example? Charles Carr wasn't married, was he? Or in any relationships?'

'Sorry. There's no dirt I can give you, and you can ask Mrs Magda about Luke.' It was friendly enough, but I kicked myself for going too far too soon. Nevertheless, it was the first indication that there was a real woman in there somewhere.

'You may not believe this, but I don't want dirt,' I replied honestly. 'I want the truth, and it's clear from his art there must have been emotional entanglements in his life. I need to

99

know whether they had ended when he came here, or whether he had others.'

She relented a little. 'Nothing I saw here. And it wasn't really a social life, just business visits and the occasional friend. The nearest the house got to having a social life was when Mrs Magda came over. The whole place cheered up, especially when she got married. They had the reception here.'

I hadn't seen any photographs of a wedding, though I'd been through such albums as there were. Magda herself would have some, I supposed. Anyway, that was a detail.

'There were women after him,' Myrtle volunteered, 'but they took one look at what he'd painted down here, and fled. Mr Carr used to laugh. He'd done *The Happening* before I came, of course, and he was into his mischief stage.'

She began to talk a little more freely about Charles Carr, and it became clear he had become as much a friend as an employer by the time he died. 'It helped me being an outsider,' she explained. 'He didn't have to talk art, just about normal things.'

'Such as?'

She considered. 'Politics. He used to have Hungarians come down to see him from time to time, those who had come over after the '56 uprising. Sometimes Americans. There was one Hungarian he especially liked, László he called him. He was about Charles's age, and had known him in the war, I gathered. I used to hear them talking about it.'

Oh bliss. Another first-class witness to interview.

'Do you know where I can get in touch with him?'

'He died, not long before Mr Carr. Mr Carr went to the States for the funeral. First time he'd gone there all the time I knew him.'

It was a disappointment, but I could ask Magda about him. There might be a family who could help. 'What else did he talk about with you, Mrs Jenkins?' There might be more nuggets to come.

She considered this. 'Food too, he liked his food. Used to grow a lot here, with Mike's help – my husband. He had a liking for American dishes, and I used to cook him a Thanksgiving Dinner now and then, with a nice pumpkin pie.'

'Did he talk to you about Budapest and his time there?'

'Never. Sometimes he'd talk about goulash, and say I never made it properly. These English recipes weren't the real goulash. He made us one himself once. I didn't think much of it, to be honest. More like soup than a square meal. Anyway, that's why he liked being with Mike and me, because he could live normally. Live in the present, not keep diving back like he does in his art from what I gather. He'd had enough of that. We were the only future he had, if you see what I mean.'

I did, and Myrtle impressed me. Fortunately she seemed to have warmed to me slightly, which was good, since she told me I could always pop in to the lodge if I had other questions, and she might have one or two pictures to show me. I pricked up my ears at that.

Even with what little she had told me so far, and the family life I had begun to build up from the archives, I was beginning to get a picture of Charles Carr before and after Budapest. The later Carr had been moulded by Budapest, either by the war or by Gréta Öszödy. I had deliberately held back from asking myself or Magda too many questions about her, such as whether Carr had known about his daughter by Gréta. If so, it still seemed odd he had never tried to visit her, in the later years of Soviet control at least. Hungary had the most open borders of the Soviet bloc, as the century progressed. Perhaps he hadn't known about her. However, Gréta would tell me everything, or so Magda had promised. So I decided to wait for that. Not long now.

When I returned to the house, I found Robin still there, though on the point of leaving.

'What now?' he asked casually.

'I'll get in touch after I've been to Budapest and have some idea of the timetable. I'm hoping I'll come back with photographs and we'll have to discuss them in relation to art reproductions.' I was aiming at brisk efficiency.

'I've already started that with Magda. Just

in principle of course, in case the whole thing...' He stopped.

'Falls through?' I finished dryly. 'Don't worry, it won't.'

'I'll chat it through with her again.'

It was the way he said it more than the exclusion that his words suggested. He was falling for her and in a big way. I bit my immediate reaction back, and refrained from pointing out that sighing after Magda really was a fairytale illusion. Magda was a princess in an ivory tower of marriage, child and husband, flying far higher than Robin could ever achieve.

Or was, I asked myself, that jealousy on my part in that I didn't want to let go of my former lovers? No, I decided. I *had* let go, and that was that.

'Of course,' I answered smoothly. 'I meant the extra photographs I might get from the Countess Öszödy which, as she was Carr's model, will have to be central to the book.'

Robin rewarded me with a knowing smile, and left.

I found I was more shaken by this encounter than I had expected. I no longer loved Robin I told myself, as the words of Charles Carr's letters danced before my eyes, and perhaps I had never had truly loved him. Oh yes I had, I was then forced to admit. *But I didn't now.* Seeing him after all this time had convinced me of that. So why was I so trembly? I would be seeing him again, but as a colleague, and I supposed that had been bound to happen some time, so why not now? After a year, our relationship should be well and truly sorted, and it had been. In two weeks, I told myself, I would be going to Budapest with David. Or correction, accompanied by David. Whether I would be truly 'with' him remained to be seen. After all, I didn't even know why he thought it was so vital that Magda did not know about his coming with me.

I checked into the bed and breakfast, and strolled down to the Crook and Harrow pub, which I had been told by Magda did very good food. I was halfway through my chicken basque when David walked in. It was the second coincidence of the day, and again one I supposed I could have expected, since it was probably the nearest pub to his home, judging by the welcome he received at the bar. His back was to me, and I waited for him to turn round. This coincidence was a great deal more pleasant than the earlier one.

I forced myself to remain calmly in my seat, continuing my meal which was indeed very good. At last The Back turned round and his gaze promptly fell on me. He frowned.

'Lucia?'

'Come and join me,' I offered, waving a gracious hand, adding a mental 'for ever'.

Rather unwillingly he did so, and belatedly it occurred to me that this might look as if I was stalking his territory, whereas it had been pure chance that the B and B was nearby. 'I take it you're here on Carr research?'

'I am. I met Myrtle Jenkins today.'

He seemed to thaw a little. 'Magda told me that she had someone from the prospective publishers coming over.'

'She did. The book designer, whom I'll need to work closely with.' I hesitated. 'Have you met him?'

'No.'

'It turned out to be someone I know. Knew rather. He used to be the designer at my regular publishers.'

He cocked an eye and I wondered if the tone in my voice had betrayed anything. If so, all he said was: 'Is he good?'

'Very good. His name is Robin Holman.'

His face changed. 'Isn't he your...'

'Go on,' I said evenly when he broke off, wondering how the hell he had known this. Only one way: Tony.

'Former partner. I'm sorry. Sorry, shouldn't have mentioned it.'

'Why not? It was over long ago.'

I flattered myself he looked relieved, but he might just have been pleased to see his spaghetti arrive.

'Tony mentioned him once.'

'Did he indeed? I wonder what context that was in.'

'General Tonyness.'

I caught his eye and we both laughed in our joint acknowledgement of Tony's little weaknesses. Then we talked, we laughed, we once again did all those things that people who are mutually attracted do, our body language coincided, our talk was of nothing but everything. I now discovered he liked old Bogart films, he knew I disliked *Star Wars*, he hated liver, I liked anchovies, he'd been to Paestum and glory of glories so had I. The pub was busy around us, but there were just we two in it, so far as we were concerned. When we strolled out of the pub at closing time, it was into a dark world which was a cocoon of warmth.

'Can I give you a lift?'

'It's only a few hundred yards.'

'I'll walk you home. Unless you prefer to jump in the car?'

'Walking is fine.' So it was on a mild September night, with the stars up above in a clear sky and the man I most undoubtedly loved at my side. When we reached my B and B, I stopped. 'I'm glad we met tonight.'

'So am I,' he said. He was very close to me and I know Budapest was in both our minds.

I was glad this wasn't my home. I might so easily have suggested we went in to 'talk about Budapest'. And, I dared to think, that had we been in his car, he might have driven me with him back to his home. It was that kind of night. He didn't even kiss me, but the wall between us had dissolved and only a word was holding us back.

Neither of us said it. Instead came his gentle: 'I'll ring you about meeting at Gatwick.'

'Thank you for walking me home.'

He gave a nod, and I knew he watched me

as I unlocked the door with the key I'd been given, and went inside alone.

December 1941

'My darling, you look so very splendid.'

Charles grinned. 'Gréta, you know very well that everyone's eyes will be on you.' His certainly were. The dark satin evening dress, the fur coat against the winter winds and the small tiara on her head.

Gréta purred in her husky voice, 'Let them. Mine will be on you.'

'They should be on Miklós this evening. Remember this is the Royal Palace, and the regent won't be that understanding.' Charles was always conscious that Gréta's husband was an adviser to Admiral Horthy, and though the situation between Gréta and Charles was well known and accepted by Miklós, who was twenty years Gréta's senior, formalities should be observed.

'Miklós is. He likes you, Charles, because you talk boring old politics so well.'

Everyone talked politics now, more specifically the politics of the war. Even though Hungary had officially remained neutral, it had provided forces to help Germany's invasion of Russia last summer. The regent might try to keep Hungary out of the war, but it was a battle already lost under the new pro- Nazi premier. The pro-Allied aristocracy were keeping very quiet nowadays even at receptions such as this, given by the regent in his apartments in the Royal Palace. Horthy himself was pro-British, or at least pro-neutrality. He even did what he could to help individual refugees, who were treated as guests rather than prisoners. How much longer could that continue as German influence grew?

Charles saw all this with a detachment born of his love for Gréta. All the while the United States stayed out of the war, he could remain here with her, her acknowledged escort. On evenings such as this Miklós accompanied them, and Charles was present in his official role, but it did not feel that way. When he was with Gréta, everything was coloured by her mesmerizing presence. It had all begun with that painting. He could not get those eyes right: he tried but the depths behind them eluded him. Gréta herself had solved that problem.

'Come to my arms, Charles, and then you can truly paint me.'

And he did, and now understood what he was trying to achieve in paint, although he had never quite done so. In a way he did not want to, for, as it was, during each meeting in love when he lay entwined in her arms on the silken sheets of her bed, he felt filled with the sure knowledge that at last he could define her mystery. Yet each time she sat for him, her eyes yearning towards him, his brush never quite conveyed what his eyes told him. The essence of Gréta herself eluded him, as perhaps it should. Uncovering the mystery would change its nature in paint. The quest made great art, not the solution.

As Miklós moved in the highest circles, Charles was able to report to his minister what the latest attitude of the all-powerful aristocracy was. This was useful since the minister was fed only the official line, but Charles knew the unofficial. Charles got on well with Miklós, and Gréta's name was rarely spoken between them.

'We are diplomats,' he had said disarmingly to Charles once. 'We know what life is, what happens around us, but it is our job to look down on it from a distance to observe, so that we may act in our countries' best interests.'

As a fledgling of twenty-four when he had first come to Budapest with the US foreign service, Charles had felt flattered by Miklós's comparison with himself, and it was only later that he realized he spoke of more than international affairs. Charles did not estimate his own future in the foreign service to be very high, he was good but not that good. Miklós's patronage was an asset.

Life in Budapest increased its frenetic headiness as each political step took Hungary further towards the abyss; it was a world that carried on regardless of the suffering so near to them in Europe, the death, the carnage and most of all the threat to the Jews. Charles saw it as the giddiness of Aesop's grasshopper blindly playing on in the face of the approaching winter. It hadn't hit Hungary yet, but it lay like a dark shadow beyond its frontiers, which no one would openly admit existed.

Charles was humble, so far as Gréta was concerned; he could not understand what it was that held her to him; he thought perhaps it was his power over paint, which she believed to be greater than it was. Maybe just his love. He ceased to wonder why as she crooned to him old Hungarian love songs in their bed, and told him tales of the Magyar history, taking him far back into romance and adventure till the realities of modern Europe receded. Each time he beheld her white body stretched sensuously out on the black sheets, he fell into an ecstasy of love beside which everything else seemed immaterial.

Their car wound up the hillside and through the narrow streets of the old quarter of Budapest called the Vár to the far end where the Buda Castle lay. Gréta lived not on the Buda Hills, as did many of the aristocracy, but in Pest, and to drive across the Danube at night with the palace so visible on the Buda citadel was an experience to be cherished. Receptions in the summer would be on the terrace overlooking the river, and even in early December looking down on the vast river was an inspiring sight.

As they walked through the courtyard to the regent's apartments, Charles paused to look at the Mathias fountain. He did so every time he came here, but never knew quite why. There was little memorable about the flamboyant 1904 sculpture by Alojos Stróbl save its sheer size. It was based on an old legend, Gréta had told him, of which there were several versions. Good King Mathias, who ruled Hungary in the fifteenth century, was outstanding as a Renaissance figure who cultivated art as well as war. One day when hunting in the forest, a peasant girl fell in love with him and he with her. But she did not recognize him as the king and when she discovered his identity she died of a broken heart knowing her love could never be fulfilled. The king surmounted the triangular shape of the fountain with his courtiers beneath him, and at the base the peasant girl sat on the right. On the left was a cowled figure with a falcon on his wrist. Charles felt a flicker of interest, as a question came into his mind but it vanished as Gréta spoke.

'Sad, my dear, is it not?'

Charles felt her arm touch his, and agreed it was.

'How lucky we are, Charles.'

'I'm the peasant and you're the king in our case,' he teased her.

'No,' she had replied gravely, 'I meant that there is nothing to prevent our love.'

The merest touch of her body, those dark eyes fixed on him, and he wanted nothing more than for the evening to end so that it might begin – in her arms. Only tonight, as he looked at the fountain wondering what the elusive question had been, there was little chance of the evening's ending in her arms since Miklós was with them. Charles would observe the formalities, have a drink with Miklós and return to his home, an apartment near the legation in the Lendvay utca not far from the City Park and the West railway station. A long way from this grandeur.

'We must remember this evening,' Gréta said suddenly. 'István,' she turned to her chauffeur who was still waiting, a respectful distance away, 'you have the camera?'

Gréta positioned herself between Charles and Miklós, taking their arms, and the moment was recorded. Did photographs carry interpretations like paintings? Charles wondered. Or did they just record facts? In fifty years' time would the world look at Gréta's portrait, or at their photograph? Would they see into the heart of both, or neither?

This evening boded to be like other such receptions, all polite words on the outside, and on the inside the real business being done. Charles was surprised therefore when the regent singled him out.

'Your Excellency.' He bowed. 'I am honoured to be here.'

Admiral Horthy looked tired, Charles thought, as though he too could see doom approaching and no way to prevent it. 'Mr Carr, may I present Mr Walter Manning. An American like yourself.'

'Glad to meet you,' Manning said, and Charles reciprocated. The admiral left them together and Charles, slightly surprised,

112

wondered what might be the reason that he had wanted him to meet this odd-looking character. He was in his thirties, Charles guessed, but his clothes, though correct evening attire, were too large for his lean frame, and bore all the hallmarks of a Hungarian tailor. No problem, there were hundreds of American civilians in Budapest. But this one was different. He was Horthy's guest – and he was British, unless Charles was much mistaken.

He was right.

'I was caught up in the Polish mess,' Manning explained laconically. So that explained his clothes, and something more.

'How did you get here?'

'Stayed around for a while, then walked.'

'Stayed around' had a familiar ring. No straightforward civilian would risk 'staying around'. This was a journalist at least, and more probably in intelligence.

'Why does the regent want me to meet you,' Charles asked him, 'and not the British staff?'

'That'll come. From what I gather, the British won't be in Hungary much longer. I'm hoping to fasten on their coat-tails to get home. Or maybe yours. I'm not fussy.'

Charles listened while Manning talked of the Nazis' treatment of the Jews in Poland and elsewhere. Of the camps set up and of the ghettos. Hitherto enforced migration had been the policy but Manning now talked of experiments on speedier methods of disposal in sealed vans with gas pumped in.

'It's coming, believe me,' he concluded.

'So why me?' Charles asked quietly. This was what they had feared, but to have it confirmed was chilling.

'The admiral wants me to tell you about my walk.'

So that was it. The regent was hoping whatever message Manning had would be relayed to the States. Horthy would know he couldn't involve the US minister in this, owing to his delicate political position, but he could ensure he was kept informed through a junior official. Charles listened very hard as Manning explained what was going on in occupied Europe, the labour camps, the concentration camps, and the increasing danger to Jews, now that emigration was no longer possible for them. Not, at least, to the safety of non-Nazi lands.

'What did he want?' Gréta asked afterwards, slipping her arm through his. 'You looked very engrossed.'

'My official face, I'm afraid. He was just another dull old diplomat,' Charles replied. He must keep his two lives apart, however hard it was with Gréta at his side.

The following day, 6 December, Charles heard the news that Britain and Hungary were officially at war. Hardly had the minister finished discussing the implications of this for the US Legation, when the devastating news came through that the Japanese had struck the US fleet at Pearl Harbor.

'This will bring America into the war; it has to,' was Charles's immediate grim reaction. So it did, as far as Japan was concerned, but the question of war against Nazi Germany remained on a knife edge for four more days, until Hitler himself decided the matter by declaring war on the US. Hungary followed suit. The minister told his staff the legation would be closing immediately, and that the regent had already paid his farewells to him.

All that night, Charles lay awake wondering where his duty lay. To return home or to stay here unofficially, go underground. He knew what he desperately wanted to do, to stay here with Gréta. To leave her seemed an impossibility too great to contemplate, and yet war had to take precedence. Could there be a role for him here that outweighed his duty to return home? The regent was a wily old fox. Had he, in introducing him to Manning, been hinting he might indeed be of more use to his country here in Budapest, than in the US itself?

Six

Immediately our taxi from the airport drove into Budapest I knew I was going to like this city. To be more accurate, it was Pest we had entered, for Buda lay the other side of the Danube. As that was where our hotel lay, we crossed the majestic river by bridge seeing the Buda Palace on the hill in all its splendour, and a huge monument of a figure waving a victory palm high on the hill.

'The Liberation Monument,' David told me. 'It was originally put there by Admiral Horthy for his son who died in a plane crash, but the Soviets hijacked the memorial and stuck a victory palm there rather than a propeller. Now it's a testament to freedom.'

'Changing times,' I remarked. 'It's a good omen for the future.'

We had decided to give ourselves a day of sightseeing on the morrow before we met Gréta, so that I could orientate myself in the city, see where Charles would have worked, the streets he would have walked, and get accustomed to the whole feel of the place. It was a good idea for all sorts of reasons, not least that I still did not know whether David was becoming reconciled to the biography or whether by coming with me he hoped to throw obstacles in my path to stop me. It was an unpleasant thought and one which I decided to ignore.

Our first evening was idyllic. I'm glad it was, otherwise I might not have had the strength to go on when trouble came. It gave me a rock to remind me I was in love with David, in love with Budapest and in love with my project. What more could I ask? It was such a good evening, laughing at the friendly, haphazard service in the restaurant, and attempting to interpret the menu. The English translations were provided but sounded so ghastly that it was almost better to struggle with the Hungarian and take pot luck. David knew a little Hungarian, it turned out, but I was confined to my tourists' handbook. I had been greatly relieved to hear that Gréta spoke very good English. Her husband had been pro-British, since he had been at school in England.

When I met David at breakfast the next day, I was bright-eyed and bushy-tailed waiting for the excitement to begin. The bright eyes were not because we had spent the night in each other's arms, for we had retreated decorously to our single rooms. With our three full days here, I had a joyous sense of plenty of time and that my steps were firmly planted on the golden stairway to happy-ever-after.

An hour later they were firmly planted on the hundreds of steps up and down to

Várhegy, the Castle Hill, or the Vár for short.

'I can see why they chose this spot for the palace,' I panted, as we finally hauled ourselves up to the Buda Castle.

'There's a lift actually.'

'Now you tell me,' I groaned.

'I thought you liked climbing uphill,' David joked.

'Mentally,' I replied with dignity. 'And I hope we aren't going to find the monsters that Charles so carefully painted in his cottage at the top of the hill.'

He took my hand. 'I don't think so.'

'You're not sure?'

He didn't answer and I wondered why. We decided to stroll round the palace and its environs before tackling the museums that the palace now houses. While I was delighting in the sunshine and David's company (though not in that order) something suddenly caught my eye. I turned – and saw what it was.

'David,' was all I managed to croak. By the palace wall in the courtyard was one of the largest fountains in sheer height that I had ever seen, but that was not what had fixed my attention. 'Isn't that the fountain in Edenshaw's garden?'

'Yes.'

It was too brief a reply not to alert me that there was something odd here. 'Did you know it was a copy of this when you showed it to me?'

'I thought I remembered it.'

'You didn't say so.'

'I wasn't sure. Now I see it, I agree, it's the same.'

'Then it must have been Charles Carr who sculpted the copy at Edenshaw. It would have been too much of a coincidence for a previous owner to have seen it in Budapest and fancied having it in his garden.'

'I suppose so.'

I hardly heard what he said. I was too busy rummaging through my *Rough Guide*. 'It says the fountain depicts a legend about King Mathias. Wasn't he one of the real goodies of Hungarian history? Sixteenth century or so?'

'Yes. Fifteenth actually. He had a formidable wife by the name of Beatrice, who astounded all her guests by having hot and cold running water in the Buda Palace. There's still said to be traces of the fights they had. Chips in the wall, and that kind of thing, when they threw things at each other. Or at least she did. She had a temper. It was Mathias who built the Renaissance castle, though it's been rebuilt and restored a lot since then.'

'No wonder he's got a fountain as a memorial.' I tried to recall what little I'd read before we came here. 'Even if he was a battered husband, he still managed to keep his end up though, didn't he, dispensing justice everywhere, fighting off invaders, encouraging the arts.'

'With a few black spots on his character, yes.'

'Legends can ignore black spots,' I said blithely, reading on. 'It says the legend is that King Mathias went hunting one day, and met a peasant girl called Szép Ilonka who fell in love with him. When she later found out who he was, she realized there was going to be no happy ending and died of a broken heart.' I looked at the fountain with its five figures. 'The guide says that the story was recorded by the court scribbler who was Italian. That's the one with the falcon.' I pointed to the cowled figure at the bottom left whom I remembered seeing in Charles's version.

'There you are, fame comes at last for all writers,' David joked, but he seemed ill at ease.

'David,' I said, determined to get to the bottom of this, 'you must have seen this when you came to Budapest before. Didn't you wonder why Charles Carr put it in his garden?'

'No, I told you. I couldn't be sure it's the same. I didn't remember it clearly – it's hardly a Michelangelo, is it?' He was clearly anxious to be moving on.

'All the more reason for it to have meant something to Charles,' I persisted. 'And it can't have been to remind him of his own love affair, because Gréta most certainly wasn't a peasant girl. If anything, I gather from Magda it would have been the other way round. Charles was the struggling diplomat-cum-artist, she was the out of reach aristocrat.'

'Why does it have to have a meaning?'

120

David sounded nettled. 'Charles probably just liked it.'

'Charles doesn't sound the sort of man to have done *anything* without a meaning in his garden.'

Now I could definitely see a flash of anger, and I was puzzled since I'd thought we were merely having a straightforward discussion. 'We don't really know anything about Charles,' he snapped – stupidly, I thought. Why was he feeling so cornered?

'*You* must know,' I said steadily. 'Shall we get a coffee?' We needed to get away from here, and we walked to a bar on the terrace, overlooking the Danube. It was a breathtaking view, but I didn't let him off the hook. 'You knew him, David, yet you haven't talked about him very much.'

'I was only just down from university when I met him again in 1990. He'd finished *The Happening* long since, and the little he was still working on was merely fun stuff.' He avoided looking at me.

'You said *again*. You'd met him before?'

'Occasionally. I grew up round there, and my parents got to know him a little, and so I did too.'

He was more in command of himself now, and I got the impression the more questions I tossed him, the more deftly would he bat them all back – apparently answered, but telling me little.

Tough. I was going on. 'He must have talked about his past life.'

'Of his early life in America, yes. Even a bit about the New York art scene after the war when he was building up his business. But never about Budapest.'

'You're an art historian. Didn't you ever ask him about that period?'

'Of course. But I was little more than a student still, full of pompous ideas and more eager to hear myself talk about my own opinions than to listen. You listen – and hear – what you want to at that age. I was busy slotting him into the art scene of the post-war period, shooting my mouth off about action painting, CoBrA, Art Informel and so forth.'

'How old are you now?'

He managed a grin. 'Thirty-four.'

'Then you were well into your twenties when he died.'

'Lucia–' he began to stir his coffee very deliberately – 'I seem to be sending out wrong messages to you.'

I went cold. What was this?

'I haven't changed my mind about the biography,' he continued. 'I still think it's a bad idea.'

'Then what,' I asked quietly, 'are you doing here? Is this why you didn't want me to tell Magda you were coming?'

He hesitated. 'Yes. And now we are here – I don't know whether you'll like this – I don't want to come to see Gréta Öszödy with you. Do you mind going alone?'

I was busy trying to take this in. 'No, I don't mind that,' I replied honestly. 'You might

122

have been a help over steering questions in the right direction, but on the other hand I might do better without distraction.' What I couldn't see was why and I had to know. He should have been as excited as I was at the chance to talk to Charles's model.

'Why did you come, David,' I continued, 'if not to meet Gréta again?'

He gave a sort of half smile. 'Because I wanted to.'

'What kind of answer is that?' I asked crossly.

'The truth. I wanted to come with you. Let me change the emphasis a bit. I wanted to come with *you*.'

The trouble with happy endings is that one has to be very sure that that's what they are and not a snare and a delusion, so I asked carefully, 'Me, the biographer, or me the—'

'You, Lucia. And a little bit the biography.'

I wanted to sing, to shout, to dance. Here I was at the top of the hill and there were no monsters to be seen.

What I did do was say weakly, 'I'm so glad.'

Luckily he thought that was funny and we both roared with laughter, giggling in a slightly crazy way. I know what we both wanted to do then, but here in the middle of the tourist part of Budapest there was little we could do to satisfy it. Instead he held my hand, then kissed it. We paid up and left our table, and he kissed me by the wall overlooking the Danube. Even the gypsy violinist who promptly rushed up to play *The Merry*

Widow waltz at our side seemed romantic. David munificently gave him more forints than he could possibly have expected, and we strolled off hand in hand, slightly dizzy from the exalted heights of being lovers.

We made the most of our new-found certainty. We lunched, we did a few tourist things, but mostly we walked, we talked and we kissed. When eventually we reached the hotel again, we smiled at each other, went into my room and became real lovers.

It was two hours later that I began to laugh.

'What's so funny?' David asked lovingly, stroking my right breast.

'I never asked you if you were married.' At that moment it seemed the funniest thing on earth to have forgotten.

'No.' He didn't laugh though. 'I was once briefly, but not now. How about you?'

'You know I haven't been. Tony must have told you. I have this problem about committing.' What a stupid thing to say now when committing to David seemed the most desirable thing on earth.

'I do, too,' he murmured. If it was meant to comfort me, it didn't. 'So, we're well suited.' And his hand moved from my breast to an even more interesting place.

Later we went out to dinner to an open air restaurant David said he remembered. It was in the old fishermen's quarter below the Castle Hill; we sat in the garden, with music playing and stars in our eyes. And I never once thought of the biography.

By the morning Charles had made his decision. He would travel with the legation staff as they left Budapest, but would take the next bus back and officially 'disappear'. With his nationality there would be no hope of getting a visa at the Kheok, the sinister building on the Ferenc József quay, which held the power of granting permission to stay – or of instant detention for those it distrusted. The latter would be the certain outcome in his case. Where to stay was more in doubt. He was sure that he wouldn't be the only American civilian to take the risk of staying in the city, since internment would be the worst thing they might face. At present, that was. If the Nazis strengthened their hold it might be a different matter. Charles, however, was a known face, so the less he advertised his presence the better – especially in view of his new role here, which essentially boiled down to 'spy'. Here in Budapest he could be an invaluable source of intelligence for the Allies if he could work out a way of getting information out of the country. He had thought a lot about what Manning had said about the plight of the Jews in Europe, and foresaw that the US with its big Jewish population would need eyes and ears in the centre of Europe.

'You must stay with us, Charles,' Gréta

naturally declared, and Miklós was equally pressing. For a day or two while he sorted out his possessions and closed down his own apartment he did stay with them. Their palace – many grand houses here seemed to be palaces – was on the Vilmakirályné utca, a beautiful tree-lined street leading to the huge City Park with its fairytale castle, museums, monuments, and zoo. It was a fair distance from Downtown Pest, and the areas which he usually frequented. He wanted nothing more than to remain near Gréta, for he knew now that heart and soul he was an artist and his future was bound up with her. Were it not for the war, he would forget his other career, but now he had no such choice.

After two days he knew he must force himself to move from the Öszödy palace. He was recognized one evening, and was stopped in the entrance hall by a known supporter of the Nazi prime minister.

'Charles Carr, are you not?'

He replied in his now fluent Hungarian that his questioner must be mistaken and broke the news to Gréta that he must move instantly.

'But why?' Gréta lamented.

'I'm an American,' he replied simply. 'I have to do war service like anyone else, and this is how I'm going to do it.'

'Then let me help you. We have influence—'

'You can't, Gréta. It's too risky with Miklós in the position he's in. You have to remain above suspicion whoever is in power.'

Reluctantly she accepted this. '*Kedvesem*, I shall be your eyes and ears in society,' she promised. 'We shall make a plan how to meet.'

Charles agreed, for he knew the die was cast. He must go to earth, like the hunted fox he soon might be. If he were seen, and if the Nazis were ever to occupy Hungary, then he had little doubt he would now be high on the list for rooting out – which as an enemy civilian agent could mean death, and at the very least the Margit prison, from which few emerged.

László was the answer. They had formed a close friendship, one that Charles was sure surmounted politics. Premiers changed regularly, László had said, and one must adapt to each new face, if one was to remain at one's job, yet still serve the greater interest of the country. That's what diplomacy meant, but nevertheless he too had to safeguard his position. He was ready at all times to go, especially since his fiancée, Katie, was Jewish. Before the war, Charles recalled, they had all laughed over the episode when the regent had confronted the then prime minister, a rabid pro-Nazi, who had declared that one drop of Jewish blood was enough to poison a character and patriotism. The regent produced evidence that the prime minister himself had Jewish blood, which was such a shock that the premier fainted and was replaced by another man. Times were harder now, and one no longer laughed at such stories.

Charles talked over his position with László, and it was Katie who had come up with a solution.

'You could live in the same block as my family, Charles. Wear Hungarian clothes and you can be a cousin up from the country. There is a small empty apartment on the top floor above them.'

He leapt at this idea. 'But I would need papers...'

'There are ways,' Katie said simply, exchanging a glance with László.

Charles told no one of his new home in Holló utca, a little street behind the synagogue, and close to where the Semmelweiss family ran a stationery business in Kazinczy utca. Not even Gréta. She was not pleased, but he was adamant. 'Very well,' she reluctantly agreed, 'then I shall employ you to be our painter – our house painter, if you wish,' she laughed.

Charles grinned. 'I'd rather paint you than your house.' Gréta, the elusive Eve, the eternal woman, and yet so warm, so much his. He hadn't yet got his new papers, and had no idea what his 'occupation' would be. He now knew what he would in reality be doing. Under his diplomatic status, he had had dealings with all the other legations in Budapest. Those of the neutral countries would remain open and there must be, he had reasoned, ways of persuading them to unofficially pass his information to their home countries whence it could reach the USA. Gréta would help him with her contacts, and that meant he could meet her and love her. Even in war, love would find its way.

* * *

The Countess Gréta Öszödy lived in Pest on the first floor of a luxurious apartment in a mansion on what was now the Városligéti fasor. Once (Magda had filled me in) this whole mansion had been theirs, but now everything was different. Even the name of the street had been changed since the time when Charles Carr had been here. I took a taxi there from the hotel, so that I could muse on my surroundings rather than where the nearest bus stop might be. David and I had crossed the Danube yesterday, chiefly to see where the US Legation had once been – the present US Embassy was very much further towards the Danube not far from the Hungarian parliament. I tried to imagine Charles Carr in this building, but it told me little. The few photographs of him in America at the time shortly before he came to Budapest had shown a tall, fairly thin, serious-looking young man, intelligent, and, I thought, a romantic. The artist of *The Happening*, however, had not been a romantic. Had the war years changed him so much, or had it been his love for Gréta that changed him so greatly?

As I approached the former Öszödy palace

129

– much changed, I imagined – I disciplined myself into the need to remember that Gréta was an old lady of ninety, and that I had to gear my questions accordingly, for her voice and stamina might be limited and give out at a crucial moment. Playing by ear was going to be important.

The front door to the house was open, so I walked in and up the central stairs to the first floor. The apartments were ranged round the staircase, but I was thrown by the fact that the Hungarian way of counting floors didn't seem to correspond with mine, and by the time I'd discovered that the countess's apartment was on the next floor up, I was well and truly flustered. Not a good beginning for a prospective biographer who needed to be in control. An elderly maid or companion opened the door, and I wondered how that had worked out in the Soviet era. I suspected that money as usual had talked and there must, I thought cynically, have been a great deal of money for Gréta to have survived first the Second World War, then forty-odd years of Soviet occupation and influence with some wealth at least intact.

I was shown into an apartment of un-ostentatious luxury. The large drawing room into which I was ushered had paintings whose obvious value I could only guess at. How had those been kept all these years? Her husband must have been a very clever diplomat, and since, I presumed, he was no longer alive, she must be worldly wise as well. Where, I wondered, did Charles Carr fit in with this husband? I wondered how I could tactfully ask a ninety-year-old lady whether she had ever had children by her husband as well as her lover. Another question that I decided to play by ear.

At first I could not see her. She was almost buried in a wing chair with its back to me and in the end it was not sight that drew me to her, but a sense of presence emanating from her that compelled me to walk towards her. That sounds strange, I know, but it happened, and afterwards, as I learned more of her, I was no longer surprised.

'Come here, Miss Cooper. Do not be afraid. Old age is not a catching disease, though it visits us all soon enough.'

I came. Her voice was husky, but unusually young for her age, and still had the traces of a musical lilt that must have wowed Budapest society for decades. Including Charles Carr. I sat down where she indicated, in the chair opposite her, and looked full at Gréta Öszödy, Charles Carr's great love. His model for *The Happening*.

She was tiny, immaculate, not in black as the stereotype I had pictured her, but in a deep rose-pink two-piece, above which shone silver hair. She was tiny with age, and she was wrinkled, but the dark eyes that studied me so closely did not show weariness with life, but a sharp interest. She was half smiling at me, displaying the same unconscious charm that Magda possessed, as though I, and I

131

alone, were the most important thing in her life. The hand that rested on the arm of her chair was wrinkled and spotted with age, adorned with rings that would have made Cartier's eyes glaze over. I wondered how – then quickly pulled my thoughts back. I was here to find out about Charles Carr, not how Gréta Öszödy lived now.

'I am glad to meet you, Miss Cooper.'

'Lucia,' I said impulsively, not knowing what Hungarian etiquette was in this respect. It seemed to be acceptable.

'Magda has told me about you, Lucia. And in particular that you are to write my dear Charles's biography.'

'With your help, if I may.'

'That will be yours, of course. Tell me, Lucia, have you ever been in love, truly in love?'

The question took me by surprise but I was happy enough to answer it. 'I am,' I told her truthfully, for a moment back to the bliss of David's arms.

'So much in love that the world lights up with his presence, and trembles when he speaks, one's feet are merely instruments to take you to him, and that all the love poems in the world were written just for you and for him?'

It was extraordinary to hear an old woman speak so, remembering and reliving her past.

As if she read my thoughts, she continued: 'One does not forget. Neither one's body nor one's heart.' Her voice seemed to become stronger as she spoke, and I was struck dumb in awe. Had I felt that about Robin? Did I about David? About David I had no doubts – but then, so once I might have believed I felt about Robin. I could not remember. But Gréta did when recalling Charles Carr.

'Will you talk to me about Charles?' I asked gently. 'I promise that I will not betray you if you do so. I will record it faithfully.' I thought of what Robin had said about my seeing the end rather than the facts and vowed that would not be true of this book.

Gréta's face lit up, and there was a warmth between us. 'Do you know, Lucia, I have never told the story in full. Not even to Magda, or my darling Klára, Charles's daughter, and my only child.'

She must have seen the disappointment written all over my face and was quick to continue: 'It must be told sometime though, for Charles's sake. And perhaps you may be the one, for it can be easier to talk to a stranger than to one's family. Magda has told me she trusts you, Lucia, and I set much store by her judgement.'

I glowed from within. The maid brought in some coffee and biscuits, and I felt myself content. The biography would be possible.

'How shall we do this, Lucia? It is a long story. I have photographs, I have portraits – you see that one there?' She pointed to one on the wall behind me, and I went to look at it. 'It was the very first he ever did of me.'

It was a spectacular piece of work, a straight

133

portrait, of a woman ablaze with light, and love of life. It was a romantic portrait, painted against an open window, the woman poised by it, but looking at the artist, holding a small dog in her arms. The artist's love for his model came across in every subtle touch of the brush. The white dress, the trees outside the window arrogant in their spring growth, the way she held the dog, so sensuously that one knew the artist and perhaps the model too were thinking of their own love. Or perhaps I superimposed my own thoughts on to it. Whichever, it was a stunning portrait.

'I've prepared some questions...' I began uncertainly, after I had told her how much I admired the painting. I was conscious of the fact that I needed to return to my own agenda.

'Questions, ah yes, but how can you have questions before you know the story, Lucia? Would it not be best to hear that first?'

I agreed, for, put that way, it certainly made sense.

'It is a long one, for I must tell it as I remember it. Now we know each other a little, I could record on tapes what I cannot tell you today and send them to you. I have more, oh much more, to tell you than my voice will allow at one sitting, and you will not wish to spend your time waiting for old age to catch up with youth. Your lover will be waiting at home for you.'

I almost laughed that he was in Budapest waiting for me, but just in time I remembered

134

that Magda was – for some odd reason – not to know of David's presence here and therefore neither must Gréta.

'Countess Öszödy—' I began, intending to say what a good idea the tapes were, but she interrupted.

'You know, Lucia, it is right you should call me by my formal name, for I come of an age where such things mattered. But now we talk of Charles, and I live in the past. Nor are there such creatures as countesses any more. For these reasons it would give me pleasure for you to think and speak to me as Gréta. The Gréta I was once, the Gréta whom Charles loved.'

I was only too happy to agree, for anything that made her remember more clearly would help me too. We agreed that she would tell me something of Charles today, to set the scene, and that tomorrow we would look at photographs. Then she would send tapes to me in London as she finished them. I had brought a small tape recorder with me, but we decided that for this introductory session I should listen with the occasional written note.

'So now I tell you what Charles was like,' Gréta said animatedly, clearly pleased that her suggestion had gone down well.

'Yes, please.' I couldn't wait to get going.

'Charles was posted to Budapest in the autumn of 1938. It was not a good time, for the Munich agreement had brought turmoil to our part of Europe. My husband, dear Miklós, was one of the regent's councillors at the time, and it was clear to us that Hitler would not be stopped by a mere piece of paper. When he invaded Czechoslovakia, well, we knew what would happen to the rest of Europe, including our beloved Hungary, unless we could manage to remain neutral. It was after Munich that many pro-British people here, including the prime minister, swung their allegiance to the Nazis.'

I could see it would be a while before we reached the delicate question I had to ask, so I decided to risk asking it immediately to get it out of the way.

'Did Charles know of Klára's birth?'

'No, my dear. Dear Miklós did not die until the 1960s, and Charles's daughter was assumed to be his – though many knew otherwise of course. Miklós was very fond of Charles, and did not mind. He too loved Klára, and Charles was no longer here then.'

She did not wait for me to comment, but went straight on to describe the pre-war world of Budapest, the literary life, the musical life, and night life and its cosmo-politan society. 'We did not know what would happen with these Nazis striding through Europe, so we young folk laughed and loved, pretending we did not care. And into it walked Charles. I met him in 1941. He told me he had seen me before that, but I did not recall it, and so I think of that day in the Károlyi Gardens as our first meeting.

'I saw this young earnest-looking man sitting sketching, and I wondered who he

136

was. He was too well dressed to be an art student, and there was something about him that made me think he was not Hungarian. A certain openness and freshness of expression. I was curious as to what he was drawing, and walked my dog behind his bench so that I could see it without his realizing it. I shall never forget that drawing. It was of an old man in front of him, staring at a child, and even in the crayon strokes there was a life and vitality that carried a message of its own. It seemed to me as if the old man stood for Budapest itself, alive, but yet somehow doomed. It is hard to be sure, whether all that occurred to me at the time, but I knew at least there was something so unusual about it that I had to find out more. So I sat by him.

'He turned to me as I spoke and his artist's eyes seemed to search me. I thought that if he looked at me so closely, perhaps he painted portraits too. He said he did, but there was a humbleness about him. He explained that he was not a professional artist, and had had little training in art, merely drawn in his spare time at first, and then become involved with other artists, especially those working in the magical realism style. He was American, he told me, and in the US foreign service. That intrigued me even more. I thought how interested my husband would be to meet him. The regent needed to know how other countries and embassies viewed what was going on in Europe, for Hitler's war was in full spate by now, and it could do no harm for

137

me to introduce him to our circle. So I pretended I wanted my portrait painted, I had no idea that it would be so good, it was just an excuse to see Charles more often. I had good looks then, and I had no need to *ask* to be painted. Artists – would you believe this, Lucia? – queued up to paint the wife of the Gróf Öszödy.'

'I would believe it, Gréta,' I said sincerely. 'They would do so now.' The shape of her face, the fine features and the life behind it had not changed.

She went on to talk of how their intimacy had blossomed, and of how she and Miklós had taken Charles to receptions at the Buda Palace where he had made a great impression on the regent. 'By that time we were lovers,' she said matter-of-factly. 'I will not tell you the details. Love affairs are much the same. Their details have the same glory to those that participate, and the same familiarity to those outside. I had not planned this; after all, I was a married woman but the closeness of the sittings gradually overcame me, the sensuousness of his hands, the way he would first look at me, and then gently stroke the canvas with the brushwork of my dress and when – forgive me, Lucia, but we are both women who have loved, *do* love – the brush reached the part of the dress that covered the intimate part of my body, he went very white, put the brush down and came over to me. I reached out my arms...' Gréta stopped, and I could see that there were tears on her cheeks, and marvelled that it had the power still to move her so much.

'I understand,' I said gently.

'I loved him, Lucia. And so it gave me such pleasure when Magda went to visit Charles in later life, and then met David.'

'David?' I repeated, taken aback.

'David Fraser. A dear boy, Charles was so fond of him. He'd known him well since he was a boy and it gave him such pleasure.'

'What did?'

'When David and Magda were married. David was so passionately devoted to her, and still is.'

Seven

'And still is.'

Those three little words blasted my legs from under me, as I left Gréta's apartment that day. I think I managed to keep a bright smile on my face, but I'm sure Gréta guessed something was wrong, though she was tactful enough not to enquire further. I hoped she would put it down to mild surprise on my part that Magda had not been married for ever to Michael Harding. I walked along the tree-lined street towards the City Park going over and over my conversations with Magda in my mind. Why had her earlier marriage

139

never been mentioned before? Why should it have been? logic enquired. Perhaps she thought Tony had told me. Perhaps she thought David had. Perhaps everyone thought I knew. Perhaps pigs would fly. Tony might not have been holding back on me deliberately, nor might Magda. The person who definitely had been was David.

In whose arms I had spent last night.

With whom I had so confidently expected to spend the rest of my life.

I bumped into a passer-by and apologized, envious that she in middle age must have had a defined path through life which I had yet to find. In the park my eye fell on a woman of perhaps my age, trailing two children and happily chattering to her companion. I stood stock still as yet another numbing thought occurred to me, making me feel physically sick.

Toby, whom I had thought to be Magda and Michael's child, was eight years old. Magda had come to Britain in 1992. Charles had died in 1994. The likelihood therefore was that he was David's son as well as Magda's. David had told me he had been married briefly – gee, thanks for the information, I thought bitterly. So briefly that he was married and divorced in time for Michael to have been Toby's natural father? Not likely.

I hadn't asked David whether he had children, so I could hardly complain, I reasoned. I did though. My conversations with him had meant past revelations time in my book, at least so far as anything that affected our relationship, and this certainly did. He should have declared his position. No wonder he still lived so close to Magda. She was not only the woman he still adored, but was bringing up his son as well. I had no problem with Toby – he seemed a nice boy – and if only the circumstances had been different I'd have leapt on the opportunity to get to know him better. After all, I made my living by writing for children, and I was no secret disliker of them. Far from it. I usually like other people's children, and I'd like to have my own. It wasn't Toby that bothered me so much as the finality of Gréta's: 'And still is.' I felt betrayed. I couldn't even plan what to do next, save that I had to go back to the hotel – and meet David. We would have to pass the evening together. And then would come the night. What then? No more love. I only had the now tarnished memory of a night when happy ever after seemed a foregone conclusion. How stupid can you get?

I wandered round the City Park, still numb with shock, and ended up by the lake staring at the towers of the fairytale castle, looking as out of place with modern architecture as the Mathias fountain in the garden of Carr's Happening. Fairytale? It should have been right up my street, but it was based upon a sham. It was a copy of the Rumanian Vajdakunyad Castle, and had been proudly built only just over a hundred years ago as part of the thousand-year celebrations for Hungary as a nation.

Like my love for David, it looked so wonderful, but it was not what it seemed.

I found David waiting in the bar when I got back. I had hoped he would be out until late afternoon, but it was only four o'clock when I made up my mind I had to stop putting off the evil moment by returning to the hotel. Not by taxi. I delayed the inevitable by a mixture of trolley bus, ordinary bus and my own two feet.

The bar was empty and he was sitting at a table looking fairly bleak. He took one look at my face and pushed a glass towards me. And a jug of wine.

'Here, have something to drink,' he said. 'It will help.'

' "A jug of wine, A loaf of Bread – and Thou, Beside me singing in the wilderness",' I recited bitterly. 'Where's the loaf of bread? And where's the thou beside me?' I hurled at him. Omar Khayyam saw life from the bottom of a wine glass, that's how he could enjoy his today. Right now, I was more concerned with my tomorrow.

'I see Gréta has told you.'

'Of course.' I tried to be icy cold, but it didn't work. 'Why, David, why didn't you tell me?' I blurted out in a very trembly voice. 'And why the hell did you come here with me?' I stopped short of the ultimate Rubicon question: *And why did you make love to me?*

He looked hopeless. 'I couldn't not come. I thought if I came with you, at least I'd be here to stand up in court, and defend myself.'

'And can you?' I hurled at him. 'After last night?'

'I didn't mean that to happen. Not till you knew. Is it,' he looked up at me then, 'so important, Lucia?'

I thought about this. 'It might not have been, if you'd told me.'

'I didn't know I was going to fall in love with you. And by the time I did, it was too late. You'd met Magda.'

'Toby is your son?' I put his 'in love with you' carefully on one mental side to be considered later.

'Yes.'

Another question hovered now. The only question, but I couldn't ask it. I wanted to ask whether he was still in love with her – but I couldn't for all sorts of reasons. In theory one can't be in love with two people at once, so this should have answered the question for me, only it didn't. Practice and history are full of people who on different levels manage to love more than one person. I'd always thought life was a series of practical and emotional events laid on top of one another and that because one had a new love it did not necessarily mean the old was auto- matically erased. It could lie unused, un- considered until it changed its base metal into friendship, it could rot away, or it could otherwise transform itself. 'And when we meet at any time again,' as the poet said, 'Be it not seen in either of our brows, That we one

143

jot of former love retain.' The durable lasts, but how durable was Magda? Magda was not the sort of person to fade gently away into history. She was too vital, too alive, too like her grandmother. 'And still is' would mean just that with her. An obsession one could never recover from.

As Charles Carr had found with Gréta.

I nearly cried out in the sheer agony of it. If I asked David whether he still loved her, and he replied yes, than that was that. I realized now that there were no second fiddles in my orchestra of love. If he said he was not, would I believe him? That was the crunch – I knew I would not. That might be my fault for not having faith, it might be his for giving me the grounds not to trust him any more.

'What now?' he asked.

I almost surrendered as I looked at him. It was clear he was in as much of a turmoil as I was. But he was bound heart and soul to Magda; I had been through that one before and there is no magic spell that can work wonders there.

'I don't know, David. I can't...' I stopped. How could I say bluntly that there would be no sharing of my bed tonight? If he was trapped in an ivory tower unable to escape from his love for his former wife, I was trapped in my own. I was the peasant girl in the forest, who had unknowingly cast my eyes at an unattainable king. I had to decide what price I was going to pay.

'I understand.' He said it gently but his

emotions had retreated behind that impene-
trable mask that he wore in the garden on our
first meeting. He, like Charles Carr, wanted
'no snoopers' in his life. How right he had
been when he said he could not commit. And
I like a fool hadn't believed him. 'What about
the biography?' he said.

I had been grappling with this as well. My
first instinct was to run for my life out of the
whole sorry mess of Edenshaw House,
Magda, David and Charles Carr. I wanted to
retreat to my ivory tower of children's writing, where a just and fair world exists, and
where sometimes, just sometimes, dreams
really do come true.

'I don't know yet.' I had the sense to realize
that I was in no state to make decisions about
that. For a start I was due to see Gréta again
tomorrow and sheer politeness made it
impossible for me to back out. Then I began
to see a way of getting through the next
thirty-six hours till it was time to go home.
'David, you told me you had met Gréta?'

'Yes.'

'Did she,' I suddenly thought to ask, 'come
to the wedding?' She would have been about
eighty then I reckoned and so it was possible.

'No. We – Magda and I went over the
following Christmas.'

'And that was the only time you went to
Budapest?'

He hesitated. 'No, I did lie about that. I
came again for a long weekend last year.
There were some paintings I wanted to see in

the museums. I'd read that there used to be a Zoffany of Garrick and Mrs Cibber in the Fine Arts Museum by City Park and I wanted to see if it was still there. I went to see her too.'

No mention, I noticed, of why he went to see his former grandmother-in-law. But then I perhaps shouldn't take that personally. Perhaps he had learned to be economical with the truth or perhaps he always had been so. I suspect the former. After all, to be charitable, Gréta lived quite near to City Park. But did I want to be charitable? Not today.

'I'll make a sort of bargain with you, David, over the biography.' I saw a sudden muscle tensing of his face. 'To take our minds off more personal matters.'

'I was thinking of leaving right now,' he said, with the first gleam of lightening up he'd so far shown.

'Hear me first.' I wanted him to go. I wanted him to stay. 'Now if thou wouldst, when all have given him over,' the poem had continued, 'From death to life thou mightst him yet recover.' 'I can't decide about the biography now,' I told him, 'and I have to see Gréta tomorrow. I want you to talk to me, not' – seeing alarm on his face – 'about your marriage, nothing personal at all. On the contrary, I want you to talk to me *genuinely* about Charles Carr as though you were actively helping with the biography.'

'And suppose there isn't any more than I've told you?'

146

'Then tell me your own thoughts about him.'

'I don't want to see them—'

'Trust me, David, I trusted you. Now you owe me one.'

He stared at me, battling away, but said nothing.

'If – and believe me there's a big if now – I go on with the biography, I shall do it with or without your help. Your choice.'

He was actually angry. I couldn't believe it. How could he have the nerve to be furious at this reasonable suggestion? Had he held back so long that he couldn't bear to think of sharing Charles Carr even with me?

Even with me? Who was I kidding? There *was* no me, however much he might kid himself he was in love. The sooner I got that into my stupid romantic head, the better.

He surprised me, however. 'I'll agree to that. I'll help you all I can. There's one condition, Lucia.'

'You're not in a position to make conditions.'

He flushed. 'Accepted, but I have no choice over this one. You'll have to believe me when I tell you I *don't* know very much. It will be the truth, that I can promise you – for whatever my promise is now worth to you.'

Oh, his anger was still there. But so was mine. I'd been put into this position by David and he alone. Moreover, I still had to work with Magda, the woman with whom he was still obsessed.

★ ★ ★

It was hard, that dinner. The restaurant where we ate up in the Vár was not romantic; it was the kind of restaurant which, although it had a few Hungarian dishes, could nowadays be found in most capitals of the world, aiming to please everybody. It was the perfect setting for a business meeting, and that's how I disciplined myself to think of it. I think David did the same, for difficult though it was to be objective, every so often we would catch each other's eye and look away again, thinking perhaps of only twenty-four hours earlier. What a difference a day makes!

'I did know Charles rather better than I told you,' he confessed, toying with a plateful of spaghetti. 'My parents lived where I now live in fact. I bought their house when they moved to the west country after Dad retired. As a teenager I fancied myself as the next Paul Gauguin, so my parents, who knew Charles through some village project, invited him to tea. I set out to dazzle him.'

I actually managed a genuine laugh.

'He was very kind,' David continued, 'and looked carefully at my daubs. I thought I'd made a friend for life, and asked him – I suppose I'd have been about twelve at this time – whether I could see his studio.'

'Precocious little brat,' I remarked.

'I admit it. Still, I was keen. Charles looked taken aback, and I see why now, but he agreed, and I went. He showed me around the studio, explained it all, talked about the pictures he was painting. The one of the butcher was on the easel, I remember.'

'*The Laughing Cavalier*?' I said.

'Yes. What he didn't show me – understandably perhaps – was *The Happening*, nor the gardens. He took me into the flower gardens one side of the house, but it looked from the house at that time as if there were nothing beyond the lawn but wilderness.'

'What did you think of him?'

'He was rather like a remote teacher, kind enough, genuinely interested, but not entirely present, if you know what I mean.'

I did, if only because David followed suit. He wasn't wholly present, either. He was remembering, which was good, but still one side remained closeted away.

'I asked him if I could come again,' David continued. 'He was rather surprised, and, I surmised, not pleased. I was a precocious little brat, as you said, but a fairly perceptive one, I think, for my age.'

'Boastful, too,' I muttered. This was easier now, we were establishing a foothold on normality.

'Accepted. Charles said I could, but asked why. I replied something about wanting to be near paint. He didn't laugh, but I think he began to take me seriously. He began tentatively to give me the occasional art lesson, and talk to me about art in general. The first was fine, the second was splendid. I got hooked because this was something we didn't do at school. He talked about the major artists as if they were old friends. He explained what each was trying to do, and he had a knack of bringing them to life as struggling people, not as names that had made it to the top.'

'So that's what set you off?'

'Yes. And it told me something about Charles as well, but not everything.'

'Not about the background of *The Happening*? Didn't Gréta talk to you about that?'

'No. She told me she never discussed it. It was too precious to her.'

'I can't believe that,' I replied flatly. 'She spent a large part of today only too willing to talk. She's putting it on tape for me. You're holding out on me, David.' The gulf opened up between us again, and stayed there.

'I'm telling you the truth.' His chin stuck out obstinately. 'That's one of the reasons I wanted to come here with you to see if she'd change her mind and talk. Apparently, she has.'

'But I suppose Charles *didn't* talk about it,' I said sarcastically. How on earth could I be expected to believe that Gréta would talk to a stranger but not to her own grandson-in-law?

'When Magda came, Charles told me he'd met her grandmother in Budapest. I was curious, and he reluctantly told me he'd been a diplomat there. He wouldn't say any more, on the basis that he preferred to think about peace and peace was Kent.'

'Didn't you think it odd that someone born in New York State needed to retreat to Kent?'

'Charles said sometimes a retreat was an advance. It all depended on your attitude.'

I gave up and went back to David's own story. 'And that's how you came to study art history?'

'I was hooked. Dreams of being Paul Gauguin had vanished. I kept in touch with Charles while I was at university and when I came down I commuted to London where I lectured. Charles was in his mid-seventies then, and so I saw a lot more of him. He was still a Mr Chips sort of character, but not exactly gentle. Or rather it was a kind of gentleness, but it had the steeliness you sometimes see in old soldiers, gained through years of being tough and seeing sights too frightful to remember – or to forget. Nothing is so important as what they went through then, and thereafter they can look on the world around them with tolerant eyes.'

'That must have been the time that Charles set up the foundation.'

'Yes, I helped him over that. And he asked me to be a trustee. You can imagine I was flattered. Magda came over in 1992 when the foundation was already set up. We married in 1993, the year before Charles died.'

'That must have made him happy,' I said, well aware I was putting a toe in forbidden water. I received my just desserts.

He looked at me as though I was betraying a sacred memory. 'We had the reception at Edenshaw House,' was all he said.

'But Magda wasn't made a trustee.' It just

came out, but I saw his face whiten.

'After Charles died, Magda became CEO,' he replied steadily.

'And what about *The Happening*?' I asked hastily, seeing the storm cloud heading right for me.

'What about it?'

'There must have been a moment when you first saw it – and when he first talked about it?'

'Yes, there was, and no there wasn't. Would you like dessert?'

'Is that a hint?'

'I'm considering my reply. I don't want to embark on that tonight.'

We took a taxi back to the hotel, and I was conscious of his sitting by me, and the wall of ice between us. Did I want to melt it? No. It was too late, I was too tired, and there were matters too deep here for me to delve into. This little peasant girl, like the one in the fountain, was beaten.

'Nightcap?' he asked perfunctorily as we walked in.

'Had plenty thanks.' I gave him an artificial smile. I thought he would take the excuse to part here and go into the bar, but no, he dragged out the ordeal until the last moment as we were outside our respective doors.

'Goodnight, Lucia,' he said, and kissed me on the cheek. I felt it burn through me as intensely as his kisses of passion the previous night. What was it implying? I had no idea, and didn't much care. Was it that he was sorry or that he wanted to keep avenues open? Either way, it was a farewell to the David I had known so briefly.

When I walked up the Városligeti fasor to visit Gréta the next morning, I was reasonably composed. At least I could concentrate on the biography now. The question of whether I would continue with it or not could be postponed until I was back in England, and meanwhile it was something to bury myself in.

Gréta, of course, was as bright as a button, even more so than yesterday, which made me feel worse. She was dressed in powder blue today, and managed to make me feel dowdy in my cream trousers and light sweater. Around her, on a long coffee table, were strewn photograph albums, and a tray across her lap showed she was eagerly prepared for action.

'I have been looking forward to your return, Lucia.'

'And I, too,' I smiled, genuinely, since I felt at home here, cocooned in her past and away from my present reality. 'Magda told me this whole mansion was yours when you first knew Charles?' I asked, when we had got down to business.

'Ah, yes. Miklós and I had difficulties in Soviet times, and it was necessary to change the old house into many apartments. We were fortunate to be able to stay here at all. I was glad for the house reminds me so much of

Charles.'

'When did he leave Budapest?'

'In the autumn of 1944 when the Arrow Cross Fascists were in power.'

'And you never saw him again?'

'The tapes will tell you all, Lucia. I must save my voice to show you the photographs.'

I had, at Magda's suggestion, brought a camera with me with which I could photograph what I needed there and then. She had borrowed it from Robin, who had nobly agreed to entrust me with it, and I had convinced Magda, if not myself, that I could use it efficiently.

At first sight the photographs looked magnificent. There were the usual slightly out of focus groups of people, some of which I hoped might include Charles Carr. There were many of Miklós and of Gréta herself – studio portraits, snapshots, formal reception photographs. Miklós looked a typical older statesman, though he could only have been in his late forties in this particular album, tall, grave, withdrawn. The photographs of Gréta stunned me, even though I had seen the portraits of her on the walls. She shimmered out of the past like a beacon flame, her beauty the more evident since they were in black and white. To my disappointment, however, there didn't seem to be any solo pictures of Charles Carr. I don't know quite what I'd expected to find but whatever it was, it wasn't there! I couldn't immediately blurt out this obvious omission, but I had to get to the bottom of it. Cautiously, I decided to begin on a different tack.

'Magda told me that you were his model for *The Happening*, and yet you said the last time you saw him was in 1944, so he was working from memory.' Gréta listened attentively as I explained – tactfully – my theory of the two sides of love. 'The dark side of love,' I concluded, 'is so often in one's own mind only.'

'There are always two sides of love,' Gréta replied to my relief, after a tense pause. 'Charles was more sensitive than most men, but have you considered that what you believe to be the two sides of love in *The Happening* might – and of course I cannot be sure – in fact be love and war?'

Why hadn't this occurred to me, I wondered? It was an interesting theory, and for an artist whose love affair was torn apart by the war, certainly possible. I would talk it over with David. Then I remembered how things were between us. Hours of happy discussion were not on the menu. Although he had promised co-operation, it wasn't going to be limitless.

'Charles did not need me physically before him to remember me.' Gréta smiled as if a sudden memory had come to her. 'He painted from his inward eye, before which I lived, I moved and I loved.'

My opportunity came. 'Do you have no photographs of him save in these groups?'

The light of mischief came into her eyes: 'Of course. Do you wish to see them?'

I played her game. 'Yes, *please.*'

Her hand went to a small album, much newer than the rest, and handed it to me. 'I kept his photographs apart. It would not do, you understand?'

I did. At least, I thought I did.

'When I knew you were coming,' she continued, 'I took them from their envelope and put them in this album.'

There weren't many, but they were riveting. Stronger than that – they *were* the biography. There was one of Charles painting Gréta's portrait, which was a must. He was laughing, not the remote figure David had recalled. Gréta was in the picture, so a third person had taken it. Miklós perhaps? Another showed the three of them, he, Gréta and Miklós, in – yes, I recognized it – the Buda palace courtyard. Gréta, in her fur coat, had an arm slipped into Charles's, and her other into her husband's. The men's top hats instantly dated the photographs and I wondered what emotions ranged behind those smiling faces. What struck me about this photo was that the three figures, though close together, looked somehow emotionally separate. I thought at first it was simply because they were all looking straight ahead towards the photographer, but it was more than that, though I couldn't quite analyse it.

'You will wonder what I saw in Charles,' Gréta said matter-of-factly. 'I was a titled woman, prominent in Hungarian society, he was a junior diplomat in a foreign legation,

156

and younger than I. So I will explain.'

I waited agog. Gréta seemed to have an uncanny knack of following my thoughts and therefore anticipating questions.

'It is easy to become a parrot in society, Lucia. One smiles, one speaks as one is expected to speak, one is on parade to be admired, to repeat what one's followers say. Charles was different. He stood outside us all, and he looked at me as though he knew me through and through. It was that Gréta whom he painted. Charles was like no one else I ever knew. and I loved him. It wasn't the kind of love that wears itself out. It grew.'

'Until the war divided you,' I concluded for her softly, when she stopped.

'Yes. Always the war. I will speak about that in the tapes.'

'Will you explain on them how you managed to see him if he had gone underground?' That was going to be a disadvantage of the proposed tape system. I couldn't ring her up every five minutes to ask questions, and anyway phone and email are no substitute for feeling one's way face to face.

In fact Gréta answered straightaway. 'It was not that difficult until 1944 when the Germans occupied the country. Until then Hungary was at war, yet not noticeably so. It was there, but in the background. Some forces were sent to help the Axis, some young Jews went to labour camps, but it did not change Budapest. Not at first. The problem was that Charles was a known face in society.

We had to change that. He grew a small beard, sometimes even a moustache too. At first he came to us as a musician – oh it was a great joke. Charles was an accomplished violinist, though amateur. So why not play in the streets? What better place to pick up the gossip of war? Better, he could play inside the big hotels – I had contacts. He played at the fashionable Hotel Gellért for example, and the Carlton and Ritz. Charles and I used to go swimming there when we first knew each other. Oh, how I remember that blue-tiled pool. In his violinist role no one recognized him from those days, fortunately. He was accepted as a Hungarian, his accent was excused as a country dialect. Look, here he is.'

And there indeed he was. The photograph I had longed for. A portrait of the young Charles Carr, but not taken in a studio. From the look of devotion on his face, it was taken by Gréta herself. No beard, in fact, but a light moustache, a cap on his head at a consciously rakish angle, as though Charles were deliberately posing as the daredevil spy.

Quickly I looked through the other pictures before I began to photograph them. There were not many, a few taken indoors, and one or two groups, one of which did not seem to have Charles in it. It was a family group, or so I presumed. A middle-aged man and woman, with two girls of about twenty and a younger boy, standing in a small garden.

'Who are they?'

Gréta glanced at the photograph, which was obviously taken about the same time as the solo one of Charles, since the paper and camera looked the same.

'Neighbours in the block where Charles lived for a time. Jewish, poor things. In 1944 – no, I will save it for the tapes.'

I wanted to ask so many questions, especially what made Charles leave? Was it the increase of danger as Horthy was deposed and the Arrow Cross seized power? That was a crucial point, because his work as an agent would surely be of even more value then, particularly with the Russians steadily advancing towards Budapest? It might even demonstrate a side to Charles's character that was distinctly unattractive – however human. I clung to the hope that there was more to this story and that it would be revealed in the tapes. All I could do now was to photograph these vital records. One thing was certain. They would set the biography alight.

'Look,' said Gréta softly, turning to one of the larger albums. 'My little Klára.'

I gazed at Magda's mother, here pictured as a teenager. Could I see a resemblance to Charles? I could not pretend I did. Nor in fact to Gréta. The face stared back at me with the sharp knowingness of adolescence and held its own secrets.

Then I could not resist asking, 'Did Charles know about her? Was she born when he left?'

'He did not know. I could not tell him for he might not have left.'

My moment had come. 'Why did he leave, Gréta?'

She looked at me in some surprise. 'I made him go, of course. I loved him and he had too much to offer to the world to die in the horrors of Budapest. He did not wish to leave – I had to trick him in the end.' Her penetrating eyes held me. 'That was the reason I did not tell him about the baby. Charles had left, the baby was Miklós's and mine. Klára never knew that he was not her father. I told Magda only after Klára's death.'

Spring 1942

There was a big difference between living here as a junior diplomat and living as an illegal citizen. There seemed no difference in Budapest itself, however. It was only nominally at war. Kállay, the new premier, was no lover of the Nazis and was eager to reassure the Allies that Hungary's role in the war was only nominal, while assuring the Axis powers that Hungary was a willing partner. This worked in well for Charles, for László had hinted that the government was unofficially sanctioning information being sent to the Allies via the neutral Ankara or Lisbon.

His new apartment was at the top of the building, above that of the Semmelweiss family. The identity papers he had been given showed him to be one Bartók Ferenc from

Tata on the Czechoslovakian border, north-west of Budapest. A particularly good name for a street musician he thought with amusement. Who would have thought that a competent artist such as himself would be 'earning a living' playing the fiddle, something that he was considerably less competent at?

'Ferenc is not one of our cousins, but a friend,' Katie had said firmly. 'That is much wiser.'

Indeed it was. For the moment the Jewish population was safe, at least in Budapest, but anti-Semitism was rising with the increased German influence in Budapest. Jewish shops were targets for fires and theft, but for the moment the Semmelweiss business in Kazinczy street had come to no harm.

His worst moment had been when he first 'arrived' here, for the Budapest system allotted a janitor or house guardian to each apartment block, and every new arrival had to register at the local police station. No residents had keys to the block (officially) save for the janitor, and no unofficial guests could stay without notifying him. Moreover the block was locked at night and no one could enter without paying a small fee.

'There is no escape, Ferenc,' Elisabeth, Katie's younger sister, had explained as she showed him his apartment. 'Tomorrow I take you to the police station.' At least it hadn't been the foreigners' registration department in Fövam Square where he had gone as a diplomat. All had been very polite and easy in

161

1938, but now in 1942 its reputation was grim. It was there, he had heard, one began to sense the other darker side of Budapest.

'That's good of you,' Charles said gratefully. Elisabeth was a lively girl of eighteen or so, and, unusually for her Jewish parentage, fair-haired. Charles had taken to her immediately, as indeed he had to the whole Semmelweiss family with whom he often spent his evenings.

'You see,' she had explained to Charles gravely, 'you must be very polite to me. They have called this part of Pest the Elisabeth City now that I live here.'

Charles had laughed and kissed her hand equally gravely. 'One day I must paint the portrait of this very important neighbour.'

Despite his new independence, he still needed Gréta financially. His former banking arrangements were closed of course, and now he must live on what little he could earn in the streets and his own money given to him via Gréta. Through her connections she drew money from her bank in Switzerland, into which his family transferred money from the States. László had been dubious about this arrangement, since he had never taken to Gréta, although he admired Miklós. Eventually he accepted the idea, however.

The new life had been odd at first, but Charles had quickly become accustomed to it, and with the change of prime minister his first opportunity came to dispatch news of real importance. Hitherto he had been building his links with the neutral legations. Now with Kállay, a patriot and anti-Nazi in power, there was a chance that a deal could be struck with the Allies. There was an air of waiting in Budapest. There were no obvious signs of war, no blackout, no food shortages – and no, thank goodness, *official* hostility towards the Jews.

'Charles!' Gréta leapt up from the table at one of the new *espresso* bars that had opened in Pest.

He frowned at the risk of calling him by his own name, but she just laughed. 'Ah, my Ferenc,' she purred. 'Forgive me?'

'This time,' he said in mock seriousness. 'You recognized me though?' Charles was disappointed. He had been growing the moustache since he had last met her a week ago, and had donned his musician's outfit for the first time, so different from his usual formal clothes with its bright necktie scarf and headdress, that he actually *felt* like Ferenc.

'Of course,' she said seriously. 'But I, *mon amour*, am your lover. Not a policeman.'

'I can tell that.' He ordered himself a coffee and sandwich.

'So where will you play, *kedvesem*?' she asked him affectionately.

'In the streets of the Vár, the markets—'

'No, no,' she protested. 'That is not where you will need to be. You must play where tongues are loose and the powerful meet. In the Hungaria, the Carlton, and the Gellért –

there you can play at tables where those in power are talking. I will arrange it—'

'But I am known in those places.'

'Believe me, Ferenc, they will not even notice a mere musician. Nor do you look as you did when we swam at the Gellért.'

'I have more clothes on,' he joked.

She reached out a hand and took his. 'Not for long, my love.'

★   ★   ★

When I left Gréta, I didn't return to the hotel immediately. Instead I took a bus down the Andrássy utca, and into what had been the Jewish quarter, and where the atrocities against the Jews back in 1944 had chiefly been centred. The synagogue was here, the Jewish Museum, and the Holocaust memorial in the Raoul Wallenberg garden, dedicated to the man who had done so much to protect the Jews of Hungary, partly through the neutral legations' protective passports scheme, and partly through his efforts at the sharp end, pulling Jews off the trains bound for Auschwitz and other work and death camps.

It was in this area that, according to Gréta, Charles Carr had lived. Why, I wondered? And how had his photograph of a Jewish family ended up in Gréta's collection? It might be a line of enquiry worth exploring, but it would be a dark one, and might lead further than the simple tale of love and loss

I'd imagined when I came to Budapest. As if to reassure myself of that mission, I went to look at that fountain once more, on my way back to the hotel. Call me stupid, call me a romantic, call me an escapist, but I thought it still had something to tell me, though I couldn't figure out quite what.

I gazed at it yet again, while other tourists milled around me. The king, the girl, the chronicler with the falcon, the huntsmen, the dogs – and the story. The guidebook told me little, save that it was the king's Italian chronicler who recorded the tale for posterity, and later poets had taken it up. What on earth so impressed Charles Carr that years later he built a replica in his own garden? I decided I would try to find further details of the legend when I returned to England. I didn't have much hope that I would find anything, since it wouldn't exactly have made world headlines, so it was odds on that any records would be in Hungarian or Italian. I could ask Magda for a translation, I supposed. Even David...

And there *was* David, appearing like an evil genie to interrupt my thoughts. I suppose it was hardly surprising he should be here since the Buda Castle is home to two art galleries.

He managed to force a grin. 'Here you are again. Are you going to write about this for children?'

'No,' I said, taking this fatuous comment more seriously than the conversation filler it was. 'This isn't a children's tale. Whatever it

165

is, it meant far more than that to Charles Carr.'

'Sighing after the unattainable?'

I was shaken at first, assuming him to be referring to me. Then I realized he was talking of Charles.

'That's all this legend means,' David continued, with a kind of desperate urgency in his voice as though he were determined to block out any other interpretation. 'Charles Carr's unattainable was Gréta. He couldn't have her for keeps because she was married to Miklós – so that's what he recorded in the garden.'

'That can't be all,' I said obstinately. 'There's more to it. Can't you see that?' His reluctance only made me more certain of my own views.

'No.'

But looking into his unhappy eyes, I didn't believe him.

Eight

Gatwick Airport is not the most romantic of places for a farewell scene, especially the sort that one hopes will never happen. Perhaps as time rolls by even airports might seem atmospheric just as railway stations with puffing smoke and parting lovers now look romantic to us. But there was nothing romantic about David's and my parting, merely a sense of desolation. Neither of us wanted this to happen, but there was no bridge that would enable us to meet in the middle of this gulf. I was old enough to know that a man still desperately in love with his ex was not something I could handle.

As we trudged beside each other with our luggage into the blare and glare of the arrivals hall, David asked, 'Any further thoughts about whether you'll go on with the book?'

There was no point in our considering whether *we* would go on with it.

'No,' I answered honestly. 'I'll have to try to look at it objectively. I'll certainly have to go to Edenshaw House again. After all, I can hardly tell Magda' – I found it hard even to pronounce her name – 'that I don't want to go on with the book because her ex-husband and I have fallen out.'

'What do *you* want to do about it?'

I sighed. 'That's unfair. Have you changed your mind about whether a biography is a good or bad thing?'

He still looked away from me, this time towards the apparently more fascinating array of hire car firms, bureaux de change and coffee shops.

'No. At least—'

I fastened on this carefully. 'Is there some doubt over it, David?'

'My honest opinion?'

'Yes.'

'I believe Charles Carr deserves a biography, but – you're not going to like this—'

'So what's new?' I muttered.

'I'm not sure you're the person to do it.'

I went bright red. It was the last thing I had expected him to say.

'I knew you wouldn't understand,' David added, seeing my face.

'You've made yourself *very* clear,' I said stiffly, hurting so much I couldn't wait to get away, and turning to do so.

'No, stop!' He grabbed my arm. 'You might as well hear me out. Look, Lucia, if I haven't managed to figure out Charles's story how can you hope to?'

'Easily,' I snapped. 'You married into the Öszödy family. You're too involved to see the story.'

'And aren't you?'

I stared at him aghast, wanting to shout out an indignant 'no', but how could I? I *was* involved. I was caught up in a relationship with David and that was colouring everything. Yet there was more to it, surely. I could treat Charles Carr's story as something completely apart from David and me. I could be objective. And then inside my head I heard those insidious words again: 'And still is.' I was kidding myself. The Charles Carr trail led to Gréta, from Gréta to Magda, from Magda to David. And I had hitched my emotional wagon to the end of this column.

David kissed me on the cheek. I felt his

warm breath, I heard his heart beat. Or perhaps that was mine, banging like the clap of doom as he whispered, 'Goodbye, Lucia.'

Back within my own four walls, I tried to see my way clear. Some hopes. They seemed to be closing in on me, taunting me. Time and time again I thrashed it over in my mind. Was David right? Was I so in love with him that I couldn't see Charles's story clearly? I'd always prided myself on being the type of woman who wouldn't be so knocked sideways she couldn't see straight, but perhaps I was wrong.

I pondered my options. It tore at my heart to think that David was slipping away from me. That one night had convinced me that I hadn't been wrong, and that 'happy ever after' had this time been in my sights. Commitment wasn't going to be a problem. How long ago that seemed now. I couldn't make David out. He was still bound to Magda, even if not legally, so what had he wanted from me? Just sex? Or had he clutched at me seeing my obvious interest and hoping I was an escape route from his problems? He'd said he loved me. So what had gone wrong? I was convinced there was more to it than my just being an easy conquest.

Options? Precious few. I considered talking to Tony but decided to put him on hold. First of all, I was hopping mad that he hadn't told me David and Magda had been married. I tried to be fair over this. Did he have any obligation to tell me? I decided he did, especially after he knew I'd met both Magda and David.

What was his game? What cauldron was he stirring now? I'd thought at first it was merely a reawakening of interest in Charles Carr, but now I wasn't so sure. Had he been doing a bit of subtle matchmaking in his old age, thinking that I might be the one to woo David away from Magda? If so, I had news for him. He'd failed. The spell hadn't worked. Maybe it needed a few more glasses of bats' blood or newts' tongues.

I decided I had to take the biography a step further, whatever my private feelings. I had to go to Edenshaw and report to Magda. The specimen chapters would be the step after that. Was I or was I not going to write them?

What were my instincts about the biography? I mused on the way down to Edenshaw, a few days later. There was no doubt there was a good story coming from Gréta and I itched to hear it. The first tape would be sent in about a week's time, so taking the time of postage into account I'd certainly have it within two weeks. Meanwhile, I could start work. I felt I had grasped the nature of the man, at least to the point where I could do the chapters of his early life up to the standard necessary for the publishers' and foundation's approval. Of course, they'd have to be improved later as I gathered new material – I realized with some unease that my mind was leaping forward as if my decision were already made.

It was strange driving down to Edenshaw again, feeling myself tugged in two directions, wanting to be part of this project and wanting to get the hell out of the whole deal. By the time I'd reached the lane for Edenshaw, however, the spell of Kent was beginning to take over. It was early autumn, the season of spiders' webs in dewy bushes, and the smell of the year's change in the air. Harvest time – except for me. For the book, yes. I had begun to look forward in an odd way to telling Magda about her grandmother and discussing plans for it. In my folder were the photographs I had taken on my camera, which had come out reasonably well. They would not be new to Magda, I presumed, since Gréta must have shown them to her when she was told of her ancestry.

I walked into the house, bright smile plastered on my face, and greeted the plump young woman at the reception desk who was beginning to feel like an old chum. Her name was Margaret, I'd discovered, and she was a vital cog in the day-to-day running of Edenshaw House.

'Is Magda here yet?'

'In her office. How did the trip go?'

'Fine.' (In parts, I thought wryly.)

I ran up the stairs, and heard Magda laughing. Assuming she was chatting to Pamela, I went straight in. It wasn't Pamela, however. It was Robin.

I suppose there was nothing odd about that

save the coincidence of his being there at the same time as I was. There were plans and photographs spread over the desk, with Magda bent over them and Robin at her side. What *was* unexpected was that Robin's hand was on her back in the possessive way that I knew well. It was one of his unconscious gestures of love.

It gave me a most peculiar feeling, but I couldn't understand why. I no longer loved Robin, so it couldn't be jealousy, but what was it? It took a moment or two to sort this one out. Then I realized that it *was* jealousy. I was jealous of Magda. Not only had she once possessed and still kept David's love, but now she was accepting Robin's too. No matter if it was explicit or not, he was stuck on her, no doubt about it. To put it in primitive terms, she had both of my men, and I had neither.

Then I shook myself for being stupid, if not over imaginative.

'Hi,' I said as cheerfully as I could manage.

Magda looked up and everything slipped back into place as her usual warm smile enveloped me. Robin's wasn't quite so warm but it was friendly enough, if a little – I searched for the word – *smug*. Poor sap, I thought. He's in over his head. Magda was way out of his league, however approachable she might seem.

'I'm so glad you came right down here,' she welcomed me. 'My grandmother said it had gone well. She liked you, Lucia. I thought she would.'

I salvaged all the enthusiasm I had gathered during my meetings with Gréta and told her about them, while Robin listened attentively. I even found myself chattering about the fountain. It was just like old times, and for a moment the aching space in my heart that David had filled received a merciful dose of painkiller.

'So where now?' Magda asked.

'The chapters,' I told her, not even thinking twice about it. Of course I wasn't going to give up. Back in the familiarity of Edenshaw House I felt comfortable again. Talking about the photographs and about the content of the specimen material, I felt back on my own turf, lulled into a world where David didn't exist. Even though he'd been married to the woman I was talking to, he couldn't invade my territory here. Or so I convinced myself.

'Are these new to you, Magda?' I asked, as I produced the photos I'd taken.

'No. My grandmother and I had a heart to heart when my mother died, and I saw them then. I think it was these photos that first decided me on coming over here. I had a grandfather I'd never met in the first place, and one who looked so interesting, partly I suppose because these were photographs over forty years old and taken in wartime. That was 1988, and there seemed little chance I'd ever get to England – Gréta told me Charles lived here, not in America.'

'So your grandmother knew all about Charles's life here?'

'Oh yes.'

This puzzled me for I had seen no letters, I realized, and I'd had the definite impression there was no contact. True, she had known all about *The Happening* but that could have been through Magda – no, that couldn't be so, because she knew exactly where Charles was. Nevertheless, I decided I would probe further, since this would be a vital area for research.

'Do you have letters between the two of them and would there be a problem about quoting from them? I forgot to ask your grandmother while I was there.' (Some biographer! I'd been so entranced listening to Gréta that my writer's instincts had deserted me.)

'I don't think so.'

'So how – sorry to push this–' I apologized, 'did Gréta know where Charles Carr was?' Why no letters? I wondered. Iron Curtain or not, letters still got through, even if censored.

'That's easy to answer.' Magda laughed, as though reading my mind. 'Hungary was not entirely cut off, you know. We knew what was going on in the rest of Europe and in the States. I presume that when the legations reopened under Soviet rule my grandmother made enquiries about Charles, and sooner or later news trickled back. He was a diplomat after all, and the intelligence work he did for his country with my grandmother's help was not inconsiderable. He must have been easily

174

traceable.'

I picked up on the 'with my grandmother's help'. This sounded promising. 'Will she talk about his intelligence work on the tapes, do you think?'

'I don't see why not,' Magda said. 'There are few secrets any more and one must remember that although there were very dark days in Budapest in the Second World War, here has been another since then that looms even larger in its history.'

'The 1956 Uprising.'

'Yes. David knows quite a lot about that.'

'I felt rather a fool,' I observed, given this perfect opportunity, and with a light laugh that didn't sound too false. 'I hadn't realized you'd been married to him. I hope I haven't caused any problems putting you on opposite sides of the fence over the biography.'

'We always are on opposite sides,' Magda grinned. 'Don't worry about that.'

Robin's eyes were watching me with great interest. After all, he knows me pretty well, and I could see him putting two and two together or at least notching up a few question marks in his mind.

'So you'll get on with the chapters then?' Magda's rhetorical question had a note of dismissal (temporary I hoped) which Robin eagerly picked up.

'Magda,' he said patiently, not looking at me, 'I've got to leave soon, so shouldn't we get on?'

I backed out, murmuring about returning

later. I could tell when I wasn't wanted. By anyone it seemed. Cinderella was back in her kitchen, and there was no sign of a fairy godmother to help me out. I was on my own – again.

Summer 1942

'What's wrong, Gréta?'

Charles had been watching her for some minutes. She had not been in a good mood when she arrived at the *espresso* bar, and the waves of irritation as she toyed with her Eszterházy cake were reaching him across the table.

His words had their effect. She put her hand on his, and her face lightened. 'I am an old crosspatch today, Charles. It's only that I am so very tired of all this pointless charade.'

Charles went very cold. He supposed he had been waiting for this to happen, surprised that she had not protested before. It was late August and the heat in Budapest was intense. Normally she and Miklós would be at their summer home to avoid it, but in times of war Miklós had decreed – to Charles's relief – they should not go. Miklós was determined to remain near the regent – just in case. He, as was Charles, was convinced that it would take but one false move on Admiral Horthy's part for Hitler to decide to occupy Hungary and the likelihood had increased with a patriot as prime minister, instead of a Nazi sympathizer.

'This heat,' Gréta complained, 'and, *drágám*, we could have such a happy time in the country if only you would come too.'

'I couldn't go, Gréta,' he explained patiently once again. 'I have a job to do.'

Her eyes flashed. 'What kind of job is that? Always you say you must live in secrecy – but why? There is no war, not here in Hungary. Budapest goes on as before. There are no SS troops here to hunt you down from wherever you live. You won't even tell me where that is. You are like a child. You enjoy playing spies, Charles, and it is I that suffer.'

'I am sorry, Gréta.' Charles felt his stomach churning. He had always feared that what he saw as his duty would clash with his relationship with Gréta. So far it had not, but it was bound to happen at some point. Even he had to admit that there seemed little reason to live incognito, and in going to such lengths to avoid the Öszödy mansion and all his former haunts. He and Gréta met now at a house on Rózsahegy, Rose Hill, overlooking Margit Island; it had once belonged to Miklós's parents, and was now untenanted, save for the staff. Gréta hated it. Even his work was hard to defend. Certainly he had a useful link at the neutral countries' legations, so that he could smuggle reports to Ankara, Lisbon or Sweden, but what was there to report? Mere tittle tattle, all hearsay and rumours. The great hopes he had had of fulfilling some useful mission were disappearing fast. He could even be regarded as a deserter rather than as an intelligence agent. So far there were distant rumbles of war in Hungary, but nothing had happened save that a small number of forces had been called up to serve. It looked as if Hungary would indeed manage to sit the war out, thanks to the regent's craftiness. However, without an active role, Charles's position with Gréta was becoming precarious.

'Why cannot you come out into the open again, Charles? Why not, I ask you? There are still some Western citizens here, they live on, as they always have, and no one sends them to the Margit Prison. If there is to be any trouble, Miklós would be one of the first to know and then you can go to ground again. Just think, Charles, if you came back to us openly, and accompanied us to social gatherings again, you could get much better information than I can give you. Charles Carr could achieve more than this Ferenc fellow you pretend to be.'

'I can't, Gréta. Not yet,' he replied gently, but his heart was pounding, severely tempted.

She pouted. 'There is someone else, is there not. You have another lover, more beautiful than me?'

'No!' Charles was horrified. 'How can you think that? Who could be more beautiful than you? And whether you were beautiful or not, I would still love you.'

She snatched her hand away. 'Then show me. Do *trust me*, Charles.'

'Trust you?' He did not understand.

'Always I am kept in the dark. You will not share my life – but you will not let me share yours either. Oh yes, you make use of the information I give you, I am useful, but you will tell me nothing of your life, not even where you live.'

'Because it is not fair to those I live with. I must keep it separate.' He was convinced of the need for that, but he was also aware of something in him that did not want to share it. His life in the closed circle of the Semmelweiss family was a warm cocoon he retreated into, embraced and treated as a family member, not as an outsider. He loved them all from Papa Jákob, his tall slightly forbidding figure dominating the table at meals with his fanciful stories and wise observations, to young Elisabeth with her impulsive loving nature, who entertained them in the evenings with her piano playing – anything from Liszt to jazz according to her mood. And there was Tibor, her younger brother, the quiet studious one of the family, who adopted Charles as an honorary older brother to be respected and admired (much to Charles's amusement). Mama Márta with her strict outer severity and her inner softness – and darling Katie, who was more often with László than at the family table, but often brought him home too. No, this was not a home Gréta would understand.

'And why is that?' Gréta's eyes gleamed suspiciously. 'Are they Jews? Is that it? You are ashamed of where you live?'

For a moment he did not know her. That she could speak thus showed a side of her he did not recognize. 'They are Hungarians,' he replied steadily, and was relieved that she acknowledged she had gone too far.

'I am sorry, Charles, forgive me. I just fear that I am losing you. There is so much I do not know.'

'You know that I love you,' he cried in despair. 'Isn't that enough?'

'It has to be. Shall we go to our hovel?' she asked softly.

Once there, in the Rose Hill house which Gréta always laughingly referred to as The Hovel, he watched her as she slipped off the light silk dress. Then embracing her he slipped off her chemise, and then the silken knickers, until she was naked in his arms. He stepped back and looked at her.

'I am beautiful, yes?' she chuckled, as she held out her arms towards him.

Oh yes. She was Gréta who dazzled him now as she had done when he first met her. Indeed more, for now he knew her, and the beauty had meaning and truth for him. He would paint her again – he had often drawn her, but he should do another portrait, here in this house. Now that he knew her, he would be able to capture the elusive quality that had escaped him the first time. Then all thoughts of paint and oils vanished as he embraced her again, smelling the white warmth of her body. He forgot what he could achieve, only what he wanted now most urgently. He laid her gently down upon their bed and was lost inside her.

Several hours later he took the tram back across the Margit Bridge to Pest. He could see that from Gréta's point of view it was ridiculous for her to drive home in her motor car, while he took a tram back into his other life, but to him it was by now second nature. The tram had become a symbol of the divide between them. Sometimes he wondered what still drew Gréta to him; he had nothing to offer save himself and his paint box, and yet she had remained his lover. He could think of no answer to this, and so gave up wondering, and was grateful that it was so. Holló street where he lived was quite a way from the Öszödy mansion so there was little chance of Gréta or her social circle seeing him there by chance. Gréta would never enter the Elisabeth City, except perhaps to visit a specialist shop.

He nodded at the janitor as he entered, and ran up the stairs. He tried to keep on good terms but not close terms with the fellow for most janitors were in with the police and information passed over was a valuable source of income. The door to the Semmelweiss apartment was open and Elisabeth ran out as he passed the door.

'Is anything wrong?' he asked sharply. Not

181

many of the world's troubles usually showed on Elisabeth's pretty face. He was used to seeing her laughing, not looking anxious as today.

'We do not know, Ferenc. Cousin János has been sent to a working camp, and there are bad rumours about them. You must have heard them. I must go to Aunt Mari to see if we can help.'

'Alone?'

'Why not? I must go anyway. If there is trouble, it threatens all the family. They must come here to Budapest. Here they will be safe under the regent's eye. He will not let anything happen to the Jews, will he, Ferenc?'

'No,' Charles replied firmly, 'but I will come with you, Elisabeth. You cannot go alone, especially so late in the day. We'll go tomorrow.'

Was this the first whisper of trouble coming to Hungary? he wondered. He had met János, and he was of call-up age. But a Jewish working camp? Szentendre, where János's family lived, was small enough for him to gather information on this, he thought. Maybe it was in the countryside, not in Budapest, that the blow would fall first. In Budapest so much could lie dormant until the volcano erupted – if indeed it ever did. Now, more than ever, Charles knew he was right to remain vigilant. However long he had to wait, and however hard it became, he had to stay here.

It was strange being with Elisabeth alone in the train, since he was usually with the whole

Semmelweiss family. With her fair hair, she looked totally different to the rest of the family.

'Who did you inherit your hair from, Goldilocks?' he teased her.

'My mother says her grandmother married into the faith.'

'Was she as lovely as you?'

She went red, and he realized he had embarrassed her. He was too used to paying compliments to Gréta and forgot how young Elisabeth was. Then he realized she must be nineteen now, and girls usually grew up quickly in these uncertain times. Elisabeth had retained the innocence of her whole family, the quality of simplicity that had first attracted him when he met Jákob Semmelweiss.

'Ferenc,' she said mock-seriously, 'you are a painter, so I shall forgive you.'

'For calling you pretty?'

'What does being pretty matter today?' she answered quietly. 'It could be a bad thing if bad times come.'

'Bad times won't come,' he said, taken aback at where her thoughts were taking her. Elisabeth was usually the carefree one, the one to console, the one to laugh, the one to care. Today with János on her mind he was seeing a different side of her.

She smiled at him. 'Once when I was a little girl, I saw a butterfly and tried to catch it. So lovely it was, I wanted it. But my mother stopped me. "Let it enjoy its day," she said,

183

"and pray that Yahweh allows us to do the same." I still pray for that.'

'So you worry about the future.' What a damn stupid thing to say. Every Jew worried about the future.

'It is part of our faith,' she pointed out. 'Always we are the outcasts, we are apart. Always looking for the promised land. I think Mama is right. We should enjoy where we are today.'

'And your cousin?'

She was silent, then said quietly, 'I am afraid that for him the day may be over. There is talk that those called to the Jews' working camps can find themselves clearing mines on the Russian front. And other tasks. Oh, Ferenc, if only the world could be happy.'

★   ★   ★

I indulged in my usual quiche and salad after some delving into the archives, and even managed to concentrate on the problem before me. There was no Myrtle here today, of course, since it was early October and termtime. That was a pity, for I'd have welcomed a chat with her. I'd have liked to know whether Charles Carr had ever talked about Gréta to her, but even as the thought passed through my mind, I realized I had another source of information on that, not counting David. After all, David was committed to helping me, but I still didn't feel like putting my head in the lion's mouth of love again before I needed to. It was going to hurt, if all I could do was take notes, say thank you very much and leave him again. Better by far to see Tony. He had worked for Charles a long time ago, it was true, but he must have had some idea of whether Charles was still somehow in touch with Gréta. Magda didn't think he was, but she was too young to know for sure herself; she would be going by what her grandmother told her. Tony had actually listened at the horse's mouth.

I realized, somewhat to my surprise, that I was still thinking in positive terms. There was nothing in my mind that said I wasn't going on with this biography, so I decided that before I left I would wander round the house and gardens again to fire myself up for the two chapters to come. By the time I had emerged from the house, I was even ready to tackle the gardens again. Even the house on the hill no longer held quite the same power, I was able to look at it objectively in all its horror. Perhaps Gréta was right, it represented love and war, not the two sides of love. I had to remind myself that I was not an art critic, but then I reminded myself I was entitled to my opinion. Unfortunately I couldn't reach one definite enough to convince me. The enigma of the murals remained intact, and would do so unless the tapes revealed an answer when they arrived.

I then retraced my steps for the walk down to the lower cottage, trying not to think too much of the first time I did this. As I walked

185

along the path, however, I passed the fountain – and of course it drew me like a magnet.

There it was, in miniature, a straight copy of the Mathias original, without anything added of Charles Carr's own vision.

Why did he do it? Was there some message here I wasn't getting? The leaves were beginning to fall now, but it was still warm, so I sat on the hump of a tree trunk and studied it. Charles had to have built it for a reason – the very fact he hadn't tried to change it told me that. What reason could that possibly have been though? It bore no resemblance to Charles Carr's story, or, I amended, so far as I yet knew it. Was he the king figure or the chronicler? Was Gréta the peasant girl or the king's wife? Perhaps he was just sighing after the unattainable like the peasant girl, had been David's obviously weak suggestion. I didn't believe that. Having seen Charles Carr's *The Happening* I couldn't believe that its creator was a weak man. The message *The Happening* put over was one of strength, so how could this fountain carry a message of weakness? And message it had, for nothing that Charles Carr had created in *The Happening* was by chance.

It should therefore be able to communicate that message to me. I was going to find it. I was going on with the book – and I was going on in my quest for David. I don't know what kept making me link the two – perhaps that Charles Carr had clearly had a mission in Budapest since it ruled so much of his later work. If he had his own quest there, perhaps this fountain was to remind himself of it. As it would remind me of mine. David was not lost to me. He was still there for me – if only I could find the key.

Nine

If I was to be in control of this quest, I knew I had to throw myself into it immediately. There was a snag, though. There is something about those forbidding words on the computer, 'New Document', let alone about a blank page of notepad, that always makes me think I shall never write again. Usually, with my children's work, I can convince myself that New Document represents bread, butter and – if I play my computer right – jam, and it works like a dream. With David, and therefore the biography, it was different. I was floundering up to my neck but ignoring all shouts from the dry land to get out of the swamp. I was well aware that the first step was to get those chapters written, and that I had to start *today*.

I managed it. I read the notes, I rekindled my interest in the subject, I read the letters from Charles's family which I had transcribed on disk, I made notes of still missing information, and then I began. I allowed myself a week, with fervent promises to Sue that my six chapters would be in the post the very next day (or day after). After all, I had little enough to do with my weekends. No friends or even family would welcome a preoccupied lovelorn Lucia. They'd seen it all before. How could they know that this time it was *really* different?

The week wasn't all peace and quiet and ivory-tower time. I had to nerve myself up to ring David on a point or two about New York art life. What exactly had Charles been involved in, whom did he admire, what did he think of the Social Realism movement, and where were his early paintings now?

It was tough, because I knew I truly had to have that input and only he could give it, since art movements were his pigeon not Magda's. Nevertheless to him my motives might be suspect. Nonsense, I told myself. I am a grown woman. I can make that call with a clear conscience. Convince me, jeered the teenager within me.

'Hello, David, it's Lucia.' The toe tested the water.

Surprisingly it was warm. I think he said something original like, 'Hi,' but I can't quite remember. I was too busy fainting at the mere sound of his voice. I managed to tell him what I wanted.

'In book form?' he asked.

'No. Just talk for a few minutes. I've read enough to get the drift.'

Obligingly he talked. And talked. And talked, with the occasional interjection from me, and a lot of scribbling on a notepad. I fell in love all over again, all the time reminding myself that he was another's emotional property. I didn't care, but at last this enchantment stopped.

A silence, then he asked abruptly, 'How's it going?'

'The work? Fine.'

'And the illustrations, photos?'

I was puzzled by this. 'Early stages so far. I think Robin's done his initial survey of the pictures and he and Magda have decided what they want to include.'

'Not you?'

'Me?' For the first time it occurred to me that writers usually have a say in what the illustrations should be, but I dismissed the thought. 'I'll be involved if and when the chapters get accepted and the book goes ahead,' I said cheerfully.

'I think you'll find it'll go ahead all right.'

'Even if they don't like my chapters?'

A pause, then he pointed out the obvious (obvious, that is, to anyone but me). 'You've opened up Pandora's box, Lucia. There are other writers.'

'That's cheap of you.' I was furious. 'Are you implying the foundation is planning to drop me if someone better comes along?'

'Not exactly. After all, you're good. I'd say you're just what they need.'

'They? Don't you mean "we"?' I asked coldly. 'You *are* a trustee.'

He didn't answer this. 'So things are moving quite briskly on the illustration front.'

'Apparently so.' I spoke even more icily. Now I came to think of it, this fast pace *was* slightly odd, since I still had to write the book, even if the chapters were accepted, so we'd be talking of a year or so before we reached production stage. Good biographies aren't written in a month. All I replied was: 'I suppose Robin wants transparencies ready for early publicity material. Have you ever published a book?' A careful hint that this was a field in which I knew what I was doing.

'Yes,' he rejoined, though politely. 'But it's true I wasn't involved closely with the publishing process – as you could be.'

What on earth was he trying to say so obliquely? It struck me it might be something he felt might clash with his position as trustee. 'I'll have a word with Robin,' I said, 'and see what his plans are.'

Another pause. 'Good idea, Lucia. They seem to be pretty close.' Then came his grand climax and adieu. 'You might suggest he doesn't get too close.'

I put the receiver down, my mind reeling. I was boiling with anger at his effrontery in telling *me* to warn Robin off Magda, coupled with a vague sense of unease that there might be something just a little strange going on that I did not yet appreciate. There was no use my questioning David any further, for he wasn't going to tell me even if he knew, and so it seemed to me the sooner I got those

190

chapters to Magda the better.

I worked on those two chapters to get them finished in the week and off to Magda. Then I tackled finishing the six chapters for Sue. The moment I got them off to her, my concern about the Carr project came back in full force, but I decided not to make any more moves till my position was secure. If there was any dirty work going on or intended, my position would be inviolable once those chapters were approved and the contract signed. Something else worried me, however. There was no sign of a tape from Gréta. She had said she'd send them direct to me, but I'd been pouncing on my post every day in vain. Was this a bad omen? I told myself not to be paranoid, but it was hard not to be now that in my mind at least this job and David were inextricably linked.

Some days everything goes right. One of them came two weeks after Magda had received my chapters; she telephoned and the day burst into glorious autumn sunshine.

'Good news, Lucia.'

'The chapters are OK?' I asked, thrilled to bits.

'Yes. I liked them – so did the publishers. Just a very few minor points to discuss.'

'And the trustees?' I held my breath knowing she had distributed copies to every one of them.

'The usual quibbles, but all minor ones, and basically, yes, the project can go ahead. The publishers are sending us both contracts

– it's a joint contract between yourself and the foundation on the one part and the publishers on the other. I hope that's all right. Since all the illustrations and paintings are our copyright and they are an important part of the book, that will make it much smoother from the publisher's viewpoint.'

A warning signal burned faintly in my mind. 'Is David happy with that?'

'Yes. He thought that was a good idea.'

I wasn't quite so sure I did, but provided the money came direct to me I couldn't put my finger on any problem with it, save that it gave more power to the foundation. As we'd discussed earlier what would happen if we fell out, however, I couldn't see this being a major issue. Indeed it was a bonus in a way. The foundation couldn't back out of the deal.

'Oh, and Lucia, I have the first couple of tapes here from my grandmother. Robin says he'll drop them in to you to avoid the risk of their going astray in the post.'

I murmured something that I hoped sounded appreciative, rang off and sat down to consider all this. First, my fairy godmother had waved her wand and told me via Magda that all my wishes (save about David) were granted, then she added that I might possibly pass a few hobgoblins on the way to achieving their fulfilment.

Not that I could see Robin as a hobgoblin, but I had a sudden panic that everything was getting out of my control. How come Robin was so mixed up in it? I shook myself impatiently. Mixed up in *what*, for heaven's sake? Some grand conspiracy to ensure that I did a good job over the biography?

Robin came a few days later. He had the grace to telephone first, which was unusual for him, but I suppose even he realized that the old rules no longer applied. It was strange seeing him on the doorstep just like old times, turning round with that familiar grin as the door opened, as though he'd just been about to leave and thought better of it. That was an illusion, as in our relationship I had been the one always on the point of leaving. Once hooked, Robin stayed hooked – and I reminded myself that apparently he was busily in the process of hooking himself to Magda. Another lost cause, but how could I tactfully point that out? And was it in my interests to do so, even if I could? I might need a friend at court.

'You've painted the hall,' he remarked, stepping inside.

'I have, O Great Interior Designer. Pray enter that you might behold fresh wonders.'

I ushered him into my living room rather than my office. He was, after all, an old friend as well as former lover and an office was too pointed a reminder that those times were over. He sank happily into the leather chair in which he had once reposed so often, and I found myself automatically pouring him his favourite vodka and tonic.

'Thanks.'

I sat on the sofa opposite him, and remembered belatedly all he had come for was to drop off the tapes. Yet he and I had both assumed this was a social call.

'How are things, Robin?'

'Not bad. Work's good. And you? How are the dinosaurs?'

'Done dinosaurs. On to alternative world monsters.'

'Glad I'm not responsible for them.'

'Tony won't be. He likes your work. So do I.'

He shrugged, flushing slightly. 'Yes, well. Odd really, I left Albion House because of you, and here I am working with you again but for a different publisher.'

'One might almost think it was planned,' I said idly.

'One might. But it wasn't by me,' he replied crossly. 'The last thing I wanted was to see you again.'

'It wasn't me either. Put it down to Dame Fortune.'

'Yes,' he said happily. 'I must say Magda's a bonus.'

'Oh.' Jerked into today's world again, I put down my glass and launched my Scud. 'Don't go there, Robin.'

'Any reason why not? And what's it got to do with you anyway, sweetheart ex-mine?'

'Because I hate to see you going down another wrong turning. Magda's not going to leave Michael for you, anyone can see that.'

'Thank you for that trust in my powers of attraction. You really know about knocking

194

self-esteem.'

'Stop,' I said shakily. 'I didn't mean it that way, Robin. You know I wouldn't ever think that. I loved you very much, for heaven's sake. I still feel for you.'

'That why you ran out on me? For the third and last time?' he enquired.

'That was my fault, not yours.' I felt desperate, wondering how and why I had got myself into this. 'I just don't want to be settled.'

'Magda thinks you have the hots for David.'

I couldn't believe this. To my horror, I felt tears come to my eyes that I just couldn't control. 'What the hell is it to do with her?' I managed to say in a trembly voice.

'Quite a lot, I think. Don't you?' I was vaguely aware of his moving, and then I was in his arms on the sofa sobbing my heart out.

'Don't, Lucia, I'm sorry.' He was stroking my hair, then kissing me; the distance between us vanished, as if our parting had never happened. I was nuzzling his neck, smelling the familiar smell of him. 'God, it's such a mess. What the hell are we to do?'

This was beginning to become all too clear, since we were closer and closer together, and I wanted nothing more than to feel his arms round me, safe back where I belonged instead of out in the wilds on some footling futile quest for David. The very thought of David, however, made me pull back, and I think Robin had the same reaction, for he grinned and went back to the armchair – rather reluctantly, I'm glad to say.

'Near miss, eh?' he observed, after a while.

'Yes. It's still there, isn't it?'

'Of course. It doesn't go, we just move on. Unfortunately,' he stared into his glass, 'we've both moved into an impossible situation. Me especially. I can't speak for you.'

'I think we're both faced with the same one – Magda, though it's hardly her fault.' Generous of me. I could cheerfully have strangled her at this very moment.

'I know I haven't a hope in any permanent sense, Lucia. She's not going to leave Michael, I wouldn't want her to because there's Toby to consider.'

'He's David's son, as well as hers.'

He gave me a compassionate look, displaying no surprise at this statement. So, everyone had known except me. 'He's settled with Michael now. There's no dispute between them over that. Toby thinks he has two daddies, that's all. It seems to work OK, and David gets on well with Michael.'

He knew all this? I was hurting inside, at realizing there was still so much I didn't know myself.

'After you, Lucia,' Robin continued matter-of-factly, 'I'm not sure I want to talk commitment myself, so it suits Magda and me perfectly.'

'But why...' I stopped. 'I see.' Magda had a marriage of convenience. 'Does Michael know about you two?'

'Not in theory. In practice yes.'

What did Robin have for someone like

Magda? I asked myself. He was fun, good-looking, kind and loving, but hardly a high flyer to match her league.

'It's not the first time,' Robin added. I took it he meant Magda had had other lovers – but then I noticed he was avoiding my eyes. My heart plummeted way past my boots.

'David?'

He shrugged. 'So she admits. They were married, after all,' he added, seeing my devastated face.

'Stupid of me,' I tried to say lightly. 'Just tell me one thing, if she's still sleeping with David – and now you – then why the hell did she bother to marry Michael?'

'She loves him, she says. And he's very rich. She couldn't live with David – too volatile. Michael gives her peace.'

'That's enough reasons,' I snapped dryly. Nay, viciously. It seemed to me my laughable quest for David was taking me backwards down the golden stairway, not upwards. Well done, Lucia.

'OK, Tony.' I had had enough of his cauldron and his magic Merlin act. Despite my intention to soldier on to get out of the enchanted thicket surrounding this biography, enough was enough. I needed help, and I was on Tony's far-from-welcome mat early next day. Before I signed that contract I needed to know what I was getting into. I had even held back from listening to Gréta's tape. 'Not a step further forward with this Charles Carr thing until I get a few explanations,' I continued firmly, as he showed me to his studio. 'You're a trustee, you told me to go to Edenshaw. *Tell me why*, or our collaboration's over. No more dinosaurs, no more alternative worlds, no monster children for you.'

'Ah.'

'And no more "ahs" either. I want to know what's happening.'

'You're writing the biography, aren't you? That's what you wanted.'

'Yes. Is it what *you* wanted?'

He considered this so long that I feared I was going to have to be taken at my word and fling him out of my life. 'On the whole, yes.'

I was playing the game on his pitch, the same comfortable old place I'd known all these years, and suddenly he seemed a stranger. There *was* more to this Edenshaw House thing. I'd called his bluff, and now I wasn't sure I wanted the result.

'Do you believe in ghosts, my darling?'

'*Ghosts?*' I repeated incredulously. 'Do you mean spooky phantoms in white sheets, or do you mean invisible or metaphorical ghosts peering over one's shoulder?'

'Any of them.'

'I suppose the latter,' I admitted unwillingly.

'Then you wouldn't be too surprised if I said I felt Charles Carr's ghost in that garden reproving me for not doing my job as trustee? Implying he wanted something of me?'

I stared at him in amazement. This wasn't

the man I thought I knew so well. Tony was being serious for the first time since I'd known him. And he needed an answer.

'In that garden? No, I wouldn't be surprised. In a way, without even knowing Charles Carr I've felt it myself. I've had a sense of unfinished business. It's different with you, because you actually knew him, so you must surely be able to guess what it might be. That's what I'm finding so frustrating, Tony. Not exactly a wall of silence, but a wall of spiders' webs I can't walk through. Gréta's the only one who's talking, *really* talking about Charles. David promised to, but either he genuinely doesn't know, or he's still not coming to the heart of the man.'

'I don't know the heart either. I'm afraid that's the truth, Lucia. That's why...'

'Why what?' I asked stonily, when he stopped.

'Why I suggested you go and have a look.'

'Why me?' I asked warily. 'What's so special about me, and just what did you think I might find?'

'I don't know, but it seems to me you're on the right path. You're writing the biography. You have a quality about you, Lucia, a sense of hopeful purpose that drives you on. You don't stop to look from side to side.'

'And that's a good thing?' I asked ironically. 'See where that's led me. I've split up from David – and his marriage is another thing neither of you warned me about.'

'Not my business,' he said easily. Too easily.

I left that, but I'd not forget it.

'This biography,' I began instead. 'You worked with Charles. Did he want a biography written?' I wasn't going to mention what David had so charmingly hurled at me.

'I don't know that we ever discussed it. He hated anyone coming to him with stories about his intelligence work in Budapest, that I do know. The few US reporters and historians who winkled him out in Kent got short shrift up to the time these matters became more open, and then he claimed he couldn't remember.' Tony looked me straight in the eye. 'Yet he had a great regard for truth.'

'Many of us do.'

'Darling, don't be touchy. I'm trying to help.'

'You might have tried earlier.'

'I might. But I knew you'd get there.'

'Where? Never-never land?'

'You're writing the biography and you're asking why one hasn't been written before.'

Had I asked him that? 'Didn't anyone want to?'

'Yes. Magda did.'

'Then why didn't she?'

'The trustees refused. And before you ask why, we did it because coming so recently from Hungary she wouldn't be up to the detailed work necessary to put into a biography, even with David's help.'

'And the real reason?' I asked sweetly.

Tony laughed. 'We felt she was too close to it with her grandmother being involved.'

'Then why not get an outside biographer?'

'David, Myrtle and myself, those of us who knew Charles well, discussed it, and we thought that since Charles himself was so reticent about his earlier life, believing the garden and paintings could stand alone, that's what they should do. Art notes and a brief paragraph of biography would suffice for the record.'

'But you and David at least must realize that they don't do that. Counting myself as Mrs Average, it mystified me.'

'And that's why we've agreed to the biography.' Tony leapt in rather too quickly.

'No go, Tony. Tell me the truth.'

'This, my love, goes no further. You never mention to anyone, not even your pillow, that I told you.'

'I promise.' This was getting interesting.

'Because recently Gréta suddenly entered the picture herself and said she wanted Magda to write the story of her life with Charles, and include his biography in it. The trustees were split over this. I felt – and two others with me – that there were disadvantages in this and the combination of personal story and biography-cum-artistic criticism might not work, especially with an involved author. So the vote was no, but at that very moment, darling Lucia, you came along. So providential.'

'No wonder Magda was so welcoming to me,' I said quietly. I couldn't blame Tony. He hadn't said a single word to me about a biography. It had all been my own idea. All Tony had done was stir the ingredients in his magic pot, then add me to see what happened.

Spring 1943

'Your musician days are over, Ferenc,' László joked as he pressed a forint into Charles's hand, then escorted him very firmly to outside where they could not be overheard. He spoke urgently. 'Listen, my friend, things move at last. Our prime minister – which means probably the regent too – feels the Nazi net draws closer. If Hungary's youth is not to be sacrificed on the altars of Mr Hitler, we must approach the British and Americans to get us out of the war now. Time is running out. You do your best but we hear nothing. These so-called neutral countries are not safe conductors for news of importance.'

'Tell me what I can do.' Instinctively Charles realized that the time had come. He could actually play a part in this war that lay siege to Hungary but had not yet struck at its heart.

'One of my friends at the ministry – his name is Veress – is in Turkey, about to meet the British ambassador at a secret rendezvous to discuss terms for Hungary surrendering. You would be a great help, since you could contact the US Ambassador there for a joint mission.'

'Yes.' Charles glowed with excitement. 'I'll do it.'

'Splendid. So you leave by train tonight.'

'Are my papers good enough?' Charles was very doubtful over this. Turkey was a long way to travel and the route lay through Nazi-controlled countries, the last of which was Bulgaria. 'What would a country musician be doing leaving Hungary?'

'We are fixing a more suitable identity.'

'Just one thing. Do I return here afterwards?'

László looked very grave. 'My friend, it might not be possible. For my colleague Veress, yes, for he is a Hungarian diplomat, but you – with forged papers – would take a risk returning, and you should decide whether you should remain in neutral Turkey or return to America to convince them of Hungary's sincerity.'

He would have to leave Gréta, was Charles's first thought, one he had to dismiss – or try to. His personal problem was a small one in the greater context of the war. Gréta would understand that. After the war, he could settle in Budapest, but now he had to serve his native country like anyone else. He would promise to return to her, and he would. Her spell was as strong as ever.

'I'll explain to Gréta,' he said to László.

'No.' His friend went white with shock. 'You must tell *no one*, Charles.'

Fool that he was, Charles thought. Of course he must tell no one, even though

Gréta was the wife of one of the regent's closest advisers. No one meant no one. What was the heartache of one man beside suffering Europe? War tore families and sweethearts apart, and ending it came first.

László watched him sympathetically. 'Miklós will know,' he pointed out. 'He will tell his wife after you have left.'

Charles clutched at this straw in relief. The parting with Gréta would be hard, especially without seeing her to explain. Leaving Budapest itself would be hard too, especially saying goodbye to the Semmelweiss family. And since the goodbye would have to be a silent one, the pain would be even greater. The thought of Elisabeth's face when she discovered he had gone, was unbearable. He'd wanted to bring his photograph of the family with him, but it was too dangerous, both for them and for him. Reluctantly he had taken it out of his wallet where it always lived.

In some mysterious way, however, Elisabeth must have discovered that he was leaving. Or perhaps it was not so mysterious. Perhaps Katie had guessed or even been told by László, for when in the afternoon he returned to his apartment complete with new papers and suit for his diplomatic role, Elisabeth was waiting for him, and merely announced that she would accompany him to the East railway station.

Now he was Gundel Béla, a Hungarian diplomat with a visa to Turkey. The beard had vanished and only the formidable moustache remained.

'I shall miss you,' he said suddenly, as the sight of the train brought the reality of parting closer.

She smiled at him. 'We have been good friends, have we not, Béla?'

'Yes,' he replied. It was true, for Elisabeth had become part of his life. He had seen her with her family as she soothed and calmed their worries; he had shared their anguish as Tibor was called up for military service with the Hungarian army, and shared their constant fear of being Jewish in Budapest. He had walked with her in the park and on the Corso, he had talked to her endlessly of America. He often wondered whether she and her family knew about Gréta and had to presume they did since László, who did not like her, must surely have told Katie, but it had never been mentioned between them – until now.

'Béla,' Elisabeth said shyly. 'I must speak, for there may never be another chance. I do know that you love the Countess Öszödy.'

He flushed with – with what? It was the truth, so why this embarrassment? Perhaps because he had kept his two lives so separate.

'But she will not mind,' she continued calmly, 'if I give you one little kiss, will she? Then I can pretend I am your sweetheart just for a moment.'

Her lips rested gently on his cheek. 'Like a butterfly wing,' he teased her. 'And now I can catch the butterfly.' On an impulse he took her in his arms. 'This is how sweethearts kiss.' He kissed her lips once, and then again, and seeing her face, again after that, and the pain of leaving Gréta vanished. The Semmelweiss family had been his own, and Elisabeth and Katie more sisters to him than Mary had ever been. And yet, with these kisses, Elisabeth was more than a sister, surely. Much more.

As the train steamed from the station, he leaned from the window, and watched her shrouded by swirling smoke drawing further and further away from him. He told himself his feelings were the natural ones of parting, that her memory would grow less even as her physical figure retreated in his view. Yet he was left with a great longing that he could not quite define, and try as he might he could not satisfy it with Gréta's image.

It was at the border that Charles realized there were problems. The Hungarian border guards came on to the train and examined his papers – which, as he knew they had been warned of his journey, he expected to be merely routine. It was not. He had been so certain nothing would go wrong, that casually he put out his hand to take the papers back.

'One moment please. These papers are not in order.'

Despite his protests he was taken from the train to the border post and forced to watch the train steam on without him. Under the eye of the guards, he was kept until the next train back to Budapest, and taken aboard it. There was no chance of escape for one of the guards remained with him for the whole return journey. It was the end of his mission.

★   ★   ★

Today the Edenshaw garden was an escape, not part of work. I'd had a business meeting with Magda to discuss the arrangements for the rest of the book and sign the contract. It had taken quite a lot of positive thinking on my part to get this far. When I first returned from that meeting with Tony, I'd every intention of throwing the whole thing up. Then I'd listened to the first of Gréta's tapes. What I heard on it about how they had met and come to love each other changed my mind. I had to know the end of the story. I couldn't just walk out on the project. Despite everything, despite the fact that the man I loved was still devoted to and sleeping with his ex-wife (for whom I was working – no, *with* whom, I corrected myself) and despite all the shenanigans that had led to my getting this commission I had to go on. I still didn't understand *The Happening*. If there were ghosts in this garden I wanted to meet them face to face. They might give me a few pointers.

It was mid-November now and a chilly one; that afternoon the sun was dying early, and with barren branches and undergrowth the garden held an air of mystery. The story still waited to be discovered. It was there waiting like Sleeping Beauty's court, ready to rise

207

again to yield its secret. I walked briskly along the paths in the Edenshaw garden, treading them for sentimentality's sake as much as anything. I even climbed to the top of the hill – and there I got the shock of my life.

There was someone there, sitting on the bench outside the fairytale cottage. He was so still I almost thought it *was* a ghost turned up to urge me on. I got my breath back when he grinned at me. The museum was closed this time of year and so were the gardens, so I had hardly expected to see anyone there – particularly this gent.

He was rather like a hobgoblin in my path. He looked like what used to be called a tramp. He was an old man of eighty-odd from the look of him, huddled in an overcoat and a baseball hat, drawing circles in the mud with his walking stick.

'Lovely day,' I said weakly.

'Sure is,' he agreed fixing his nationality right away. So he was an American tourist, even if he did look more like a hobo. 'You going in this place?'

'No,' I replied. 'I've seen it before.'

'What' yer come up here for then?'

I'd humour him. 'Just to get to the top of the hill. Like the Grand Old Duke of York,' I added. Not that he would know that rhyme, I thought belatedly.

Oh yes, he did. He shouted with laughter. 'Good to meet you, Duchess.'

I waved cheerily, and set off down the hill again. I didn't know it then, but I'd just met

Cousin Luke Casey.

Ten

The second tape, no less than the first, had intrigued and fascinated me. It was a completely different experience to listening to Gréta in her apartment, where I could occasionally interject a question of my own. Now I could hear her voice undistracted by the need to get everything down in note form, since I had the tape to refer to. I found myself beguiled by the soft voice, which although it had aged still suggested what a corker she had once been – and still was.

This period was frustrating both for Charles and for me. We both longed to do something more active in the struggle to see this war finished. Little bits of information from here and there might have been valuable if they ever reached the eyes for which Charles intended them, but we were young and longed for the grand gesture. Charles used to tell me that this was what intelligence was like, a series of tiny pieces contributing to the whole jigsaw, but I was impatient. I know how much my dear Miklós longed, as did the regent, to extricate Hungary from the war, and this was

1943 when talk of Allied invasion of Europe
was in the air.

Most of all I longed to see Charles happy
and fulfilled, and at last it seemed about
to happen. I managed, through Miklós, for
him to be sent on a mission to neutral Turkey.
I did not want to lose Charles, far from it, but
I could see that I would lose him in a different
way if he continued in his frustration. He
might throw away his life in some desperate
act of foolhardiness, in his determination to
make his mark. The mission to Turkey was a
dangerous one, but I forced myself to let him go
through with it.

What if he did not return, you will ask? I
was prepared for that. I was sure that our love
was so strong that Charles would return to me
after the war, even if it was too dangerous for
him to return immediately. He was to leave by
train, and I knew I would not even have a
chance to say goodbye for there was so little
time. As it proved, this did not matter. I heard
next day that Charles had been turned back
at the border. He had forged papers, of course,
and they were recognized. Our own guards
turned him back. I could not help being a little
glad for myself, but for him it was a terrible
blow. He felt such an opportunity could never
come again.

I saw him the following day – and I sensed
he despaired of his undercover work ever being
of value. He told me he had just one guard on
the return journey to Budapest, and he had
easily managed to escape him without his true

identity being compromised. Poor Charles. He was certain he had been betrayed. I could not understand this. Betrayed by whom, I asked myself? Budapest was full of spies, professional and amateur, but we had both been so careful, and there was scarcely time in this episode for both betrayal and effective measures being taken to stop him leaving.

And then I realized that there was one way the secret could have been known. Although he would not tell me where he lived, I knew of the Jewish family there – you recall, I showed you the photograph. The Jews at that time were always ready to curry favour with influential pro-Nazi sympathizers as a precaution. What better than to warn one that Charles was on his way to discuss Hungary's unconditional surrender to the Allies? You saw the photograph of the Semmelweiss family. Charles had given it to me one day, and I kept it to remind myself how easily it had happened. The smiling faces must have hidden a devious purpose. I have always blamed that family for everything. Charles was never quite the same after that failed mission. Of course I cannot be sure, and it might not be that Charles himself had told the family where he was going. He was friendly with a young Hungarian diplomat who was engaged to one of the Semmelweiss daughters, and he could have discussed Charles's mission with her. I cannot believe that Charles would have been so foolish as to talk about it. He was so very strict over such matters.

There the tape came to an end. I couldn't wait for the next instalment. The theory about the Semmelweiss family certainly made sense, and I wanted to know more. Much more. There had been more on the tape about Gréta's relationship with Charles, but it was the Jewish part of it that stayed with me. Charles's life in Budapest was beginning to take shape in my mind, now that I knew there was a connection between him and the tragic history of the Jews in the city. I had been in the Jewish area, seen the memorials, visited the synagogue, sniffed the atmosphere of those times for myself.

By today's standards the spy network of the Balkans sounds the stuff of Ruritania, faraway *Boys' Own* adventure tales of derring-do, but from biblical days such work has all come down to betrayal, dangerous missions, and agents disappearing without trace, and still does today. Only its face changes. Ankara in the Second World War was full of agents and double agents, and so was every neutral city. The difference was to me that in Budapest the centre stage was taken by Charles Carr.

From what little I knew of him, I tried to put myself in his shoes, rather than see him entirely through Gréta's eyes. What effect, I asked myself, had the failure of this operation really had on him?

Spring 1943

It had been all too easy for him to escape, Charles reflected bitterly. He had not been handcuffed and in the crowd of passengers leaving the train at Budapest he was able to throw off the guard and run for his life. His *life?* he wondered. It was hardly a challenging escape. It was almost as if someone wanted him back in Budapest.

He went to an *espresso* bar to have a coffee while he thought about his next step. Was there any reason he should not return to his apartment? He had not told the janitor he was leaving, only the Semmelweisses could know. So why not go back? He needed to see László urgently to discover what had happened. Surely he would know or find out exactly why the Hungarian guards had turned him back? Was the mission annulled? Could be. Perhaps one of the fascists in the government had discovered the project, and stepped in. If so, why was he left at large? Answer, he reasoned: he was operating on behalf of the regent and prime minister. And if this were the correct solution, he would be under surveillance from now on, and probably not only as diplomat Béla.

Budapest was a leaky bucket. Everyone had a different agenda, personal, political, racial. Which particular agenda had come into play over him? And was it safe to contact his former colleagues? He reasoned it must be – carefully. Either he would have had a stronger guard on the way back to Budapest and be in the Margit Prison by now, or he was permitted to go 'free' though it was possible that Ferenc and his musical activities were now known to the powers that be. Which meant that so was the existence of Charles Carr. So be it. Provided he remained aware of that, and aware that trust in others could mean disaster, he would be safe. But it didn't stop him thinking.

He returned to his apartment, greeting the janitor with *'Jó estét'* as though nothing had happened. He hoped that his 'diplomat's suit' would be taken as Ferenc's Sunday best. What did it matter if not, since he must already be on the official suspect list?

Instead of announcing his return to the Semmelweiss family, he went quietly to his own small apartment above them, looking glumly at the intentionally disordered kitchen that had been meant to suggest that Ferenc would shortly be back. For the first time since his arrival almost five years ago, Charles felt a stranger in this city. He had thought he had grasped the core of it, but now he knew it had slipped from his hands – if he had ever had it at all. The worm of war had worked its way through the flesh to the heart of Hungary.

There was a knock at the door and he hurried to it, expecting Elisabeth, though he could not understand how the news would have reached her so soon. It wasn't her, how-

214

ever, but Katie. Katie was completely different in looks from Elisabeth. She was tall, strong, and dark, taking after her father, rather than her mother's side of the family whose fair hair and slenderness Elisabeth had inherited. Usually Katie was the calmest of them. Nothing ruffled her. But today her face was full of anxiety.

'May I come in, Ferenc?'

He ushered her in, and waited for her to speak, hoping for some clue as to what was happening. 'I have a message for you from László,' she continued.

Thank heavens for that at least. 'What?' he asked sharply.

'He says it is too dangerous for you to meet yet. He will contact you again, but not for the moment. Do you understand?'

Charles did and was chilled by its implications. I am on my own, he thought. 'Can you tell me why?' he asked quietly.

'I do not know,' Katie said miserably. 'I suppose he does not understand what has brought you back. His colleague Mr Veress is safely in Turkey.'

'Nor,' Charles replied, 'do I. I was expecting him to tell me.'

This was the worst of news. László obviously suspected he had been brought back for a purpose. Turned, they called it in intelligence circles. His life would be spared on condition he became a double spy and bit the hand that fed him. Oh yes, he understood. 'I have to prove myself clean, is that it, Katie?'

'I do not know,' she repeated, 'but something strange is going on.'

'Over me?'

'I think it is wider than you, Ferenc. László is concerned because the regent's and prime minister's desire for peace with the Allies is not that of everyone, and the fascists in our country may win.'

'He thinks I may be an informant for them. Or rather that I have been forced to become one.'

'Yes.' She could not meet his eyes.

'And you? Your family?' He could hardly bear to ask.

'To us, you are Ferenc, and we love you. We know you could never betray anyone, of that we are certain, and I think László believes that too. But he is nervous of some of your friends.'

She spoke so reasonably that for the moment he did not grasp what she implied. And then he did. Anger, loyalty, fear jostled with the need for a calm head, and he managed to reply.

'László knows I need sources of information, and he knows that is dangerous. Tell him – and your family, Katie – that I too am always aware of this, no matter whom I'm with. Man or woman, prince or' – he stumbled over the last word – 'lover.'

As she gently shut the door behind her, Charles felt abandoned. Always before he had been able to retreat to the inner self within him, questioning the world with the artist's

216

objective eye, and he could re-emerge strengthened. Now it seemed more a refuge in which he should remain, even though to the outside eye he would appear the Ferenc – and Charles – it had known. Only there lay safety. Outside raged the terrible suspicion that had come to him and had now been given food by László's wariness. If it was not a leak inside the Hungarian Foreign Ministry, then there was only one person apart from the Semmelweiss family through László himself who could have had information on his mission. Had Miklós learned of it, and through him Gréta? The thought tore at him with sharp pain. He had to ask himself that if this monstrous thought were true, whether betrayal would have been for personal reasons or political. The latter was the worse to consider because of the implications it carried. He could not, would not, believe it, and all night Gréta's image alternately lulled and destroyed his dreams.

Next day took on a kind of normality. Everything began to slip gently back into place with Papa Semmelweiss cracking his terrible jokes at dinner, Mama Márta agonizing over the overcooked carp, the prayers for Tibor's safety, and Elisabeth sitting quietly, glowing with pleasure to see him back and stealing the occasional glance at him – which of course he noticed. As he listened to their ritual prayers he began to relax, and to realize the monsters were in his mind, not at this table – nor in the Öszödy mansion.

The following day he went to the café in the Vár where he usually met Gréta. It would have been their next appointment, the one which he should have been unable to attend. He knew she would be there, guilty or innocent, for the news would have travelled fast. Little doubt of that. He watched her before she caught sight of him. She was at a table on the sidewalk, unconscious not only of him but of ogling passers-by who stopped to address a second look at her, even though she deliberately dressed plainly for their meetings. Dressed as she was in an old mackintosh and beret, her bearing and vitality still seemed a symbol of the old world of Budapest.

Her face sparkled, as he came over to her, kissed her and sat down as though nothing had happened. And though he was aware deep inside of his suspicion, now it seemed ludicrous. He could not talk of what had happened, and in any case it was unnecessary.

She must have picked up something in his manner for after a while she said, 'Ferenc, there is something you wish to talk about, is there not?'

'Perhaps,' he replied guardedly.

'You must not be cross, I heard through Miklós that there was a failed attempt at contacting the Americans – it was yours, was it not? Somehow I was sure of it.'

'Yes.' He could not bring himself to say more. The stupidity of his thoughts combined with his determination on reserve held him back.

'But you are back – and free, thank God.'

'Yes.'

She turned that penetrating look on him. 'You think I might have been involved in that? That I love you too much to let you go, even for the sake of Hungary?'

'I did wonder, Gréta.' It seemed stupid now, trivial. 'Put it down to my arrogance,' he said lightly.

'No, it is not arrogance. In fact, I *could* have done it, but even had I known then where you were going, I would not have done such a thing. Not to you, Charles. I know how important this is to you. How could you imagine I would take that away from you? If we love each other, then we shall be together somehow, somewhere, sometime. I believe that. I have to. Even if you had gone, I would know you would return to me as soon as you could.'

His worries had been for nothing, and he now felt ashamed of his suspicions, even though he knew every possibility had to be thought of. He watched the rise and fall of her breast under the pink silk blouse she wore, and the black high-heeled shoe swinging on the end of her crossed silk-stockinged leg, and desire so strong overcame him that all he could reply was: 'Shall we go to the house?' The words came out huskily, haltingly, and she took his hand in hers.

'Yes, Ferenc. Let us go, and be thankful that you are here again.'

It was Gréta herself who some hours later returned to the subject again. 'Who could have betrayed you, Charles? You must be very careful now.'

'Someone in László's ministry,' he replied sleepily. 'It must have been.'

'Are you sure you told no one, Charles? No one at all?'

Even as she said it, he remembered Elisabeth's sad face as the train had left Budapest.

'No one.' It was the truth, but only the letter of the truth. The Semmelweisses must have known, but he couldn't believe that the family had betrayed him any more than Gréta herself could have done.

His greatest anxiety now, if his every move was going to be watched, was how to carry out his former task of forwarding information through the neutral legations, and for some days after his meeting with Gréta he did little, uncertain of his best path.

It was Elisabeth who solved his problem. The family had been discussing it – even Katie, she said, and it was agreed that Elisabeth could take over the delivery to the legations.

'No,' had been his instant reaction when she suggested it.

'What safer bearer could you have?' she asked practically. 'No one would suspect me. I can take them in the van with Papa's deliveries from the shop.'

'I can't involve you,' Charles said flatly. Since his return he had realized that Elisabeth was becoming a part of his life that had nothing to do with war and betrayal. She was almost a part of himself, reflecting an ideal of life to which he clung in the face of the turmoil around him. Elisabeth's simplicity and goodness shone through his life. His love might belong to Gréta, but she was of the world he saw around him, the world in which he moved. Elisabeth was in his dreams. He couldn't analyse exactly why this should be so. Perhaps he still might find the answer through his brush. He had drawn her in pencil many times, but in paint he might manage to convey the truth of Elisabeth from the unknown inside himself to canvas.

'As Jews, you are suspect anyway,' he urged her fiercely, horrified by her offer of help. 'How could I let you become deeply involved in my work?'

'Charles' – she was deliberately using his name instead of Ferenc, he realized – 'you treat me as though I were a little girl still. I am not. I am nineteen, a woman and I have as much right as you to decide how I shall serve my country. My family – and all of our race – are in great danger. If Hungary surrenders and leaves the war, we may be safe. If not...'

She did not need to continue, for Charles knew all too well what would happen. Sooner or later the deportations and labour camps to which the rest of the Jewish population in Europe was being subjected would come to them also.

Gradually she quietened his objections and

after the whole family had agreed to it, Charles gave in. It was his rational mind that told him it was a reasonable risk. What bothered him is that he was aware that far more than reason was involved here.

★   ★   ★

Life can turn unexpected corners, and this one was very unexpected indeed. Here I was driving down to Kent for a dinner party at David's home, where, he had casually told me, Magda would also be present (no mention of Michael) and another guest he wanted me to meet. Joy at the ice being broken between us, no matter for what reason, was soon replaced by more practical concerns. What could I possibly wear that could compete with Magda? There was only one answer. Don't even try to compete, I told myself – several times, since my mind was racing through my wardrobe with increasing desperation. Christmas would soon be here, so I ended up with the faithful black velvet and dangling bits of jewellery. Competition was a waste of time. I could only be 'my own sweet self' as my father used to say – and still does when he wants to annoy me.

Worse than what to wear was how to endure the whole evening. I would be a witness to David's devotion to Magda, and even the fact that I was back in the ring to fight another round was poor compensation for that. I could cope, I told myself feebly. Then I put it another way. Would I want to miss out on this opportunity however painful it was going to be? After all, David must have some particular reason for wanting me to be there, he couldn't be doing it just to taunt me. Even I wasn't as paranoid as to believe that.

Every lorry seemed on a crusade to block my passage, and by the time I arrived at my B and B I was already running late. I'd arranged to get a taxi to David's, since he had delightfully offered to run me back afterwards. By the time I arrived at his home, I was half an hour late and the last to arrive. David opened the door, and I had my bright smile ready. I thrust my votive offering of wine at him, gabbled hello and apologies happily, slid out of my coat and prepared for battle by becoming anonymous for the evening. The role I had decided to adopt was fly on the wall.

One look at Magda in a floaty pale lemon evening dress (in December?) made me realize that I was on the right track with my plan, but one look at the other guest and I was hooked. It was the hobo I had met at the top of the hill in the garden.

'Hi there,' he greeted me in an un-eightyish kind of way. 'If it isn't the Duchess of York.'

Magda looked mystified but smiled politely as I laughed. 'We've met before,' I explained, 'though we didn't fully introduce ourselves.'

David made haste to make amends before the hobo could speak. 'Lucia, this is Luke Casey. Lucia—'

'Luke?' I yelped. 'Cousin Luke of the Carrs?'

'Sure am.'

I then remembered something that Pamela had told me ages ago – that the 'ancient cousin' turned up every so often and that Magda dealt with him.

'That's wonderful,' I said with genuine enthusiasm. 'Do you mind if I grill you?'

'The only grilling to be done this evening,' announced David grimly, 'is my cod steaks. Work can wait.'

'This isn't work,' I whipped back. 'It's pure pleasure.'

'I guess the host has right of way.' Cousin Luke didn't look too disappointed.

I saw Magda smile at David as he passed to go to the kitchen and thought for a moment that she was going to follow him in. She didn't. It was immediately obvious that she knew Luke of old and they chatted away about everything under the sun except Charles Carr, while I longed to get to grips with what he could tell me about Charles. At last there was a pause into which I dropped an inane conversational gambit.

'Are you over here just for a holiday?'

'Last stage of the bum,' he informed me laconically.

'Luke is a wanderer,' Magda explained. 'He spends half his time in Georgia, the rest wandering round the world.'

'Not much longer, I guess,' he said ruefully. 'Time catches up with slow walkers.'

'And you knew Charles well?' I asked.

'Sure did.' He grinned at me, as if he knew just how tantalizing I found this, since he had no intention of continuing.

I listened quietly throughout that meal as Magda, David and Luke talked about America, especially Georgia – where they had all too obviously all been together. Every so often I caught David's eye resting on me thoughtfully, but I couldn't tell why. Maybe he was just being a watchful host. Why had he brought me here if he didn't want to talk shop about Charles Carr, I wondered. Just to enjoy his cooking? It was good, I granted him that. The cod had a tapenade crust, accompanied by a mash to die for. It was preceded by an onion soup with a touch of orange. I quickly identified it as a Joscelyn Dimbleby recipe – another sign of David's and my mutual good taste. It was followed by a fruit crème brulée, which I attacked with gusto, wondering meanly whether it would do just a little bit of damage to Magda's slim figure.

Every so often someone would toss me a bone of conversation – chiefly Luke, or Magda to be kind – while David, it seemed to me, addressed the minimum directly to me, almost as though he found this as hard as I did. But perhaps I was being over-fanciful. These were three strong lions in the Carr camp, and I was still the outsider – even though I was supposed to be on the inside now.

If it hadn't been for all this going on – or

not going on – I could have felt at home in David's dining room. I liked it. There wasn't a lot around that was personal, but what there was had a friendly atmosphere, the pictures, the few photographs, and relaxed table arrangement. It was the kind of room to spend Christmas in – but I quickly switched my thoughts away from this pipe dream.

At last I began to feel I had a place in this dinner party as Luke told stories of his trips round the world that had us in fits of laughter.

'Have you always been a traveller?' I asked casually.

'I guess,' he answered. Don't go any further, the atmosphere once more suggested.

This time I did. 'So you could tell me about Charles's life before the war? Not now, of course.'

'Guess I could,' he agreed.

'And during the war?' Now I felt I really had put my foot in it, though Luke answered readily enough.

'I flew with the US Eighth Air Force, Duchess.'

That put the kibosh on my hope that I had a ready-made witness for the war years.

'And after the war?'

'Travelled the world taking in old Charles as I did so.'

'In the fifties and sixties?' I asked, mindful of *The Happening*.

'Maybe.'

Now why should he be so cautious? True,

he didn't know me well, but Magda and David were vouching for me. Nevertheless the door was slowly closing – though I sensed it might still be ajar.

Around ten thirty, David drove Magda home to my surprise. It appeared he'd picked her up too, as Michael was childminding. It occurred to me, unfairly, that surely she could have driven herself. However, their jolly little ex-marital drive home at least gave me a chance to talk more to Luke, who turned out to be staying with David.

'You're writing this biography. That so?' he asked.

I realized how bright Luke's eyes were. Like Charles Carr's perhaps, the eyes of an artist. 'Yes. Tell me, Luke, do you paint?'

'Nope.'

'Or write?'

'Nope.'

'So what do you do to record your trips round the world?'

'I just looks, Lucia.'

It was a good answer, and I thought a truthful one. 'And you knew Charles well?' I asked again, not knowing quite how to get through this stone wall.

'Yup.'

I suddenly realized he was still sizing me up. It was an enormous relief. That's what this whole evening had been in aid of. His short answers hadn't been hostile, but to stall until he'd reached a decision. 'Will you talk to me about him?'

'Why don't you talk to me about him first?'

This surprising suggestion took me aback and I was about to say that wasn't the biographer's job, then I changed my mind. Maybe, in this case, it was.

I thought very hard about what to say. 'So far – that's from the letters, the work, and what little everyone has been able to tell me so far – he was a man with deep passions both about his work and about the woman in his life. A sense of humour that wasn't always apparent. Totally dedicated to one thing, and to the need to convey it in paint to himself, rather than anyone else.'

'Do you like this fella, Lucia?'

'I think so. There are too many gaps to be sure yet.'

'Such as?'

'There's still a big gap for me between the Charles Carr as he was at the beginning of the war and the one who returned to Europe to paint it.'

'And how do you reckon to fill it?'

'I'm waiting for the rest of the tapes from the Countess Öszödy – that's all the evidence I have on the war years.'

'That all?'

I was being grilled now, apparently in the most casual way.

'No,' I replied. 'I can't use that alone. The story has to make sense in my mind by tying in with *The Happening*.'

'And what if it don't do that, Lucia?'

'I don't know yet. I could put Gréta's

228

account in, but make it clear it's one person's account and there's no corroboration.' Perhaps it was the glass or two of wine I'd taken, but I did my best to imagine how I would feel if I couldn't make head or tail of the man I was writing about. I'd be seeing him through Gréta's eyes only – with a bit of help from others. Would that satisfy me? 'I don't know,' I repeated. 'I'd have to decide whether I still wanted to go ahead with the book. Do you have a view on that, since you knew Charles after he came back from the war? You could tell me your impressions.'

'I guess I could at that. But I can't make everything come right for you if it ain't there.'

At that moment David came back, and raised his eyebrows, obviously amused to find me hunched forward deep in conversation with Luke. 'You haven't wasted much time.'

'I guess she thinks with a man my age she'd better get right down to it as quick as she can,' Luke answered laconically.

'How long are you here for?' I asked him hopefully.

'I'll stick around for a while. A week maybe.'

'A week? I'll need you for months,' I shrieked in frustration.

'I'll be back, Lucia.'

'Do you have e-mail?' I asked desperately, seeing a prime source of information flying out of the window.

'Nope. Don't have no phone either. Just have these two feet. I'll be back, darling girl.

David, one of those whiskies of yours will suit me fine.'

'Darling girl?' David repeated, as I hopped into the car, wondering how the temperature was going to be. 'You seem to have scored a hit.'

'When is a hit a miss?' I muttered crossly. 'He's going to talk in his own time and not mine. He's going to wait till I've written it all and then tell me I'm wrong. I need a go-between. Will you do it?'

I saw his face in the darkness, staring at the road as he negotiated a sharp bend.

'I don't do go-betweens. You want to know what I think?' he said at last.

'The truth?'

'And nothing but, I promise. I'm sure Luke knows a lot more than he's letting on. He wanted to try you out, and then see what the result was. Now he'll really test you.'

I could have wept in frustration. What *was* all this? 'But if he knows, for example, what Charles was doing in the war, why the blazes won't he tell me?'

'My guess is that it's because it's the foundation's book, as well as yours. He's a wayward old cuss. If – and it's only if – he knows more about Charles Carr than you can find out elsewhere, he might choose not to be a lone voice in the wilderness among a lot of prickly cactuses. He might prefer to take my line – that the paintings and garden are enough in themselves.'

I thought of Luke as I had first met him on

the top of the hill, and it seemed to me David might be right. He was obviously a law unto himself and had nothing to lose by keeping quiet.

'He *looks*, Lucia, he told you that,' David continued. 'He does not judge, the past is the past, and the world goes on. That's his philosophy.' He drew up outside my B and B.

'But the truth? Wouldn't he want that told? Suppose I get it wrong?'

'What, as Pilate once observed, is truth? Different things to different people. His view of Charles might not be anyone else's.'

'Oh, David.' I spoke as I felt, in despair. I was beaten. I would go round and round in circles getting nowhere at all. I must have slumped physically too, for suddenly I found myself in David's arms. He was nuzzling my face, kissing me, but mostly holding me very, very close.

'Go on, Lucia. You can do it. I know you can. Don't give up.'

He was forcing energy back into me. Now, when I was on the point of throwing in the towel, David was the one wanting me to go on. It didn't make sense.

'Why?' I asked.

'It has to be done.'

I struggled to get my thoughts in order, and how hard it was with him so close to me. 'Why do you want me to do it?'

'Prove me wrong, Lucia.'

I didn't have a chance to ask what on earth he meant by this because I was smothered by his arms, and he was kissing me to such purpose that I couldn't speak even if I wanted to.

'Why is it,' he muttered, 'that neither your place nor mine is ever available?'

Eleven

March 1944

Elisabeth was still not home. Charles had returned to his apartment after an anxious walk by the Danube during which he had battled to convince himself there was nothing wrong. Yet there had been a curious atmosphere in Budapest. There were fewer people strolling the streets than there would normally be on a Sunday, and a general sense of tension in the cafés. He'd thought about stopping at an *espresso* to see if anything were amiss, but he didn't. He was too anxious to discover if Elisabeth had returned in his absence.

Yesterday she had gone to visit her uncle in Buda, Papa Semmelweiss's brother Zoltán, but she should have come back last night. Charles felt the same sickly fear sweep over him as when she was making her 'deliveries' to the neutral legations. There were informers within them, as there were everywhere. He had tried to stop her, because her face was becoming 'known' which was doubly dangerous for a Jew. All she would say was that it was 'for Tibor'. Nothing had been heard from him since he left for the Hungarian army a year ago, and everyone knew what had happened to the Hungarian Second Army in Russia last summer. It had been all but annihilated, and now hope had faded even from Mama Márta's eyes.

What concerned Charles about the work he and Elisabeth were doing was that it seemed to be achieving nothing. Prime Minister Kállay's policy of trying to convince the Western Allies that Hungary's heart was not in co-operation with Hitler, save in trying to prevent eventual Russian domination, was falling on deaf ears. There were, thanks to Veress, the diplomat with whom his failed mission in Turkey should have been shared, now two B2 transmitters in Budapest, but though messages were getting through the British secret organization SOE, and therefore to the British Foreign Office, nothing was happening on the political war front. Worse than that, Charles had received news yesterday that the OSS, the US counterpart of SOE, had dropped an agent into Hungary four days ago, but the chief of them had been unlucky and been captured immediately he landed, although there was no news of the other. If only, Charles thought in frustration, he had been able to get to Turkey himself.

Instead the plan had been foiled from the beginning – though how and why he still did not understand.

He rushed up the stairs to the Semmelweiss apartment, only to find that Elisabeth still had not returned, and the atmosphere was more tense than when he had left. However, someone else was waiting impatiently for him, his friend László, who rose immediately on seeing Charles, and with a nod to Katie he followed Charles quickly upstairs so they could talk in private.

'Elisabeth?' Charles asked sharply, as he closed the door behind them.

'There is no news. We can only wait. Or, rather, you can,' László said quietly. 'Charles, I must say goodbye to you.'

'Why?' Charles already feared the answer.

'Have you not heard? Fine spy, you are, Mr American,' László tried to joke, but his face was strained. 'The Germans will reach Budapest any moment. Hitler has told the regent he will occupy our country, and they crossed the border at dawn. My friend, the war is beginning. We pay the price for our anti-Nazi prime minister. Kállay and the regent together are too much for our jittery Mr Hitler, now he begins to lose the war. He fears the Russian advance and this is the result.'

'But you?' A thousand questions and a thousand fears raced through Charles's mind.

'I have no choice. I will be on the Gestapo's list without doubt for I am linked to Veress.

234

Our Turkish adventure is still remembered by my pro-Nazi colleagues. Veress has already left Budapest, and Kállay has sought refuge in the Turkish legation.'

'And Katie will leave with you?'

'No. I am travelling alone. Much though I wished to take her, she insists her coming would endanger me. I might cross the border, but a Jew could not, she says, and I fear rightly. I said I would stay, but she would not have it. I would be dead in days, and we both know it. She tells me it is my duty to go, and that too I know. There is a plan that some kind of Hungarian government in exile might be set up in the United States.' He looked straight at Charles. 'You should come with me, Charles. Will you? You too run a great risk in remaining here.'

'I cannot – what about Elisabeth?' Even as Charles noticed László's surprised glance, he realized that it had been Elisabeth, not Gréta, who had come to his mind first.

'Remember you too are known, Charles, even if only as Béla.'

'Gréta will protect me.' Charles sounded stiff even to himself.

László was silent for a moment, then burst out, 'Yes, Charles, she will protect you, while she wishes. But remember that Miklós is Horthy's adviser.'

Charles felt the anger boiling up inside him, all the greater because László expressed the niggle of doubt he had faced and dismissed. 'You have never liked her, László. You do not

235

know her.'

'I see her, Mr American. That is wiser.'

'And just what do you mean by that?'

'I see her using men, playing pro-Nazi against patriots, playing Horthy versus Fascist. I see her using you, Charles.'

Charles hardly recognized his own voice, as he struggled for control. 'You fool, László, of course she does. How else would I get my information?'

'And who questions the information?'

'I do.' He was losing objectivity. He knew it, but could do nothing to persuade those grey eyes staring at him for once so seriously that they saw a different Gréta, that they were biased by the maelstrom of Budapest life into suspecting everyone, however unjustly.

'Take care, Charles. Not just for yourself, but for those I love. Trust *no one*, it is safer that way.'

Safer than what? Charles thought savagely. The Margit Prison? The Gestapo? The canvas of his mind was covered with images of grey anonymous-looking buildings lining the streets of life. Behind their walls who knew what dangers lay? An individual person was only a pinprick beside them.

'You must look after the Semmelweiss family, Charles. It's too late for Jewish families to leave together. The borders will be sealed against any such attempts.'

'And what will happen to those who remain here? The regent must still have some power, and he is sympathetic to the Jews' plight.'

'Who knows, dear friend. You can still come with me.'

'I cannot. If the balloon goes up, I need to be here.'

'Oh, it is going up, American, and once it is there no one will be able to stop it. The rumour is that our friend Adolf Eichmann is on his way to Budapest,' László said quietly. 'Forgive me, Charles, but I must ask you. You have said nothing to Gréta of where you live or with whom?'

Charles flushed. 'No.' Even as he said it, he remembered her petulant 'Are they Jews?' 'She suspected they might be Jewish,' he told László steadily, 'but I gave her no clue as to where I live or as to whether they were or not.'

László looked at him sharply. 'Then promise me, Charles, that if – when – the time comes that this is necessary, you move out of that apartment block.'

'I do promise.' Charles was cold with apprehension. Eichmann was the most feared Nazi by the Jews, because of his obsession with expunging the entire Jewish population from all German territories by deportations to work camps, or worse, as some whispered, death camps.

László embraced him, tears in his eyes. 'Wish me good fortune, Charles, and take care that Béla and Charles Carr have disappeared for ever. You must be Ferenc, if you are to remain alive.'

After he had left, Charles tried to think. The

last instruction was easy enough. He was still Ferenc, the musician, but even as Ferenc he was associated with Gréta. He could not concentrate, or see a clear path before him, because there was a more immediate fear to grapple with: what had happened to Elisabeth? He went to join her family in their apartment, but unable to bear the waiting, he decided to go to Buda to Zoltán Semmelweiss's home to see if she were still there.

He was hardly outside the apartment block, however, when he saw her hurrying along the narrow street towards him; her face was almost hidden in the hood of her coat, but her identity was unmistakable. In a moment she was in his arms, and he was hugging her close to him, so great was his relief.

'Where have you been?' he asked fiercely, now his fear was calmed. 'We have been so worried.'

She remained in his arms, without drawing away. 'There has been trouble, Ferenc,' she whispered. 'All is well with our family at the moment, however. You have heard what is happening?'

'The rumours about Eichmann? Yes.'

'No rumour, Charles. He is here. He has said he wants to have his headquarters in the Hotel Majestic. We heard the news of the meeting between Hitler and Horthy last night, and that is why I did not return. There was a meeting of our elders in my uncle's home. We have been fortunate so far in Budapest, thanks to the admiral, but now I am

238

afraid that we butterflies are trapped indeed.'

She tried to smile, but there was little point. They both knew the threat that faced the Jews if Eichmann had his way.

Charles's trepidation grew. The Majestic was on the Schwab Hill, one of the best areas of Budapest, with many splendid houses. It was an open declaration that the old upper classes of Hungary would no longer wield power here.

'No harm shall come to you, Elisabeth, or your family. I will make sure of that.'

'Even you cannot promise that, Charles.'

'You called me Charles,' he remarked, to avoid acknowledging the truth of what she said.

'That is how I think of you, and always have. So when we have little time left, why should I not say it – when we are alone.'

'Don't think that way, Elisabeth.' With his arm still round her, he looked down at her face. The fair hair tumbling over her cheek, a tiny spot on her chin, the finely chiselled features, and the eyes that looked at him so steadily. He knew the face so well, but felt he had never seen it before. Now he, too, had come home at last.

'I love you, Elisabeth.'

The four words seemed to come out of a great truth inside him that had been working its way to the fore for a long time. Far, far too long. In his mind, images of her swirled around, as if he were dreaming a painting, and merging with the reality here in his arms.

He would keep this moment for ever, and one day he must paint those images that were searing themselves into his life.

She laughed. 'So here we are, darling Charles. And this is much more important than Eichmann at this moment, is it not? For I love you, as I have loved you so long.'

The images in his mind were circles. One of light, blazing out with images of Elisabeth, and another of darkness doing its best to push its way through, to divide him from her. But it did not succeed, and it finally retreated.

'We must catch the sunlight while we may, my love,' he whispered. 'Shall we do that?'

'Yes, Charles. Oh yes. And when it goes we will tell ourselves it has only disappeared behind a cloud.'

As he left the Semmelweiss apartment that evening, his inner happiness struggling with his fears for the future, he remembered that tomorrow was his day for meeting Gréta. Gréta seemed another life now, but he knew he must deal with it. He was too clear-headed to think that the chains that had bound him for three years could be lightly broken; he had a duty to them and to her. It would not be easy to part from Gréta, but until he had done so, he could never be free to be completely with Elisabeth. Could one love two women at once? Could one love overlie another, and if so, was that because his love for Gréta was different, was his love for her the call of the flesh alone? He had not thought so,

240

and he did not think so now. It called so sharply, however, that it would present itself as an enemy to be conquered. Conquered, it would be, however, for only Elisabeth could be his meaning for life.

★   ★   ★

On my desk before me was the photograph of that blessed fountain that so mesmerized me. Once again it had virtually thrust itself before me. Quite by chance, I'd come across a different version of the legend. In this one, Ilonka had been chasing butterflies in the forest when the king caught sight of her, and she was no peasant girl, but the daughter of impoverished gentry. In the best traditions of properly brought-up young women, she invited this anonymous handsome hunter back to tea and to meet Daddy. Not to be outdone, he suggested they popped up to see him in Buda, one day, but he didn't leave his address – or name.

Naturally enough, when they got to Buda, they couldn't find him. Until one day when a royal procession goes by – and lo and behold – Ilonka recognizes her beloved, and sadly creeps away to die of her broken heart.

There was one other vital difference in the two versions of the legend. In this new version, the cowled figure with the falcon and dog was not the court chronicler but the court jester. And that threw up even more questions as to why Charles Carr put the fountain in the garden. Which version did he know?

I decided to get on with what I *did* know. I was getting on splendidly with the biography, or at least its first draft. Everything might change of course as my research continued. I felt curiously isolated, however. I was well used to working at home, but I suppose I had come to think of this biography as a joint quest involving several people as eager as I was to discover the full story. I had expected that Magda would ring up from time to time and perhaps even David, just to see how it was going. At the very least I had expected Tony to take an active interest. No. It was left for Robin of all people to do that, for he was still my postman for delivering the tapes.

I had got over my irritation that these were still sent to Magda. At first I put it down to the vagaries of an old lady, but then I began to wonder whether this was so, since Gréta bore little resemblance to a vague old lady. She was as much in command of herself as Magda was. Probably she sent them to her granddaughter so that she could listen to them first. Was there anything wrong with that, I asked myself? Surely it was natural that Magda would want to listen to her grandmother's story? And yet it bothered me. There was – unless I was getting paranoid – a hint of control about this that I didn't much like, yet there was nothing definite to complain about.

'Come in,' I said brightly when Robin turned up on my doorstep at the appointed time. This was usually when the sun had just gone over the yardarm – not that Robin's much of a drinker but it was a good excuse to settle down for a chat. And chat is what he appeared to want that day.

'Here it is.' He tossed the usual padded bag on to the table; it was addressed to Magda and had been opened. So what, I told myself firmly.

'Have you played it?' I asked politely.

Robin looked surprised. 'No, should I have done? I'm only concerned with pictures, as you know.'

'Yes.' I withdrew my prickliness, and we chatted of this and that, but nothing in particular. Nonetheless, knowing him so well, I felt there was something he had come to talk about that wasn't yet lying on the table with the padded bag and our glasses of wine and fruit juice. At last it emerged.

'You don't fancy a trip to Paris, do you?' he asked casually.

I was naturally dumbfounded. 'Work,' he added agreeably, reading my expression correctly.

'How can it be? I thought you were working hard inside your new lady love's glove over this?'

Robin appeared to be finding the bottom of his glass extremely interesting. 'I am.'

'Then why not take her to Paris?'

'You're the biographer – and I'm not *taking* you. I'm asking if you'd be interested in

243

coming with me.'

'OK, tell me why.'

'There's a Charles Carr painting in the Pompidou Centre that I'd like to see and thought you might like to do so too.'

I assimilated this. 'But why me and not Magda?'

He shrugged. 'I don't know. And that's an honest answer. I found out about the picture quite by accident, not through Edenshaw House, and when I investigated its provenance I found out that it's on loan from Magda herself.'

'So? Very generous of her.'

'Yes. The odd thing is that amongst all the hundreds of pix and photos I looked at of his work at Edenshaw that one wasn't amongst them. I'm quite sure of that.'

'Why didn't you ask her about it? Probably it was sub-standard and she didn't want it at Edenshaw.'

'It can't be that, or the Pompidou wouldn't have taken it.'

'True. So what did Magda say when you raised the question?'

'I didn't.' He looked amused at my look of astonishment.

'Why ever not?'

'Again I'm not quite sure. I think it's because of its subject matter.'

I suddenly became interested. 'And that is?'

'From the reproduction I saw, it might have something to do with that fountain you're so keen on.'

I was hooked now, but cautious. 'Why should that influence discussing it with Magda?'

'I've been through the records of Carr's work – and that one wasn't on it. As you're so keen on sniffing Carr out, I thought I'd mention it to you first.'

'Magda won't like it if she thinks we're ganging up on her.'

Robin just looked at me. 'Are you a man or a mouse?'

I giggled. 'Stupid of me. I'm the biographer, I have control, right?'

'I wouldn't be too sure of that.'

'Hello, what's this? I thought you were your lady's true and faithful knight?'

'I am. I am infatuated. So infatuated, I want you to hold my hand and say there's nothing odd about this painting.' He was grinning, but I could see he was serious, which puzzled me. I longed to ask what he thought he wanted out of his relationship with Magda – if relationship it was – and whether they were sleeping together. I couldn't of course. All I could do was hold his hand, as he requested. That, I decided, I owed him, so I made up my mind.

'All right. I'll come. Single rooms, right?'

'Darling Lucia.' He took his revenge. 'You are not irresistible. I'd only thought of a day trip with Eurostar. It's cheaper that way.'

'Done,' I said promptly, 'and I'll stand lunch. How about that?'

'Sounds good. Play your cards right and

245

I might buy you a sandwich on the train going back.'

I plunged into the next tape, as soon as Robin had gone. I would think about fountains and Paris later. I had developed a habit of listening to the tapes once to get the general impression and replaying them for the note taking. Gréta's story had reached 1944, now, and I knew from my other research that this was the time when the war really hit Hungary.

Gréta's voice came over clearly and evocatively, taking me back as usual to my ill-fated day of love in her city:

I was helping Charles as much as I could by providing him with information straight from the Buda palace, but there was most certainly an informer somewhere in his circle. An American agent was even dropped into Hungary, but was arrested immediately by pro-Nazis. The coincidence was too great. Then on Sunday 19 March, 1944 the worst happened and the Germans occupied Hungary, ruling it from Budapest. The regent stayed as the country's figurehead, but our anti-Nazi prime minister had to flee from Budapest. He managed to reach America to be a figurehead for an emigré Hungarian government.

In Budapest itself the Germans ruled everything and we, who were anti-Nazi, were powerless – and punished for it. Immediately terrible restrictions were placed on the Jews in Budapest, and deportations from the provinces to the work camps at Auschwitz and elsewhere began immediately. It was hard for Charles and me to meet. We did so, but I knew that we had to be very careful. I tried to persuade him to leave, but he refused. I then tried to persuade him to hide in our palace, but again he refused. Our home on Rose Hill, where we used to meet, was commandeered by the Nazis, and so we used the Öszödy palace for our meetings. Charles would come through the rear entrance, and our staff – such as were left to us – were loyal. But one day, Charles did not arrive, and I was very worried, so I went to his apartment. I had never been there before, and was eager to see it – and to see his neighbours, the Jewish family, whom I suspected of being his betrayers to suit their own ends...

Something struck me as odd about this, and I replayed the tape. At last I worked out what it was. I was sure that when I was with her at her apartment, or on one of the tapes, she had said Charles was so security conscious that he would not allow her to know where it was.

It was a small detail, and there must be some explanation. Probably in the emergency these rules had changed. I made a note of it, however, and decided to ask Gréta or Magda about it when I was next in touch. And that would be when I had returned from Paris and cleared up that little oddity too.

It was strange travelling with Robin again. In our three years together we had visited Paris twice, for long weekends, and had had a whale of a time. Robin is at his best in foreign cities, since he has that easy English casualness that doesn't offer challenges but merges in with whatever is going on. We took an early train from Waterloo and were in Paris by eleven o'clock. Paris means different things to different people, but I know that to us both that day there was a distinct sense of what might have been between us, probably because we were remembering our earlier visits. I wouldn't say that David vanished from my life, but he was certainly suspended for the day.

As Robin and I queued up for the museum, just as we had for the Musée d'Orsay when we came here to celebrate (a euphemism for consummate) our love, I felt nothing had changed in Paris itself. Only we had moved on, although today it seemed as if it would be mighty easy to move straight back. Just as well we weren't staying the night. We had fought our way across the forecourt in the March winds through groups of tourists watching jugglers, dancers and acrobats, and after the queue disgorged us into the museum, we then fought our way up the escalators to the fifth floor where the modern art museum was.

We deliberately did not ask for the exact whereabouts of the painting we were looking for, although we had checked beforehand that it was indeed on show and not in store. We just wandered around until we found it. This was not hard for it drew me from across the room as soon as I glimpsed it.

'It's there,' I cried, louder than I had meant, to a roomful of tourists, who looked at me in surprise as if the human voice were entirely out of place in an art museum. Robin seized my hand and we raced across to look at it. It was indeed by Charles Carr, and it was of the fountain. It needed study, because representational it was not. Not overall, at any rate. Robin was right, though, the figures were unmistakable even though they were not in the same positions or costumes as the sculpture itself. Interestingly enough, it was painted as late as 1993, not during the time of *The Happening*. It was more the post-modernistic style of the late 1970s and 80s in its apparent rejection of any distinct pattern, and the use of different complex images on the theme. The forest was represented but fought for dominance with the figures who seemed to be lost within it, not looking at their surroundings or each other, and each with his or her own agenda. It was a sort of *Midsummer Night's Dream* in paint. The king was nude apart from his crown; the foresters' faces almost hidden by their hunting gear, cloaks, and horns; the chronicler – or jester? – seemed to be diving for cover in the bushes; and as for the peasant girl – Robin and I just looked at each other, our hands still clasped though who was helping whom I could not tell. The peasant girl was a swirling ethereal image of fair-haired beauty that was more Pre-Raphaelite than modernistic. In one hand a butterfly rested, and a gentle sunbeam of light curved round, catching her fair hair with a sweet sadness that caught at my throat.

'So what does it tell us?' Robin asked me presently over lunch, by which time I had regained the emotional strength to pore over the catalogue.

I had expected the title of the painting to be *The Fountain* or Hunting or some such thing. Instead it was given as *Unanswered Questions*. Interesting. So Charles too had seen puzzles in the fountain – or were we both seeing questions where none existed?

'And it's just as you said,' I concluded, ' "on loan from Magda Fraser, 1997".' My heart skipped a few beats over that one.

'And what does that tell us?'

'Either Magda was given this by her grandmother and decided to donate it to the museum, or it was bequeathed to her by Charles Carr.'

'Or presented as a wedding gift,' Robin said gently. 'She donated it in the year of her divorce, though I don't understand why she gave it away, since she was so involved with Edenshaw.'

I could not meet his eye. 'As I said earlier, generosity. Perhaps the Pompidou asked for a memorial of him.'

Neither of us believed it, and the onion soup suddenly seemed less delicious than I had expected. I was beginning to have un-comfortable thoughts about *The Happening*. And that threw a question mark over the biography itself.

Twelve

I left it a few days before I paid my next visit to Edenshaw. I had to discover more about the background of that painting, but first I wanted to be sure I saw the puzzle in perspective – if puzzle it was. Unfortunately I left it too long. By the time I walked into Magda's office, it was all too clear the ball was in her court. It's fair to say she might not have seen it in the same light as I did, however, for she seemed the same as usual.

'Robin tells me you had something you wanted to ask about the picture I gave to the Pompidou.' She merely seemed slightly sur-prised.

Nothing like having the rug pulled out from beneath one's feet, I thought, annoyed with myself as much as Robin. Never apologize, never explain, I reminded myself.

'Yes, it was really interesting,' I managed to say enthusiastically, despite my whirling thoughts. 'It's such a late picture and out of keeping with what Charles had been doing for so long.'

'That's why I didn't want it hanging here.'

'So it belonged to the foundation.'

'No.' Magda surmounted this one very easily or was I just imagining things? 'My grandfather gave it to me when I married David. He wasn't satisfied with it, since it didn't belong either to his later work or to *The Happening*. Yet he liked it.'

'It was good of you to loan it then.'

'Perhaps, though not *so* good,' she added, laughing, 'since I have to confess I don't much like it myself. Why does it interest you so much? There's no mystery about it. David and I were splitting up and dividing our possessions. I work here and have the benefit of all my grandfather's other work, and I thought Charles would have liked to have one painting hanging in Paris.'

Magda still looked at me inquiringly, so I more or less had to go on to explain just why it interested me. 'It's because it's based on the fountain in the garden.'

She laughed. 'Ah. The Mathias fountain again. Hideous, isn't it?'

'The painting, the copy or the original fountain?'

'The original, and so that makes the others unattractive too.'

'Unless Charles had a special reason for painting it. Surely he must have done or he wouldn't have bothered to sculpt the fountain in the garden.'

She sighed, with a slight note of exasperation. 'He did like it, but there's nothing odd about that. If you'd asked me before I'd have told you. It was his idea of how to record his own story for generations to come, summing up *The Happening*, if you like. *The Happening* records his passion for my grandmother, the fountain records Mathias's love affair – both were doomed to tragedy, one by death, the other by separation. The broken heart is the same.'

I spoke without thinking. 'But Charles doesn't seem to have made any attempt to meet your grandmother again after the war.'

'What is this, Lucia?' Magda asked good-humouredly. 'I've explained already. My grandmother was a married woman and the child so far as everyone knew, including Charles, was Miklós's. How could he go barging over there even if he could get a visa? It wouldn't have been fair.'

My bridges were burnt now. 'But after Miklós died?'

'People get old,' Magda replied. 'It can be easier to let things be. Charles wanted to remember their love as it was. OK?'

'Yes.' That made some kind of sense. I remembered Browning's poem 'The Statue and the Bust', which I'd thought daft at school. It is about a lady and her knight who never plucked up the courage to elope together. As the years passed she stuck a bust of herself up at her window, so that the knight could see her at the peak of her beauty as he galloped by. Finally he erected a statue of himself at the peak of his manly power in the street below for the same reason. *And* I remembered the cruel story of Charles Dickens, who re-met his first love in middle age and, presented with a plump middle-aged frump instead of the slim chick he remembered, he promptly ran screaming from the room. There's artists for you. But was Charles Carr really as immature as all that?

We chattered on for some time, and then I took my leave. I had a date with some quiche and I offered to stand her lunch, but Magda declined. As I was leaving, I suddenly decided to do a Colombo and pop back into the room with one last question. 'Oh, one thing puzzled me on the last tape, Magda – something simple, I'm sure. Your grandmother mentioned going secretly to Charles's apartment block, but she also told us Charles had always kept the address from her.'

I had caught her off her guard. I saw a definite flash of anger in those lovely eyes, and for the first time I glimpsed the steel beneath the velvet. Perhaps again I imagined it, however, for all she replied was: 'As you say, easily explained. My grandmother gradually became involved in the Semmelweiss affairs. She was helping Charles protect the Jews of Budapest. Zóltan Semmelweiss was one of the Jewish leaders, so eventually she must have known where Charles lived.'

Easily explained indeed. So why the anger? Probably simply because I was pestering her on a busy day.

'Wouldn't it be better to leave these details

till the end, Lucia?' Magda continued. 'I'm no writer but it seems to me you should get the story down in draft and the tying up of such details could then be done at one time. My grandmother's a game old bird, but it's going to be tiring for her if I keep ringing her up with every detail.'

She was quite right, that would be more sensible. Nevertheless the memory of her choice of words: 'I keep ringing her up', lingered. I was the biographer, wasn't I?

Much as I wanted to give Robin a piece of my mind for spilling the beans about our visit to Paris, it had to wait. There was no point calling him on my mobile, and indeed it might be better not to call him at all – if the unease that had set in after my discussion with Magda lingered. Assuming it wasn't down to being just a bad hair day, it might be better to have him on my side, rather than alienate him.

So I set forth for the restaurant for a calming piece of quiche. Did I say calming? How wrong can you be? The first person I saw as I marched in was David.

May 1944

'You have been avoiding me, Charles,' Gréta observed.

How could she still look so beautiful, so poised, in the midst of war? Charles felt oddly detached, seeing her with the artist's questioning eye rather than the lover's. It was strange to be here in the Rose Hill home again – and it would be the last time, so Gréta said, because the Germans were intending to move into it.

'There has been much to do,' he answered quietly.

It was true, albeit an excuse. The nightmare of the last few weeks had been so intense he had told himself that she would understand why he did not come. In a matter of weeks, the Budapest they had known had vanished, probably for ever, and instead a reign of terror had descended on them, chiefly affecting the Jews but involving all the old order of Hungary, save for those pro-Nazi. The threat was inexorably drawing nearer to Budapest where the Jewish population were living in fear, unable to leave. There was nowhere for them to go, and their fate seemed certain to follow that of the Jews from the provinces in their cattle trucks to Auschwitz. The terrible yellow star had to be worn by every Jew and each Jewish home had to display it. Jewish businesses, including that of Papa Semmelweiss, had now been taken out of their control, and the owners themselves reduced to menial labour.

Their janitor was now virtually their jailer, and Charles himself was looked on with marked suspicion since he was known to spend much time with the Semmelweiss family. He continued to do so, but was aware he was sticking his neck out. He had promised László to leave if the situation became critical and instinct told him that moment was approaching. Elisabeth, to his relief, was no longer able to make deliveries to the neutral legations, and he himself met his contacts outside the legations. Now that Hungary was occupied, it was essential he remained free so that the flow of information could continue. The world should know what was happening here to the Jews, and what was happening politically, for that might affect the Allies' invasion plans – which must surely now be well advanced. His realization of this and of the fact that the Germans now must surely lose the war made the predicament of the Jews even greater.

'You are still avoiding me, Charles.'

Gréta spoke lightly, but he could read serious concern in her face. He had been her lover for three years now, and still when he looked at her the grip of desire instantly seized him. 'We cannot go to our little house for that is in Nazi hands now, Charles,' she continued, 'but we could go to the Öszödy palace.'

Charles interrupted her quickly, in case his resolution gave way. 'You know how much I want to, Gréta, but I can't. Not for the moment.' He knew he was being disloyal to her in his love for Elisabeth, and that he must tell Gréta, but not here, not at a café. He owed her that. 'I can't come to your home, Gréta, and you know this is no time for lovers.'

'It is the *best* time for lovers, Charles,' Gréta replied. 'For we do not know what will happen, how long we may have. There are informers everywhere.' She paused. 'You are worried about those Jewish friends of yours, aren't you, Charles?'

He looked at her warily. 'Yes.'

'They are in a bad position. I will help you to help them if I can. The regent is still regent after all, though his power is little. I know he wants to help the Jews if he can.'

Charles was appalled. He was determined to keep the two sides of his life separate, and he did not want Gréta to endanger herself. On the other hand, if she could really help the Semmelweiss family, how could he refuse at least to listen? 'You must not compromise yourself or Miklós,' he said sharply. Suppose Gréta asked him for the Semmelweiss address? In view of László's warning, he did not have the right to give it to her even if he himself decided there was no risk.

'Charles, I have something very important to tell you, and that is why I am glad you came today. You have a cousin called Luke, do you not?'

Gréta always had the power to shock, and this question came out of the blue, out of a past long behind him. He had never spoken to Gréta about his family save in general terms, so how could she possibly know of Luke? 'In America,' he replied shortly.

'Not in America. He is here in Budapest.'

Charles's immediate disbelief was replaced with caution. The last time he had seen his young cousin was before he left for Budapest in 1938. Luke could only have been sixteen or so then which made him about twenty-two now.

'Don't worry. He is safe at the moment,' Gréta continued.

'It can't be my cousin. Be careful, Gréta,' Charles warned her, 'he may well be an imposter.' If Charles Carr was on the Gestapo books, then the arrival of a 'cousin' might well be a ruse to draw him out of cover.

Gréta leaned forward. 'Our contacts have checked him. I have brought a photograph with me.' She pushed a picture across the table, which Charles took. It showed a young man with rugged good looks who might indeed be an American, though he looked more like a young hillbilly. It could, he supposed, be Luke, but he couldn't be sure.

'He was dropped near Lake Balaton on a mission with your OSS in March. His leader was captured, but your cousin Luke is a resourceful young man and escaped. He was found on an estate by some friends of ours, and sheltered, for they are pro-West, of course, but he could not remain there long.'

'So where is he?' Charles asked in foreboding. This was beginning to sound all too real. Luke was a young daredevil when he was a boy, just the type for the OSS.

'He is under the enemy's nose. He is with me, in the Öszödy palace.'

'Are you mad, Gréta? Is he in uniform?' Charles was appalled.

'He keeps his identification on, but not his uniform.'

'Thank God.' Without identification discovery would mean he'd be shot out of hand. As would anyone sheltering him, as Gréta must know full well. 'You can't keep him there. It's too dangerous.'

'No, we just have a new Hungarian gardener, that is all. Poor man, he has been dumb since birth.'

Charles eyed her sharply. Surely she could not believe such a masquerade could escape notice for long?

'So now you will come to the Öszödy palace to see him – and me.' Gréta smiled. 'I do this for you, Charles, and so does Miklós.'

He kissed her hand, truly grateful. Luke – if it was he – presented him with a major problem. He could not leave him to fend for himself, or to be looked after by others. He would have to be involved. 'Does Luke know about me?'

'Oh yes. But not, dearest Charles, as Ferenc the musician. He knows of our love.'

Charles was thinking furiously round all sides of the problem. This could, if László's warning about Gréta was true, be a trap, but if Luke were really there it would clear up once and for all whether Gréta was a true friend or using him as a political chess piece. 'Thank you, Gréta. Can I see him?' He had made his decision.

'Of course. And Charles, you need a new apartment. You cannot remain with these Jews. You cannot help them if you are seen as one of them. There is an apartment near us—'

'No,' he said gently. 'You may be right, but I should not be near you. The information I pass on partly depends on you, and now so does Luke's safety – if it is him, of course. I must be sure. These are two reasons, and there is another.'

'Which is?' she laughed.

'My feelings for you.'

He couldn't say love, for he didn't know whether that love was past or present. He needed time to think, and made an arrangement with Gréta to come to the Öszödy palace the next day.

That evening Charles came to a conclusion. The time László had foretold was indeed here. He must move away from the Semmelweiss family, for apart from his work there was also Luke to think about. But how was he to tell them that though he would be making sure of their safety, he was going to move away? In the end it was solved for him for Katie came to see him late that evening.

'I told László that I would join him, Charles. Now I want you to send him a message through one of the legations that I cannot do so. And please tell him that I love him.' She sounded so calm, so in control, yet Charles knew her better than that.

'You always knew you could not leave,

261

didn't you?' he asked gently.

'Yes. I would have endangered him if I'd left with him, and now I cannot because of my family.'

If Katie saw no hope, what hope might there be for Elisabeth? Fear at what might be ahead seized hold of him, and he forced himself to put it to one side.

'Forget me, Charles. What will you do?' she asked.

'I should move from this apartment.'

'That is sensible,' she answered immediately.

He was relieved that she understood. 'I don't want to go.'

She ignored this. 'You will need a new identity.'

'In fact I might need two, one for me, one for – let's say a fellow American, but I can arrange that myself.'

'There is an apartment I know of near the Opera House in Mozsár utca. That would be safer than here.' She hesitated. 'I do have one request, Charles.'

'Anything, Katie.'

'Please take Elisabeth with you. She has fair hair, and does not look Jewish. With false papers, she at least may escape what is to come. She could pass as your wife, if you had no objection?'

Objection? He felt dizzy with sudden happiness. 'Only *pass* as my wife? If she wished—'

Katie shook her head. 'A formal marriage service would draw too much attention to

262

you both.'

He went to embrace her. 'Thank you, Katie. Would your parents object?'

'No. I have discussed this with them. And,' she smiled, 'with Elisabeth.'

He kissed her on both cheeks, and once lightly on the mouth. 'For László,' he said, and felt her tremble in his arms.

★ ★ ★

Seeing David sitting there in the Edenshaw restaurant, once again oblivious to my presence, I felt a wave of emotion sweep over me. He was reading a newspaper, and his face bore that concentrated closed-in look I remembered so well, loved so well. Ridiculous really, when we had been at loggerheads for more than fifty per cent of the time we had known each other, but I still felt I knew the real David who would emerge to stay for ever if only I could reach him. This is the heffalump pit of every frustrated lover, I suppose, at least the female variety. All I can claim is that I knew it was true in my case. For some reason he was guarding his stumps as if he were all set to regain the Ashes. All I had to do was produce a googly to catch him out.

I selected my quiche at the counter, chose my salads with great care, picked up a bottle of water, paid for my trayload and proceeded to slide it gently on to David's table. Then I sat down opposite him.

To do him justice, he grinned after he got

over the shock, which took him about two seconds. 'It's a fair cop, lady. Have you been stalking me long?'

'No. I have a job to do, remember?'

'Ah.'

'Now that you're here though...'

'That sounds ominous.'

'It might be,' I conceded. 'I've been to Paris with Robin.'

He looked dumbfounded, and it had to be real. He couldn't be that good an actor. 'Um,' he managed to gulp.

'So I suppose you know what I'm here for.'

'I imagine so,' he said drily. 'But as we were fairly well washed up anyway, I'm hardly surprised.'

'What on earth are you talking about?' I was truly not with him.

'Robin. I presume you've got back together. Sensible of him. Maybe of you too.'

I couldn't help it, I began to beam with happiness. 'Actually, no, but thanks for minding.'

He scrabbled to regain ground. 'I don't.'

'Too late.'

He glared at me. 'So why this jolly trip to Paris?'

'The Carr painting in the Pompidou Centre. It was a wedding present to Magda, so she said, but I assume you must have known about it.'

His face changed, it went quite white, but I didn't think it was with anger. Not at me, anyway. 'It was a wedding present to both of us actually.'

'The credit for the loan was to Magda Fraser only.'

'True. I was feeling so wretched at the time of our divorce I said she could keep it. OK by you?'

'I'm writing Charles's biography, David. The painting's relevant,' I said gently. 'I just wish I'd known about it earlier.'

'Why on earth? Ah, that fountain again.'

'The Pompidou call the painting *Unanswered Questions*, which isn't a name they would dream up for themselves. What do you imagine the unanswered questions are?'

'I don't know, I didn't know, and I didn't *want* to know. I'm sorry, Lucia, but that's how it is. The answers to the questions lie in his work, and if one hasn't the wit to work out what they are, then Charles wasn't concerned that you should know them.' He spoke not angrily but rationally.

'I feel like the poor sap in the Grimms' fairy tale who has to think up an unanswerable riddle before he gets to wed the princess,' I offered brightly. Or prince in my case.

'The princess being?'

I chickened out. 'The biography of course.'

'Lucia?' David was looking at me in appeal. 'Shall we stop pussy-footing around scoring points? I did wonder what that title *Unanswered Questions* referred to. I even had my own ideas about it, but the way ahead for them looked pretty murky from where I was standing. I couldn't take it, for all sorts of reasons. My son, for one, and for another—'

'Magda,' I answered for him.

He held my gaze. 'Yes.'

Whichever way I turned, I fell over Magda. Or Gréta. Perhaps Charles Carr had felt the same. Well, there had to be a way through the thickets, and I had by all the rules of fairy tales to find it myself if I was to reach my happy ending. This was obviously David's underlying message.

Very well, I would. 'David,' I said, 'that first time I came to Edenshaw, you took my mother and me round the gardens, but you left us to make our own decisions.'

'So?'

'Do you think you could do that again? Now? I want to have a look at that fountain, and see if I reach the same conclusions as you about the unanswered questions.'

'I'm not wild about the idea...'

'Then get wild, or don't come.'

Perhaps it was the flat note of certainty in my voice, or perhaps the challenge, or perhaps even because he wanted to come of his own free will, but whichever, he thought for a moment then replied, 'All right. I will.'

'You've had some more thoughts on the questions?'

'No, but for the first time I feel like facing them. Does that sound crazy?'

It didn't. David was already getting to his feet and folding up his newspaper. 'Hang on a minute,' I said mildly. 'I need a mug of tea before I face that lot.'

The March weather was still cool. Nevertheless, it was a good time to be in the gardens because there were signs of new life everywhere, which seemed a good omen. Bulbs were forging upwards, wild snowdrops and anemones in flower were carpeting parts of the ground. There were even swelling buds on the chestnut trees.

'Before we go to the fountain,' David suddenly asked, 'can we take the same route as last time?'

'Go up there?' I looked up with foreboding to the top of the hill. 'The last time I went up, I met Cousin Luke – only I didn't know who he was then. It was fairly creepy.'

'I'm sorry about Luke,' David answered, as we climbed up – in my case panted. I had got out of condition over the winter, which comes of working at home. 'He has a mind of his own.'

'Do you know his story?'

'No. All I do know – or rather suspect – is that although he just says he was in the Eighth Air Force, in fact he was in Budapest during the war.'

I almost missed my footing in shock. 'And he won't even talk about it?'

'Nope. Believes in the past being the past.'

'Oh great,' I snorted with feeling. Was there anybody around here who *would* talk?

'It was your idea to take the biography on,' he kindly reminded me.

In return I reminded him, 'Others had had the idea before me. Including,' I added,

'Magda.'

'Tony's been talking then. Forget that, will you?'

I was narked. 'I'm hardly likely to raise the subject in general conversation. But I can't help wondering.'

'Wonder on, my fair lady.'

I fumed and decided to try to ignore this in my wider interests. 'Why did you want to come up here?' I asked when I triumphantly reached the top.

'I want you to look again at the painting inside. You didn't spend long in there last time. Come in with me.'

'I intend to.' No way did I want to face it again alone.

So once again, I went in to face the monstrosity, the dark side of love.

'Did you notice the words?' he asked me.

'What words?'

He pointed and I could understand how I could have missed them. The monster was wearing a thin belt of gold, and on it some words were painted. I squinted at them: *Et in Arcadia ego*. 'Old Latin tag,' I remarked to show my knowledge of things classical. 'Doesn't look much like Arcadia he was enjoying.'

He did not reply, and I decided not to question him. He clearly had some purpose in mind, so I held my peace (just). We trooped right down to the bottom of the hillside again and round to the cave, with the other painting, the one on the fair side of love. This too bore some words on the tiny narrow belt. ' *"Et ego in Arcadio"*,' I read out. 'Same tag.'

'No it's not. Do you know any Latin?'

'Enough to translate that. Anyway, it's used on countless old pictures and things. It means: Even I have lived in Arcadia.'

'Right. This one does mean that. The other doesn't. It reads *"Et in Arcadia ego"*.'

'So?'

'The order change in the words gives it a vastly different meaning. *"Et in Arcadia ego"* refers to death or the devil serpent, so the tag means: Death is found even in Arcadia.'

I thought about this. 'So how does that affect the meaning of these paintings? It seems to fit with the idyllic cottage proving to have hell inside it, but what's the significance?' I caught sight of his face. 'Don't you dare say you don't know,' I howled.

'I don't know.'

'Just for that,' I told him vengefully, as at last we reached the fountain, 'I need co-operation. *Real* co-operation.'

He looked at me seriously. 'I'll do my best, but because – if you must know – Magda and I had a fearful row about the Paris picture, the result has been that this fountain turns me off. The full size one in Buda I can take, but the fact that Charles sculpted this copy makes me queasy. And don't ask me why – I can't explain it.'

He actually looked physically sick again, so I forgot all about vengeance. 'You can walk on, David. I'll do it alone.'

He gave a funny sort of nod, I presume in gratitude, and took me at my word. Through the skeletons of the barren trees I could just see his red sweater moving as he paced up and down the path to keep warm – or was it in tension? I dragged my thoughts away from him, and turned to look at the fountain.

When I had first seen it, I had taken it to be an afterthought that Charles had added to the garden. Now, with the consciousness of that Paris painting done so late in his life, I began to see it as a centrepiece. It could hold the key to the story of Charles Carr in Budapest. I studied the sculpted figures, none of them looking at each other. First the girl who in both versions died of a broken heart. She wouldn't do that today, she'd go all out to grab the king, probably even if the king were married, though I wondered what King Mathias had thought of it all. Had he remained aloof staring into space, as he appeared? Was he in love with the girl, or was it a one-sided affair that the second version of the story suggested? Was he married at the time or between his two wives? Did Ilonka truly love him or was she a gold-digger?

I had looked Mathias up in reference books; his first wife died leaving him without children and the second, the formidable Beatrice, survived him but again did not have children by him. Were they happy marriages? Those marks of smashed china in the palace decor did not suggest the latter one was ecstatic, though who could tell? Maybe it was a

270

Taming of the Shrew situation. But if he did not love his wife perhaps he *did* love the peasant girl. Or perhaps he loved them both. This was possible too. Romance would have it that the king's marriage was one of alliance and that the peasant girl was his real flame. Even in version two he could have nobly ignored his own heart in the interests of marriage and state.

I studied the chronicler, or jester, who so far as I could find out could have been the only one who recorded this tale for posterity, then I looked at the girl herself, blind to the true situation and trustingly getting in over her head to the point where the king could do nothing to prevent her fate. Did he even know about her love for him? Or did he know all too well and have her bumped off? The latter left a nasty taste in the mouth. I went further. Mathias left a natural son, John. Perhaps his mother was the peasant girl, and she died in childbirth. My reference books were silent on the question of John's mother. And perhaps the truth was immaterial anyway for Charles's purpose – and now mine.

The fountain meant unanswered questions for us both, for only the chronicler knew the truth. A nineteenth-century poet had written about the legend too, but he too would have relied upon the chronicler. And suppose, I asked myself hollowly, he was a jester after all? Suppose the Snark *was* a Boojum? I was beginning to feel in Lewis Carroll land, and the worst of it was that all my unanswered

271

questions must remain unanswered because the controlling power had been in the hands of this chronicler jester.

I felt a surge of adrenalin. I was on the right track at last. I was sure of it. What is a biographer's fatal flaw? To fall victim to one side of the story only. For too long, I had relied on the infallibility of one person's word: Gréta Öszödy. On the fountain sculpture the chronicler was turned away from both the girl and the king. He saw only his own power. Perhaps he was the jester too – though that cowled head did not suggest it – but either way he stood outside the story. He could manipulate, he could juggle the facts, and *so could Gréta*.

'David,' I cried out shakily as I physically staggered out to join him. 'I've got it.'

He didn't make any fatuous joke about not giving it to him, instead he gave me a searching look. 'Are you sure?'

'Yes, and without even having to ask you. I know what Charles Carr saw in that fountain, in that story, why he put it here.'

'What is it?' There was a tremble in his voice, as if he were half fearful, half excited.

'You won't like this. What I've been writing is Gréta's story and not necessarily Charles Carr's. She is the court chronicler, and the jester, and how can we rely on him? There's no corroborative evidence. Suppose King Mathias sacked him? Suppose the chronicler tried to seduce the peasant girl and when she rejected him didn't pass on the king's message that he loved her? Suppose he was

Beatrice's chronicler, not the king's? Suppose he was her spy? Suppose the jester decided to tell it his way?'

'Suppose,' David interrupted gently, 'you stop talking just for a moment.'

'Why? I'm sure I'm right. That means there's a big question mark over the big love affair. Charles couldn't have known Gréta would be *our* chronicler/jester, so he must have seen it as applying to their relationship. Oh David—'

This ended in a squeak, since he just took me in his arms and kissed me in passion, relief, love. I don't know which it was but it went on and on until I said feebly, 'We can't. It's only March.'

'Sex doesn't have seasons. It's not against the bye-laws if there's no one else around.'

'But—'

There were no buts. He was absolutely right. It was the first time I've ever made love in an anorak, but by golly if it's as good as that every time, it won't be the last.

It didn't change anything of course, I told myself afterwards. He was still Magda's emotional possession, but at least I knew he wanted me. He wanted to break free of that enchantment, if only I could find the way to release him.

Thirteen

We went back to David's home. He even had an open fire, which with a little persuasion perked up sufficiently to toast a couple of stale crumpets he found in the kitchen. He refused to talk further about Charles as we strolled hand in hand through the garden. From time to time we glanced at each other and smiled, but mostly we were content with our own thoughts – which speaking for myself were temporarily ignoring biographies and obstacles that stood in the way of future happiness. If it was time for Cinderella to flee from the palace, I didn't notice it. Midnight struck but I stayed right on with Prince Charming.

Certainly David came nearer to that image than at any time since I had known him. Sitting on the floor side by side before the fire – well, you could almost dignify it with that name – we were reduced to the same level, and perhaps that loosened our tongues as though it were easier to talk thus than walking upright with the mask of everyday life upon us.

'We need to talk about the biography,' I was

eventually forced to mention.

'We do.' David frowned. 'Not too much though.'

'Perish the thought,' I answered lightly. That was the problem in a nutshell: no one – save perhaps Gréta – would talk 'too much'.

As a reward for my sarcasm, he chucked a cushion at me, which carried away my last bit of crumpet, but gained us a breathing space.

'There's no point,' David maintained, 'in my rabbiting on with all my guesses and wild fantasies. You need to finish it, get down the story as you see it. I'm more biased than you.'

'Of course,' I agreed. He saw Magda at every turn, and where he saw Magda he saw Gréta close behind.

'I used to think I was round the bend wondering about the exact relationship between Gréta and Charles, so it's a relief that you're thinking that way too. You have to believe me, Lucia, I don't know any more than you've found out so far. And nor does Magda.'

He's conditioned into protecting her, I immediately concluded, but wisely did not comment.

'I couldn't even be sure that there was anything else to learn – from Gréta's point of view,' he continued. 'It was Charles who puzzled me.'

'In what way?'

'I suppose it was *The Happening*. Basically I thought as you did, that it must represent the two faces of love, even though so far as I could work out from Gréta, the only dark side

275

of love to their affair was their separation, and the fact that their last days together were dangerous because of the terrible time Budapest was going through.'

'Just how dangerous, though? And was it dangerous for *them* or for the Jewish population – especially the Jews we know he was close to?'

'I don't know.'

'But Luke has been coming here all those years. Doesn't he know? Surely he must have said something, especially if you're right and he was in Budapest in the war?'

'He won't speak to you, he didn't speak to me – or even to Magda. It's just my guess he was there too.'

'Based on what?'

He thought about this, and eventually said, 'The fact he keeps coming to Edenshaw even though Charles is dead, and the fact that each time he visits he goes round *The Happening* several times, studying it, especially the garden.'

I remembered him sitting on the bench outside the cottage on top of the hill with its terrible contents. So that hadn't been a one-off, it was his routine.

'He relives the past, without wanting to talk about it. Odd,' I remarked.

'Luke *is* odd. And anyway, it's not that odd. Plenty of former soldiers shut up like clams on the subject of their experiences.'

I agreed, and dropped the subject, turning back to surer ground. 'Would you tell me

276

about the painting in the Pompidou, if you can?' I asked. 'I don't want to force you because it obviously upsets you.'

To my surprise he answered immediately, 'Yes, I'd like to do that – now.'

A warm glow – not from the dwindling fire – spread through me.

'I told you we had a row about it, Magda and I,' David began. 'That was an understatement. You know what Charles's last words to me were? I should have told you but you seemed to be doing well on your own, and as they didn't make sense to me at the time, and still don't, I'd half forgotten them. He said, "Mathias was a fool. But so was I, David." As soon as I saw that fountain the first time I went to Budapest, I realized that it was the original of the tiny one in the grounds at Edenshaw, and that it must have some importance. I connected it after a while with Charles's comment but couldn't see what he was getting at. I suppose I was too clouded being married to Gréta's granddaughter by Charles, and knowing Gréta through Magda rather than coming direct to her, as you have.'

'Have I?' I wondered about that, because I too had met first Magda then Gréta.

'I don't mean,' David said carefully, 'that Magda was deliberately keeping any great truth from me. I'm still sure she doesn't know any more than I do what happened in Budapest.'

Of course not, I thought savagely. He would think that. I had to fight this prejudice to some extent, however. 'She must know the story so far as it's revealed on all the tapes, even the ones that Gréta hasn't yet sent to her, even though she denied she'd told either Magda or her mother.' I remembered what she had said to me in her apartment – but how could I rely on 'the court chronicler' for truth now?

'So, that gets us no further. Agreed?'

Oh yes, I had to agree. Magda was out of the frame, Gréta was in it. These seemed to be the boundary lines for whatever basis we were continuing on, but it was a bleak prospect for any real co-operation over the biography.

He seemed to read my mind. 'That's why I don't want to talk *too* much, Lucia. You're the biographer – you have to get there.'

'But what,' I asked, foreseeing a pit ahead large enough to take several heffalumps, 'if my biography comes to a head, with something that Magda doesn't like?'

'Magda,' he replied in his 'I am an objective trustee' sort of voice, 'is not the foundation. The trustees have the last say.'

'Precisely,' I answered. 'And you are one of them.'

David took the point immediately and he didn't look happy about it. 'You mean, if Magda can't accept what you decide is the truth because it comes out anti-Gréta?' And when I nodded, he answered me. 'Sweetheart, I'm a trained historian. I can look at the evidence, no matter how hard it is.'

278

Sweetheart? Oh happiness. 'Thousands couldn't,' I pointed out nevertheless.

He laughed. 'Even if I were George Washington's wife I could believe he was innocent of cutting down that cherry tree if the facts proved it.'

He seemed to have forgotten he wasn't still married to Magda. Stop it, Lucia, I told myself. Don't make inferences that might not be implied. Unfortunately inferences often aren't, but they are valid all the same. David might love me, but he was still emotionally hooked in to Magda or at least to their joint life, because of Toby. My spirits had descended from up to down, and now down even further in seconds.

'So let's go back to that painting, shall we?' he suggested.

'Is this for the record? Shall I give you a source note?'

He hesitated. 'Not for the moment. See what comes out in the wash.'

Right, so he didn't want to upset Madam. I'd have to live with that – so far as the biography was concerned. Whether I could live with it in my private life was another matter.

'I loved that painting from the moment Charles gave it to us,' David said, 'even though I don't go for the fountain itself. Unfortunately, Magda didn't. I don't know why, but she hated it, and could never give me a valid reason. She kept saying the perspective was wrong and that the symbolism of the figures didn't mix with the realism of the forest, but I thought there was more to it. I put it down to the fact that Charles had made it clear that the painting was primarily for me. He gave us other presents too, so this isn't as strange as it might sound.

'As soon as Charles died, and the trustees began to discuss which paintings should be hung and which not, I was anxious to hang this one in Edenshaw House. She wouldn't have it. She said it wasn't part of *The Happening* because of the time he painted it, and it wasn't akin to his later work. It was a sort of hybrid going back to the past, and therefore had no artistic validity. And she certainly wasn't going to dignify it with a room of its own in the house.'

'Pardon me,' I asked politely, 'but what status did she have? I thought she'd never been a trustee.'

'That's right. Charles didn't want both of us to be trustees, and made that quite clear. However, he did want me to be one, for that had been his first intention all along. Magda was miffed about it, but as Charles made his wishes clear in writing there was nothing she could do.'

'Except become CEO.'

'Yes. That seemed reasonable to the trustees.'

'And to you?'

'I'm one of the trustees.'

'Don't prevaricate.'

'I was against it – simply,' he added quickly,

'because I was a trustee. I couldn't give any other reason. She, everyone agreed including me, would make an efficient CEO and she has done so.'

I couldn't argue with that. Everything I had seen about Edenshaw House (apart from the flaky paint on the gates) was done with professionalism and efficiency.

'So, back to the painting again,' David said – not too pointedly. 'She wouldn't hang it in the house, so she suggested a museum. I refused to let it go as it had been a wedding present, and she couldn't give it away without my agreement. It got fairly nasty' – David was fairly pink at this point – 'but it blew over, and the painting hung in my study. When we split up, though, it was a different matter. We neither of us had much money' – that surprised me, for Magda seemed the sort of woman who would never opt for love in a cottage – 'and she demanded the picture. When I refused, because I knew she wanted to get rid of it, she threatened to take Toby and deny me access to him. He was only three, but she'd been willing to leave him with me originally.'

'Oh David.' I didn't trust myself to say anything more, because what I had in mind would have overstepped our boundary with a vengeance.

'So I had to let her have it. I have to say in Magda's defence that I had not behaved impeccably myself. I'd been having an affair with someone else – I'd been pretty miserable

281

when I found out about Michael.'

I had gone cold. An affair? 'So what went wrong over Toby?' I managed to ask.

'Magda took both the painting and Toby. My affair had broken up and she argued that I had no stable home in which to rear him, and then that I was a disrupting influence on a child so young.'

'But that's terrible.' I was appalled. 'How can you...' I broke off, without saying 'still love her, still be mesmerized by her'. The answer was obvious. Magda was one of those women whose power over men transcends whatever they do to them.

Luckily, David misunderstood. 'How can I bear to leave Toby with her?' he finished for me. 'She's a good mother, she loves him, she runs a wonderful home and he's happy enough there. She's reasonably good over access as it's worked out.'

I bet she is, I thought. She's into control. The bleakness in David's tone did not escape me, but it reinforced what he had claimed for himself. Whatever his own pain, he could still see something objectively (apart, I thought savagely, from Magda). This boded well for the biography at least.

'Although I gave in over the picture, I made damn sure she didn't destroy it – in a particularly bad row she threatened to do just that. Instead I insisted that she loaned it, not donated it, to the Pompidou where I could easily ensure that it was actually there.' He took one look at the expression on my face.

'People take strange attitudes when they're divorcing. They behave out of character. I regret to say that I threatened to get her ousted as CEO if she couldn't produce that painting at any time the trustees demanded to see it.'

Out of character? Generous on David's part, I thought. Then I pulled myself up. If David could be objective, then so could I. So far Magda had done nothing to justify any feelings on my part towards her other than gratitude and admiration. Not much anyway. The one question I would have asked David – but couldn't since it was against the rules – was why the marriage had broken up. And this, I supposed, partly depended on why they got married in the first place.

May 1944

Charles was determined that this would be his last appearance as a street musician. Tomorrow he would slip into his new identity and move into the new apartment. Today, coming to the Öszödy palace to meet a gardener, Ferenc seemed the more sensible choice. He'd arranged through Gréta to meet Luke in the garage – not that Miklós ran a car any more. It was still in the garage, waiting for the war's end, and provided an ideal place to meet since the garage was unfrequented.

Charles was nervous about the meeting, only half convinced that this could possibly be his cousin. Even questions about family details could not provide absolute proof. If Luke had been captured and tortured, as only the Gestapo knew how, any stooge they put in his place might be as fluent as the real Luke in the family affairs of the Carrs. Worse, Luke might have been 'turned', his every move monitored by the Gestapo.

Charles's first glimpse reassured him that this was indeed Luke. Tall, lean, untidy shock of brown hair falling over his face, moustache – they could be anybody's, but the eyes were the daredevil eyes of the boy he remembered.

'Hi, Charles.' Luke kept his voice down, but his excitement was obvious. He was pacing around the garage with pent-up emotion. 'Gee, it's good to talk again in God's own language.'

'Luke.' Charles embraced him with relief. 'What are you doing here, you old devil? No, don't tell me. I know. You couldn't keep your fingers out of the butty tin, eh?'

Luke grinned. 'Only the brownies, Cousin Charles.'

That was reassuring. It was the right answer for the lad he remembered, and hardly an incident that Luke would have recalled under torture. Even so, Charles decided to take care.

They chatted amicably about family matters for some time. Charles found it hard to stay on guard since the talk of the past, particularly with Luke's casual quips and jokes, took him away from the problems of the present. One of Luke's comments worried him though. 'Your dad's real upset about you, Charles. Most of the family reckon you're a deserter. Guess they'll think that about me too. We'll have to stick together when we get back, eh?'

Charles battled to put this disturbing news aside, while he dealt with more immediate issues. 'After what Uncle George did in the last war I don't think we'd qualify for an Oscar for Best Villain.'

Luke blinked. 'Who the heck is Uncle George? I never did hear of that guy.'

'I'm damned glad. He doesn't exist.'

Luke laughed. 'Satisfied I'm your cousin, you old bull-shitter? Suppose I report back to the lovely Gréta that you're not the real Charles Carr.'

'I'm too dull for anyone to impersonate me.'

'You reckon so? What happened to the painting?'

'I haven't done much recently. Too much else going on.' Charles was lying. He had done drawing after drawing of Elisabeth, trying in vain to capture her on paper or canvas. Her appearance was simple to convey, but how could he portray her loving heart, not just for him, but for life and everyone around her?

'Gréta showed me the paintings of her. Why none recently?'

'Something called a war on, Luke.'

'You could have fooled me, soldier. I just

dropped into the middle of this mess. You know the Carr speciality. I fell on my ass, still got the bruises. You fell on your feet it seems. Good for you.'

'In what way?'

'Gréta's told me about you and her.'

'I keep that apart, Luke. War and love can make an explosive mix.'

'She's keen on you, Charles. Only damn thing is, I sure as hell can't see why.'

'Thanks for your confidence.' Luke was looking at him with the keen observation Charles remembered from their earlier meetings. He had been the sort of boy who could go to the movies and come home talking about the odd characters in the audience.

'Only joking, Cousin Charles,' Luke shot back promptly. 'But you must be one hell of a lover for the lady to keep up her devotion throughout this political mess. Watch your back, won't you?'

'You've been here six weeks or so, and you talk about *my* back?' Charles asked drily. 'I've been watching it for six years.'

Luke shrugged. 'That may be as well. Gréta tells me you want to get me out of here. That suits me. It makes me kind of nervous living in a place like this.'

'Why?' Charles guessed the answer very well, but he wanted to see whether his instincts were the same as Luke's.

'You know what we Yanks are like,' Luke replied carelessly. 'We trust our own backyard

286

and no one else's. There are too many Germans visiting this place for my liking.'

'Of course. Miklós remains close to Horthy and to refuse to entertain them would put him in a dangerous position. Besides, that's where I get my information from. And before you ask,' Charles continued steadily, 'I did say information and not misinformation. Horthy is pro-West, so is Miklós, and therefore so is Gréta. OK? They are not feeding me German propaganda.' He was still certain of that, if only because he made a point of double-checking where he could.

Luke grinned, and held his hands up in surrender. 'Sure, Charles, sure. Just testing. All the same, I reckon you're right. I'm better out of here.'

'You can move in with me the day after tomorrow.' Charles hesitated. It was the last thing he wanted, but he had no choice. He trusted Gréta but her household was too big, and the risk to Luke – and therefore himself – was unquantifiable. 'There are only two rules. First, Gréta should not know where you and I are living. We've talked about it and she understands why it's better that way.'

'OK by me.'

'Second, there are two bedrooms, but there'll be three of us living there. And this is something that it's vital that no one but no one knows. You and I share. The second room is for my wife.'

Luke spluttered in shock. 'Charles, you old devil. I never knew you had it in you. Head in the clouds, my Aunt Jemima. You not only have the Countess Öszödy worshipping at your feet, but a secret wife too. I presume she's secret from the countess?'

'Yes.'

Luke looked very serious. 'Is there more to this, Charles? A wife and separate rooms? I know what's going on round here. There's talk amongst the servants. Is this woman Jewish?'

'She's my wife, Luke. That's all you need to remember. Her name is Elisabeth.'

As he walked home, he turned over and over in his mind whether he had been wise to take Luke under his wing. Luke was smart, it wasn't going to take him long to figure out what was going on. He trusted Luke, but he was in danger of breaking his own rules on not letting his right hand know what his left was doing. Yet he didn't want Luke under Gréta's roof, and Luke could never cope alone in this city, or even if they could arrange it, outside.

⋆   ⋆   ⋆

I stayed with David that night, our second whole night together, and next day the sun shone both literally and in my heart. We were indeed meant for each other. We liked the same kind of cereal. And we both liked tea not coffee for breakfast. These small details somehow assumed an immense significance, as did the laundry basket overflowing with

288

dirty clothes, the cork message board in the kitchen with its scraps of paper bearing messages to himself: kitchen paper, washing-up liquid. They meant nothing individually but added up to a home, and one in which I felt *at* home. The drawback was that part of the owner was missing – the part that still, despite all the terrible times their marriage had gone through, belonged to Magda. The witch's spell was still unbroken.

I went back to Putney, and shut myself in my ivory tower to finish the biography. Spring began to turn into summer before my writing caught up with Gréta's tapes. I found it hard to write, since I now had this deep unease about whether Gréta's word alone could be relied upon. I felt reasonably happy up to 1944, but from now on material other than Gréta's testimony was sparse. I had general histories of Budapest at the time and one or two memoirs of the period, but nothing on Charles himself, save what Gréta had told me. I had a few letters from other family members in the States, but apart from con-firming that Charles was doing intelligence work there, nothing was added to the story. Apparently he had spoken to the head of the American legation telling him he was going to remain in Budapest, which was as well since rumours began to fly around that he was shirking his duty to join the armed forces. His father had been convinced of it, and it had been Luke's mother who dug out the infor-mation after the war that he had indeed been acting as an undercover agent, and that his information had been vital in gaining a picture of Hungary's political intentions.

I cursed the fact that Luke was so difficult to deal with. Talk about Macavity the Mystery Cat. I was sure there was a story still to be told about the Semmelweisses, Charles's neighbours. I went to the Wiener Library in London, and contacted Holocaust historians, in the hope that the name of Semmelweiss in Budapest might ring a bell. All I found out that could have a connection with 'my' Semmelweisses was that a Zoltán Semmelweiss was one of the Jewish leaders on the Central Jewish Council set up by the infamous Adolf Eichmann the day after he arrived in Budapest, the purpose of which was to convey his barbaric orders to the Jewish population.

Could this be the man Charles lived near or with? I couldn't work out which from Gréta's tapes. Whichever it was, something seemed to change in 1944, probably at the time that Eichmann arrived.

As for David, he didn't just vanish once more from my life, leaving me alone while I solved the riddle that might win me my prince; life isn't quite so unfair as that. Nevertheless, he didn't encourage me to drop in at his Kentish home when I visited the Edenshaw archives. Instead, he preferred to come to Putney, where we made do with my single bed, and he made himself useful. He even cooked from time to time – I remember one dinner party with Mum, Dad and Tony who all thought it great and beamed at us, as though we were an established couple. If only! We talked of everything under the sun, even discussing Edenshaw and Magda was within bounds, although matters of interpretation were not. Tony remained a nodding Buddha throughout, eating his Thai stir-fry sagely, and saying yes and no at intervals. He did loosen his tongue to talk a little about the 1960s and how *The Happening* got painted. On Charles's frustrations and successes over this he was very helpful, about its subject matter he was not. Possibly, to be fair, because he didn't know any more than we did.

I listened avidly to Gréta's next tape, brought, to my surprise, by David. I wondered whether he had been making some kind of point to Magda and if so whether I could rejoice at this. Rejoicing had to wait, however, as it emerged she had merely given it to him to post. (What, I wondered, had happened to Robin?)

'I had to give Charles some important information that his cousin Luke had been captured on a mission and was living with us in secret at the Öszödy Palace,' Gréta's voice told me. 'The regent knew, but no one else up to that point.'

Luke! So David was right, and Luke had been in Budapest. What's more, he was living under Gréta's roof and therefore would know whether or not we were getting the true story – unless, of course, she fed the same line to him at the time as to me now. I acknowledged

I was getting ahead of myself here. I had no proof that I wasn't getting the true story, just as there was no proof that the court chronicler was not telling the true story of the peasant girl and King Mathias.

Nevertheless, I was cock-a-hoop and whooping with joy at this breakthrough, and as a result almost postponed listening to the rest until I met David again. Then I thought better of it. This was work, and although David might be my personal pivot, he should not be the pivot on which the biography should turn.

Gréta continued:

I wasn't sure what I felt about Luke. I was convinced, as Charles was not at first, that he was Charles's cousin and so he proved to be. Nevertheless there was something about him that I didn't take to, and I was glad when he left our roof and went to live with Charles in his new apartment. One heard of many strange things in those days. After all, the leader of his mission had been captured immediately he landed, and it seemed a miracle that Luke could have escaped in uniform and speaking no Hungarian, and that he should have landed on an estate of a family so anti-Nazi. No one escaped the pro-Nazi Hungarian political police or the Germans when they arrived in our country. The Gestapo were adept at getting what they wanted, and might well have 'turned' Luke to do their job for them. I tried to warn Charles of this possi-

292

bility, but he was oblivious to the danger. I could do nothing more, except hope for Charles's sake that I was wrong. All the same, I was more careful about my own meetings with Charles, and chose the time and place very carefully so that there was no danger we could be seen by anyone. I also stopped giving him much valuable information about the regent's plans, for it was too dangerous in these German-controlled times.

I began to feel slightly sick, after the tape finished. Now where was I? Before I had made my own mind up about Gréta, here was she planting the idea that Luke was not trustworthy.

I dithered about it, but in the end decided that until I had all the tapes from Gréta, and knew the full story on whether her fears about Luke had been justified, I could not decide how to present it. After all, I had to remember that Luke was alive and there was the law of libel to consider. While I was waiting for the last tapes, I would concentrate on the middle years when Charles was actually painting *The Happening*. I could at least use Tony's material for that. The full meaning of *The Happening* could not be determined until I had heard all Gréta's story – *and* Luke's story, even though I hadn't the slightest idea when he might turn up again. I tried to talk to David about him, but he was of no help. He didn't know Luke's address, so I was left with the nephew, who might perhaps pass on a letter – if he knew the address.

I decided I wouldn't draw David in any further. This was one for Magda, and it might be tough, so I chose my time carefully. I told her how the book was going, and then asked her if she had listened to the tape. She had.

'So, what do you think about Luke?' I asked her.

'I was taken aback,' she replied frankly. 'But if my grandmother says there was something fishy going on, it's probable that there's some truth in the story and that she'll develop it. We'll have to wait and see.'

'That's what I thought too, but how do you feel about that? You know Luke, and even if he were a baddie, we can't say so in so many words without concrete evidence.'

'Then we omit him.'

It sounded so easy, put that way. And so it might be depending on how the story worked out. Being me, however, I couldn't leave it at that.

'But suppose it comes to a question of your grandmother's word against Luke's?'

Magda actually laughed. 'Luke is a crazy old man. My grandmother still has all her marbles.'

'That doesn't affect what happened in Budapest.'

'It affects what happens now,' Magda pointed out. 'Whose word do you accept? My grandmother's, of course. Luke's out to lunch mentally.'

'And suppose I can't go along with that?'

'You'd be crazy yourself.' Magda yawned. 'I hope you do see it that way, Lucia, because that's the way the foundation will.'

'The trustees—'

'Will go on the facts, not theories. There's a history of the Öszödy family in the archives from which you will see that their honourable conduct throughout the war is a matter of record. They were loyal supporters of Horthy, anti-Nazi and later anti-Soviet.'

'But who wrote the history?'

'Lucia, what the hell has come over you?' Magda was beginning to get angry, and perhaps rightly. 'Are you implying my family were some kind of double agents? You're here to write Charles's story and he wouldn't thank you for attacking my grandmother. I'd hate to think we'd chosen a biographer of the "must find a dirty scandal to spice it up" variety.'

I was down and almost out for the count, but I still managed a cool: 'You haven't. I'll look at the facts and make a judgement.'

'Don't let it be a judgement on the lines you're thinking about or the book will be thrown out.'

'The trustees decide that.'

'Quite. I think you'll find that they'll be on my side in this.'

'David—' I began like a fool.

'Will vote for whatever I think's right.' She said this with supreme confidence. Whatever he had said to me and whatever his intentions might be, I had a sinking feeling that she

295

might be right.

Summer 1944

'So now I am your wife, Charles.' Elisabeth laughed as he took her into the apartment.

'You are.' He kissed her lightly. 'But you will sleep here in this room, I sleep in the other. After the war, darling, it will be different. When we can truly be married.'

'Dearest Charles,' she said soberly, 'there may be no after-the-war for us. These identity papers say I am Elisabeth Lotz and I want to be with you now. Do you not want that?'

'More than anything,' he said fiercely, his heart and mind churning. 'But I can't let you do it, *kedvesem*. My cousin Luke is coming to live with us. There is nowhere else for him to go.' He told her the story and she listened in silence. 'According to his papers, he is Lucas Belarov, a Rumanian and my cousin.'

'Is this safe for you?' she asked anxiously.

'Yes, I think so.' He hesitated. 'He was befriended by the Countess Öszödy, but he cannot remain there.'

Elisabeth went very still. 'She was your great friend, Charles. Does she remain so?'

He met her eye steadily. 'Not as she used to be. Not now there is you.'

'Does she know about me?'

'No.'

'That is good, Charles.'

'I have to tell her, Elisabeth.'

296

'It might not be wise.' And when he looked at her questioningly, she explained, 'Tell nobody anything unless essential. And this is not.'

He knew she was right, though everything in him fought against the deception. But this was war. The secret would be kept.

Fourteen

I took the only step forward I could. I wrote to Luke via Charles's nephew in the forlorn hope that I might get a rapid answer. If Luke presented an entirely different side of the story from Gréta's, or even if he merely told me she was lying, I would know where I was. I could suggest in effect the readers of the biography should make their own choice. Otherwise, I might be being led deeper and deeper into the quagmire without even having the certainty that I was in one.

The tapes were still arriving from Gréta, and Robin once more reverted to his job as carrier. It seemed an entirely voluntary action on his part as they could easily be posted, but I decided not to be flattered.

'There seems to be a lot of work to do on the illustrations for this book,' I couldn't help observing, on this visit. 'Odd, when it isn't even written yet.'

'There is, just as I expect you have a lot to do in the archives at Edenshaw.'

I grinned. 'Touché.' All the same, I had never made any secret of my interest in David, whereas Robin was ambivalent about his in Magda. I could hardly ask him if he was back trapped in the honey again, but I feared the worst. There was, once again, a smugness about him that suggested to me – no, Lucia, don't go there. Then I rethought the sense of this embargo. Why on earth shouldn't I? Surely in my private thoughts I could dream up what scenarios I liked? My favoured one, which had instantly come to mind, was that Robin hadn't – until he showed signs of restlessness – actually been admitted to Magda's bed. Now he had achieved this honour, a detectable smugness was the result.

I had to keep reminding myself that I *liked* Magda, and had no evidence so far, apart from irritation on her part that I was doubting her grandmother, to change my mind. I had heard from David his side of the marital breakdown, that was all, and no judge would condemn on that alone.

'Have you listened to this tape, Robin?' I asked casually. I don't know what made me put this particular question since he hadn't taken much interest in any of its predecessors. He'd said he had better things to do than listen to old war stories, and that his job was to put over Charles Carr, artist, in the best way he could.

'I have actually,' he replied, taking me by

298

surprise. 'I happened to be there when it arrived.' I might have swallowed that, if it hadn't been for the fact that I noticed he was avoiding my eyes. I wondered what the tape contained, but deliberately didn't ask him. If I was in for some kind of shock I preferred to face it alone. Alternatively, it might just have been he was remembering the roll in the hay they'd been enjoying as it came through the letterbox. I took my wicked thoughts hastily away from that mental picture.

'Cup of coffee before you go?' was all I asked, but the moment he had left, I flew to the tape.

I have come now to a painful part of the story of Charles and myself, but there is no avoiding it. We had been lovers, close lovers, for over three years. It was inevitable that war should bring problems, and we had done our best to surmount them. Now it was getting increasingly difficult. By July 1944 the Jewish problem had become one of the two dominant aspects of the war in Budapest, thanks to the presence of Adolf Eichmann and the SS. The other one was the Allied air raids that were now beginning, sending us all into panic and depriving us of sleep as we sheltered in cellars.

Charles was very concerned with helping the Jews and I too did what I could. Early that month two important things happened so far as the Jewish population was concerned. Our regent, urged on by his advisers of whom Miklós was one, and several of whom were

Jewish themselves, was at last able to intervene in the persecution. He refused to allow any more deportations of Jews to the concentration camps, as had been happening in the provinces. The Budapest Jews had many other hardships to endure but not that worst of all prospects to face. Eichmann was furious of course, but our regent had been very cunning, thanks to Miklós's advice. Such deportations required large numbers of the Hungarian gendarmerie to be brought in from the provinces to administrate the procedure under the supervision of the SS. The regent quietly sent them back to their homes, and Eichmann knew there was no way he could handle the deportations with just his own men in Budapest. Hitler, with his eye on international opinion, decided to let Horthy have his way, and all looked hopeful for the regent, the Jews and Hungary itself – especially when at the end of August Eichmann left Budapest.

The other event of early July was that a man called Raoul Wallenberg came to work in the neutral Swedish legation, setting up a department to issue Swedish passports to such Jews as could obtain them. The numbers had to be limited, of course, but they would enable the bearers – with luck – free passage out of the country. He persuaded other neutral country legations to follow suit and did much good work in alleviating oppression against the Jews all over Hungary.

I am sure that Charles was deeply involved in this too, because of his friendship with the

300

Semmelweiss family and because he already knew the neutral legations through his earlier work, especially the Swiss legation. Wallenberg took many Jews to work directly for him, which saved their lives, and in helping him, Charles did not need me so much. He had a new identity, and with great sadness I realized that to continue to meet might be foolish. We should at least cease to be lovers until the war was over. With the Allies having landed in France and the Russians advancing from the east, that could not be long. Afterwards we could make plans for the future. There was Luke to consider too, for he also became involved in Wallenberg's work.

After I told Charles of my decision, which he reluctantly accepted, I went home and looked at the portrait he had first painted of me. It was magnificent and how little we had thought then of what war might do to us. I cried. I tried to be brave for Miklós's sake, and for the sake of Hungary, which needed anti-Nazis such as we were to stand firm. What we were doing was for the best, but it would be agony to see Charles – as I might sometimes have to do if I had valuable information – knowing we could no longer share our love.

The tape continued much in this vein, and when I switched it off, I was puzzled. It was interesting but I couldn't think of anything that would have warranted that slightly shifty look in Robin's eyes. Perhaps I'd missed something, or perhaps the shiftiness had to

301

do with Robin and Magda rather than the tape. It couldn't have been caused by the Louvre painting affair because he and I had a blazing row on the phone about his telling Magda about that. It had resulted in our shouting at each other and mutually declaring we couldn't imagine what had made us stick to each other for three years, and it had ended with a sort of apology from Robin and a sort of acceptance of it from me.

So that look continued to mystify me. I even insisted on playing the tape to David when he next came.

'Seems OK to me,' he said, though there was some doubt in his tone. 'It's just the story of the break-up.'

'She says *she* broke it off,' I began, anxious to get this right.

'Even if he did the breaking off, the version on the tape could be put down to face-saving on her part. She wouldn't be the first person to want to do that.'

'True. I think the jury's still out though.'

He glanced at me. 'Objectivity, Lucia, remember?'

'I do. I'm so objective, I want to spit. OK by you?'

He laughed, but I didn't feel I could take much more of this lack of direction in the biography. I was getting distinctly edgy. I could see this going on for ever, and then what would happen? I would have to take Gréta's account for gospel and just make clear that the biography was all based on her account. Magda would be happy. Justice would be satisfied. But I wouldn't. And nor, I suspect, would David – principally because I was not. And if neither of us was convinced that we had the full story about Charles, even if the biography were published, Magda would have won hands down. However irrational it might seem, I would see her image between myself and David for ever. He would remain in thrall just as he was now. Perhaps this was crazy of me, but lives can turn on moods and details – and often there's no going back.

July 1944

Charles realized he was shaking with tension as he went into the Káro lyi Gardens where he had arranged to meet Gréta. It was chilling to see children still playing and people strolling here as though nothing was happening. Because, he supposed, for many of them, nothing was. The presence of the Germans, the oppression of the Eichmann Kommando and the Hungarian gendarmerie who carried out his orders, did not affect the majority of the population, only the Jews who were afraid to leave their homes, who all had their own stories of atrocity and horror on the streets.

The air raids affected everyone though. Not many yet, but they would not stop until the Soviets reached here, and what would happen to Hungary then? What would happen to *him*, come to that? Should he stay or go? That didn't lie entirely in his hands. It depended on whether Elisabeth could or would come with him; even if they married there might be doubt about that. He suddenly felt an intense homesickness for his Buffalo childhood home, even though he knew he could never return there. He could never have the sense of freedom he would need, where the pressures of the family business would close upon him once again. Not New York either. Somewhere else. He decided he would go to seek the green grass and hills of Kent in England. Its red roofs and the quiet of the Kentish valleys had left their mark on him, when he visited it once before the war. There he could be happy with Elisabeth. He'd had enough of capital cities and the two faces they presented, the Janus of the glitter of the successful and the Janus of the grinding misery of the fallen.

Kent was a far-off dream with many problems and nightmares to be faced, however – one of which was Gréta. He had to tell her they should no longer meet, whether as lovers or as colleagues. He could see her waiting on the bench, that slim, still figure, carved upon an eternal landscape of his memory. As soon as she glimpsed him, she would stand up and stroll away. He would slowly follow until they reached a café or other rendezvous of her choice, one not frequented by police or SS. Today followed the same routine. When at

last they were sitting at a café on the Teréz
Körút, Charles found it hard to talk naturally.
All the sentences he had planned, all the
endearments and reassurances he had re-
hearsed, vanished from his head beside the
reality of Gréta's presence.

At last she asked, 'What is wrong, Charles?'

And so he told her, finding words at last to
talk steadily and rationally, trying to ignore
the steel in her eyes, the iron resistance to
what he was telling her must happen.

'There is more than the war involved here,
is there not, Charles? There is someone else,
someone you love more than me.'

He was not going to pretend otherwise.
'There is, Gréta,' he said gently. 'I love you, as
I have always loved you. But now I love her
too, and she needs me, as you do not.'

'The Jew.' She said it impassively, no hate in
her voice, merely an observation.

Charles did not reply, for it made no difference now.

Gréta remained like a coiled serpent, ready
to spring. Then suddenly she relaxed, and
was the Gréta he had always known, as she
laid her hand over his. 'It is the war, Charles.
Don't worry. I have Miklós, you have your
Jewess. Pray God we all come out of this
alive. I am not so blind. I am married, and
you were bound to meet and marry someone
yourself one day. So it is now. I have been
fortunate for three years after all.'

He looked at her white hand on his and the
beautiful face that he had never entirely

captured to his satisfaction on canvas; there was always something that eluded him. For the first time, however, he felt alienated from her, his usual battle with desire did not come and though everything she said was meant to be consoling, it failed to strike through to his heart.

'For the sake of this war, Charles, we must stay in touch. Because we do not love together does not mean we should not work together. We are at a dangerous time, now the regent has shown his hand by stopping the deportations. We have enemies enough without you and I being enemies too.'

He reluctantly agreed they could continue working, but inside he felt less certain she was right. Who are our friends and who our enemies? was always the question to be faced. To his relief, Gréta did not ask again where he was living, nor what he was currently doing. That made things easier, for he had far-reaching plans for himself, for Luke, for Elisabeth, and the fewer people who knew the better.

* * *

I was still dissatisfied with what I was writing, aware that I should be feeling an inner conviction that I knew Charles's story for sure during the war, and it didn't come. Nor did any letter from Luke. Correction, there had been in a way. Only it didn't come to me, and it wasn't a letter. It was a postcard of a former silver mine in Colorado, addressed to Magda. She showed it to me and I read: 'See you sometime, kid. Tell the Duchess to carry on.'

'What does he mean by that?' she asked curiously.

'I wrote to him with a few questions and asked if I was on the right track. That's what he means.'

She asked me what the questions were, in case she could help, and I quickly invented a new set. I decided I needed to keep my lines of inquiry straight. I cursed Luke for being a difficult old cuss. Maybe – I had to bear in mind – he was also a *deceptive* old cuss. He could have been there in the vital period. Suppose he had caused trouble between Gréta and Charles? Suppose he was a double agent, as Gréta suspected. Talk about out of my depth. I began to feel the waters were closing over my head, especially when I heard Gréta's next tape.

By the end of August of 1944 everything seemed to be calming down. Eichmann left Budapest after his plans for one fell swoop to deport the Jewish population had been foiled, and there were increasing rumours that the regent was about to seek a separate peace with Russia and the other Allies. Before that, though, terrible things had happened. I missed Charles so much, for I only saw him very rarely, but there was nothing I could do about it. I tried to help him by keeping my ear even more firmly to the ground, and by passing on what I could gather of the German plans.

Miklós and I made a policy of friendliness towards the Nazis though our hatred of them was well known to the regent and our friends – such political deception can be essential. Charles was by that time working in the Swedish legation where Raoul Wallenberg was doing his best to help the Jews of Hungary with his passport scheme and machinations. I still used to meet Charles in the Káro lyi Gardens and I did not think I was under surveillance, though Charles might have been because of his connection to Wallenberg.

I was afraid that the Semmelweiss family might betray Charles – Zoltán Semmelweiss was on the Central Jewish Council and had Eichmann's ear. Miklós told me that he was brother to the man whom Charles had be-friended, so I suspected that one of the daughters had made a play for Charles and had succeeded in alienating his affections from me, by seeking his sympathy for their plight. I had not thought Charles could be so naive, but realized he must be missing me.

I hoped he did not speak too freely about me to her, for that would put me in great danger, not to mention Miklós, but I could not get Charles to understand this. He merely said he never talked about me to her, but I did not believe him.

And then there was Luke. I still mistrusted him, and Charles said little about him.

I began to feel deeply uneasy about increasing references to Luke, wondering where it would lead. It wasn't the only reason I had for concern. When David next came to see me, I sensed there was something else on his mind, and though he discussed the relative merits of our having a weekend in Dieppe or one in Dorset with apparent enthusiasm, I could see it remained, so I asked what it was. I was becoming depressingly aware that it was nearly a year since I'd fallen in love with him, and that I seemed to be getting nowhere fast.

'I'm not sure,' he replied helpfully. 'I know I said I wouldn't get mixed up in this, in order not to influence you, but there's something you ought to know.'

'And it is?' I didn't like the sound of this at all.

'Your chum Robin is spending a lot of time at Edenshaw.'

'I know,' I said, relieved that this was all. 'He pretends he's there for the pictures, but we know what he's really after, don't we?'

'Do we?'

'Of course,' I answered blithely. 'Magda. I think mutual eagerness might have moved a step forward.' Too late I realized this was tactless, and hastened to redeem the situation. 'I mean they've done the paintings and they're on to the photos now.'

It sounded weak even to me, and David wasn't fooled. 'You mean they're sleeping together,' he stated flatly.

'I've no idea whether they are or not, but I did get the impression that might be the case.

I'm sorry, David.'

'Sorry, why? Magda and I are divorced,' he said. 'And in case you hadn't noticed, I'm sleeping with someone else too.'

Oh, I had noticed, believe me. Again that seemed to end it, and again I was wrong. I hadn't forgotten Robin's insinuation that David was still sleeping with Magda, but I'd pushed it right to the back of my mind, but even with his present reaction, a tiny niggle remained.

'Anyway, it wasn't about your former paramour's bedding arrangements I wanted to talk,' David continued. 'I wanted to warn you to watch your back.'

'What on earth do you mean?' I stared at him as if he were cuckoo and he went rather pink.

'Maybe I'm seeing more to this than there is. I may be biased, but don't be too trusting at Edenshaw.'

'About whom? You know I'm wary of Magda and I have no problem with Robin. Look, David, explain, will you?' I was beginning to get really worried.

'I'm probably imagining bogeys where there are none, but I have a feeling Robin's doing more over this book than just the pictures.'

'What on earth *can* he be doing?' I frowned, not understanding this at all.

'When I went to Edenshaw yesterday, I walked in on Pamela unexpectedly in the archives, and found Robin there. She was

310

saying to Robin, "Here's your copy of the tape".'

'You must have misheard. She was just giving him the tape for me.'

'Perhaps, but I didn't get that impression, because she was writing on the label.'

Puzzled, I went to the pile of tapes on my desk, and picked them up. They were all labelled with Gréta's distinctive handwriting, including the most recent. There was no sign of Pamela's handwriting.

'So what, anyway? Perhaps he needs copies for the pictures so he knows the full story.'

'Why doesn't he talk it over with you? He can't need to know all the details. *Does* he talk it over with you?'

'Look, I thought I was the paranoid one round here. What on earth are you implying?'

'Back-up,' he replied.

'Copies, you mean, in case the original goes AWOL?'

'No. Didn't you tell me you'd had a conversation with Magda about what would happen if you couldn't go along with Gréta's story?'

'Yes, but that was all "what ifs". She understood that perfectly well, and we agreed about what we'd do.'

'Magda is great on back-up. She likes to know where she's going. It's tough for me to say this, Lucia, but if the book got dropped for any reason and if push came to shove between you, wouldn't it help Magda's case if she had a back-up plan?'

311

'Which is what?' I still didn't follow.

'Another biographer. Remember I warned you earlier about that?'

That was blunt enough even for me to get the point. The penny dropped with a re-sounding clang. 'Robin?' I squealed, bursting into laughter. 'Oh come off it, he's not a writer. How on earth could he do all the research and what-not necessary, let alone construct and write a book?'

'Maybe he'd have a helper. Think about it, sweetheart. That's an awfully pretty back of yours, and I'd hate to see a knife right in it.'

August 1944

Every day Charles insisted on going with Elisabeth to Raoul Wallenberg's office in the Swedish Legation on the Gellért Hill in Buda. Her papers showed her to be Lotz Elisabeth, a Hungarian of Swedish descent married to Lotz Károly. The place on her jacket where her Yellow Star had been removed seemed glaringly obvious to both of them, and each journey was a tense time. Under the brilliant and indefatigable Wallenberg, the neutral legation passport scheme was growing, and Charles, while nominally at the Swiss Legation, acted as part of Wallenberg's intelligence network on what was happening in the Jewish quarter. He had the latest news via Zoltán of what Eichmann was doing on the deportation situation, and most of all when raids were being made to round up Jews for labour camps or worse. Speed was of the essence, for if news reached Wallenberg in time he could act quickly to intervene. If any of them recognized Charles Carr from former days they never revealed it. He himself hardly recalled what it was like to be Charles Carr. Elisabeth was employed in administration in Wallenberg's Department C, and was desperately anxious to get her family passports to safety, but so far they had refused. It would be more dangerous to try to leave, they thought. Everything would be all right. Zoltán had Eichmann's ear – what need had they of other help? Papa Semmelweiss was convinced, Katie was not, and nor was Charles.

It had been agreed that the safest plan for Luke was to stay put until the Russians arrived, as they surely would. Meanwhile, he carried false papers, and worked at the Swiss Legation with Charles, where his lack of Hungarian would not stand out and his schoolboy German and French were rapidly improving.

Their apartment had become a home, of which Elisabeth was the centrepiece. The intimacy was both blissful and close to the unbearable. Charles did not know whether he welcomed Luke's casual undemanding presence as a prop to his own discipline, or resented his sharing of Elisabeth's company. Sometimes they would visit the Semmelweiss family, coming through the back entrance with an illicit key in the hope of avoiding the watchful janitor's eye, and always leaving before night fell. He would not let Elisabeth go alone, for fear he never saw her again. Jewish girls were often seized from the streets and never seen again. Betrayal was a constant fact of life.

At their own apartment, Charles could at times pretend this was a normal family but then as night drew near and he would have to separate from Elisabeth, his body was afire with love of her and he knew the pretence was useless. He thought he was keeping this to himself, but he had not succeeded.

'When are you going to put that girl out of her misery, Charles?' Luke asked one night in the darkness of their room.

Charles froze, then a great relief swept over him as he decided that talking about it might help. 'If you mean what I think you mean, I'm not.'

'What the heck are you waiting for? For Hitler to burst into tears and say he's sorry about this mess?'

'A marriage certificate,' was all he could think of in answer, but the words sounded pompous and unreal even to Charles himself.

'Not possible and you know it. Too dangerous.'

'Then I can't make love to her as though there weren't a war on. She's even younger than you, Luke.'

'What's age got to do with it? Her family

thinks she's sleeping with you already. She wants to. The only person who doesn't want it is you. How the heck do you think I feel, stuck in here?'

'You're a fool, Luke,' Charles replied angrily. 'What if she became pregnant? You think that would be a good thing *now*?'

'It's up to you to make sure she doesn't.'

'Not so easy.'

'Halfway's better than never getting off the starting pad,' Luke said laconically.

'Even if I did, there are other factors,' Charles unwillingly admitted.

'Gréta? I reckon I could take over your meetings with her – if they're still necessary.'

Charles was glad of the dark, which made silence easier. Such an easy way out of his predicament had never occurred to him, and even with it put before him, he felt reluctant to take it. Fate would surely pay him back in other ways if he accepted Luke's offer. Only now did he realize how great the strain had been. Their meetings had been as frequent since they ceased to be lovers as they had before, because there was so much happening about which they needed to be in constant touch. He agreed with Gréta over that, but to be with her, to remember the past, and then to walk away, was always hard.

Sex and desire were part of love, but he knew now that he no longer loved Gréta, so why the constant tug towards her when he was with her? Everything in him yearned for Elisabeth, so why was it whenever he was

315

with Gréta he wanted her physically as much as he had always done? And she knew it. She could tell the effect she was having on him, and he could read the triumph in her eyes. She didn't, he sometimes thought, even care when every time he walked away, the remnants of control forcing themselves into bringing him home to safety – and Elisabeth. While he still saw Gréta, there was no way that he could morally make Elisabeth his.

He had thought there was no escape from this torture. Gréta was at one remove from the regent himself. She knew his plans, his thinking, any new blow that might come upon them. Charles had believed he could not forgo those meetings for the sake of his own private happiness. But with Luke's suggestion, now there was a possibility.

'She'd be hurt,' he said.

Luke chortled. 'Hurt? That's one tricky woman you have there, Charles. Do you know she follows you?'

'*Follows* me? What the hell do you mean?' Charles was instantly alarmed.

'Remember when we met at the legation the other day? Gréta was watching you from the other side of the road. Remember I took you out the back way? I knew you wouldn't believe me so I didn't bother telling you.'

'You're mistaken,' Charles retorted angrily. 'Gréta wouldn't do that. What reason would she have?'

Luke didn't respond, and his silence infuriated Charles even more. He could guess what

316

Luke was thinking, that she had been there in the hope Charles would lead her to where he lived. He was mistaken though. That would be petty, and Gréta was never that. She must have had some innocent reason for being there, or else Luke was mistaken. Nevertheless the thought of not having Gréta as a complication in his life was too tempting, and a great weight seemed to roll off him as he thought it through and made up his mind.

'OK, Luke. I agree.'

'Good.' From his mumbled reply, Luke was already half asleep.

Charles insisted on explaining the new routine to Gréta himself, and to his relief she accepted the situation without fuss. 'Until the war is over, Charles,' she added. 'And then we will see things clearly again. Perhaps you will wish to marry your Jewess, perhaps you will not. We shall see.'

'The war must be over soon.'

Mere words to him, for he knew the day would never come when he could or would want to return to Gréta. As he walked back towards the apartment, he felt free for the first time for many years, as though a chain had been unshackled from his mind, his heart and his body. He could love Elisabeth as she deserved.

He found her in the kitchen when he returned, preparing their evening meal.

'Can I help? It smells good.'

She glanced round at him, perhaps because of some change in his voice. 'It is mutton and cabbage you can smell. I was lucky to get some today. It is a *good* day, *kedvesem*. You can help me mix dumplings if you wish.'

If he wished! Charles laughed. Dumplings suddenly took on a new and glorious mysticism. He would even paint dumplings, to try to capture that elusive charm.

'Let's pretend we're in America,' he said, cradling her in his arms, 'strolling down Broadway. I'll take you there on a trip when this war is over.'

She laughed. 'And what shall we eat then, Charles? Mutton and cabbage?'

'No. We shall eat...' Charles considered, going back to his youth – what did they eat in America? 'Apple pie,' he pronounced. 'And once a year a Thanksgiving Dinner of turkey and pumpkin pie.'

'What is pumpkin?'

'Pumpkin is...' Charles could not explain it, so he waved his arms around, while Elisabeth considered this.

'That is a big cheese,' she decided.

'Very well, Big Cheese Pie then.' He whirled her round, caught up in the mood of the moment.

'I like to eat more than once a year,' Elisabeth said gravely. 'Every day shall be Thanksgiving Day if we can have them together.'

'And the nights,' he said lovingly with her once more in his arms.

She looked up at him, eyes full of hope. 'We could have our Thanksgiving Dinner before we go to America, dear Charles.'

'But not our nights.'

'That too,' she said shyly. 'Luke is not always here.'

He caught his breath. 'You are sure, Elisabeth?'

'Oh yes. I am sure. After all, Charles, I cook cabbage for you as any wife. I should have the pleasures too.'

'I think...' He could hardly bear to say it, or to delay his happiness a moment longer, but he had to. 'We should have your papa's blessing.'

'*After* I am your wife,' she said firmly. 'And, Charles, this stew may be cooking for some time.'

Three hours later Elisabeth stirred in his arms. 'Poor Ilonka,' she murmured happily.

'Who?'

'The peasant girl on the Mathias fountain. Do you know it?'

'Yes.'

All he could think of was Elisabeth, the feel of her body in his arms, the brightness of her hair lying across her face and chest, and the knowledge that soon they must move, for Luke would return. 'Why poor Ilonka?' he asked, to delay the moment.

'She never caught her butterfly. And I did, despite what Mama told me. But I will live. The butterfly is alive. It always will be, won't it, Charles?'

'Always living, Elisabeth. Always living.' He felt tears in his eyes and wondered why.

When Luke returned from the Swiss Legation, he brought bad news. Perhaps he had sensed the different atmosphere, or perhaps he needed fortification before speaking, but he left it until after they had eaten before breaking it to them. 'Eichmann has struck again,' he told them.

Immediately they were back in the everyday world of nightmare, and Charles felt Elisabeth's hand slip into his.

'Tell us,' she said.

'He's arrested three of your leaders, Elisabeth.'

'Which?' she asked fearfully.

'Petö, Stern and Wilhelm. They are with the Gestapo.'

'And my uncle?'

'Some other council members have managed to get out of Budapest, but I don't know about Zoltán.'

He's taken the worst, from our point of view, Charles thought. Nightmare closing in once more, for these three men were closest to the regent. 'This must mean Eichmann plans to defy the ban and get the deportations started again. Another Kitarsca.' There had been a notorious incident a month earlier in mid-July when Eichmann nearly succeeded in getting 1,500 leading Jewish men deported by train from the Kitarsca internment camp. For internment, read labour. Deportation meant Auschwitz, and Auschwitz, everyone now knew, meant death.

For the next two weeks Charles's overwhelming happiness with Elisabeth was set side by side with the rocketing political situation and the fear of the Jewish population. And then the unbelievable happened. The regent managed to get the Jewish leaders released, Eichmann's plan was thwarted, the pro-Nazi premier was replaced by a Horthy patriot, and on the last day of the month Eichmann left Budapest. Nothing changed radically for the Jews, for the Germans still occupied the country and the capital, and air raids continued, but a ray of hope that Hungary could still escape to rule itself now opened up once more – as one had in Charles's heart now that Elisabeth was with him.

Fifteen

David's suspicions seemed to numb my brain. The thought of Robin acting in cahoots with Magda sickened me. I had believed that everything was all right again between us, but now I had to face the fact that he might have merely been waiting for a chance to get his own back on me for running out on him. No, I dismissed this thesis impatiently. I *knew* Robin; he might get sucked in to such a scheme, but he wouldn't hide it from me. Then I remembered he'd said nothing about it when he came to my flat on the last occasion.

I nearly picked up the phone to sort it out on the spot, but I resisted the temptation. For once in my life I knew I had to play smart. If there was something to David's guess, then my best policy was to lie low. A row at this stage, before any definite evidence was on the table, meant the 'villains' (if villains there were) could simply say I was round the twist. Furthermore they could claim I was unsuited for the great task of seeing the wood for the trees so far as the biography was concerned – in which case they might hand the project to Someone Else. True, I wasn't paid by the foundation, and in theory could still write a Carr biography, but without access to Edenshaw archives and illustration material for the book, it would look a sorry thing.

I wasn't going to take the risk. After all, this wasn't just a book to me, this represented my future with David. I was still sure about this, even though there was no rational connection. It was like the old folk song: 'On yonder hill there stands a lady, who she is I do not know.' All the poor sap had to do to get this unknown lady to wed him was to get round the problem she'd been conditioned into by her dad: always to answer no. (And pretty deep psychology there, I thought.) The sap tries to fight it but the same negative answer always comes back at him. So, he turns into a wise guy and presents his proposal with something to suit himself *and* her.

In this case I was the sap, and David the unapproachable object of desire. Shall I go away, David? I amused myself by asking. And I swear I heard a resounding No! in my head as well as my heart.

Nevertheless I was aware that everything was waiting on me – or rather on the biography. I almost began to dread the next tape arriving, for it would indicate battle lines might have to be drawn. Fortunately, David was intuitive over this, and once again acted as courier in view of the fact, as he anxiously explained, he had put the bee in my bonnet and didn't want me stinging Robin – unfairly, he added after a moment, which made me giggle.

Moreover, he said he wanted to hear the tape. 'Why this time?' I asked. 'You didn't before.'

'Gréta told Magda this would be the last. It has the rest of the story on it. I want to be here, whether it biases you or not.'

I took this as a great leap forward. It was, I told myself, a committal of sorts. 'Don't speak,' I ordered him. 'Don't utter a word. Right?'

'Understood.'

And so we put the tape in my hi-fi. For the first time the sound of Gréta's voice made me instinctively recoil – which must surely be prejudice on my part. I was seeing bogeys where none had yet been proved to exist.

Gréta's voice was as sweet as always:

The false hope that had seemed to be offered to the Jews by the departure of Eichmann at the end of August was cruelly crushed six weeks later. The Buda Palace was a difficult and tense place to be during those crucial weeks. The regent kept his own counsel with a very small circle of trusted followers, of whom of course Miklós was one. With his permission, which stemmed from the regent himself, I gave as much information to Luke as I could. It was strange dealing with Luke, for as you know I did not entirely trust him, though for his lack of moral fibre rather than for political reasons. He was, I suppose, genuinely fond of Charles, and grateful to him. Nevertheless I missed Charles greatly, both as a lover and for our working partnership. I told Luke to pass on to Charles the momentous news that the regent was determined to seek peace with the Allies, and the first step for that would be an armistice with Russia whose troops were advancing rapidly towards Hungary. The Nazis of course still occupied our country, even though Eichmann had left Budapest.

I was desperately worried though, because the Buda Palace was not safe – the Nazis had their spies there, and there was no way of telling whether the regent's plans were being leaked to the Nazi authorities. And if word did reach their ears, the outlook for Hungary, especially for the Jews, was poor. Not that the threat to them had ever gone away, even in this six-week calm. The regent had been forced to agree with the German authorities that all able-bodied Jews of both sexes should be gathered in labour camps outside Budapest in order to work for the German war effort, and only by great cunning did he manage to ensure that this never actually was put into operation.

And then came 15 October, when catastrophe arrived and the nightmare began. The regent had sent a mission to Moscow to discuss the armistice, but it never arrived – and it seemed probable that the Nazis had got wind of it and intervened. Not knowing this, the regent had taken a brave step; he broadcast on that Sunday that an armistice was to be agreed with Russia in the expectation that the Hungarian army would take over Budapest, and with the Russians so close they would support him. Alas, the Nazis had ensured that this would not happen – they kidnapped his son, and faced with that, and the fact that there was no sign of army support, Horthy surrendered himself to the Germans and was deported. What happened then was the worst of all worlds: the Arrow Cross, or the Greenshirts as they were known, who were the pro-Nazi thugs of our country, took over Budapest; the next day Eichmann returned. The putsch against the Budapest Jews had begun. All this happened in little more than twenty-four hours.

For those of us who had been close to the regent, it was a terrifying time. We were isolated, but it was the Jews who were the immediate victims. We political enemies could wait – though not for long. I managed to get an early word through Luke to Charles that the Semmelweiss family should find a refuge elsewhere, and Charles immediately took them into his new apartment. I'm afraid it was in vain for the family disappeared. The Arrow Cross gangs roamed the streets plundering and murdering Jews at houses marked with the yellow star. Charles's apartment was not marked, of course, but the family vanished. Was it chance? Was it planned?

I was grief-stricken for Charles, as he blamed himself for leaving them in the flat. I reasoned with him that had he been there he would have shared their fate, whatever it was. He would be immediately suspect too, and his accepted status of working for a neutral legation would be no defence. He came to me at once, and all that night we talked and talked at my home. Finally Charles agreed that he must leave Hungary immediately if he could manage it. Before that, we had one last night together – Miklós was still at the Buda Palace, but even had he been at home he would have understood. He too loved Charles.

Oh, that night. I never forgot it. Such tenderness, such memories, such joy clutched from chaos and destruction. That was the night – Gréta stopped for a moment, a choke in her throat – *that I became pregnant with Klára. The following day he left. He said he would see me again when the birds returned in the spring, but alas that proved impossible. Hungary was part of the Eastern bloc, and*

travel was difficult, particularly for an
American with Charles's past as a diplomat.
It did not matter. I had Klára, and I had
Charles's love, and he knew that he had mine.

I looked at David when the tape finished.
'Well?'

'You first.'

'All too beautiful.'

'Maybe it was.'

'But you don't think so.'

'No.'

'Nor do I. Wouldn't any woman want to let
the father know about his daughter's birth?
And that bit about the birds returning in
spring – perhaps I'm reading too much into it
but...'

'*Madame Butterfly?*' he picked up.

'Yes.'

'Would Charles really have talked like
Pinkerton walking out on Madame Butterfly?
Far more likely this is Gréta romanticizing
afterwards.'

'So?' I was dubious about this. 'It doesn't
invalidate the basic truth. If women are con-
demned for hyping up their lovers' last words
in their imagination, the crime rate's going to
shoot up rather high.'

'Romantic little soul, aren't you?' He flicked
my hair and kissed me on the nose.

'Patronizing chauvinist,' I retorted amiably.

'I admit my faults.'

'Generosity itself.' Then I got serious. 'Tell
me, David, is this the story you heard from

Magda when you were married to her? And if so, what did you think of it then?'

'Roughly the same. I always thought—' David frowned – 'that it all sounded too pat, this great love affair, but I might just have been cynical. After all, Gréta and Charles had been together three and a half years, with an apparently complaisant husband whom we are always being told loved Charles greatly. On the other hand, looking at it now, I wonder. Gréta was a married woman of thirty-two. Charles would have been thirty by 1944. He would have been in his mid to late twenties when he first met her, and those are volatile years in anyone's life. It's possible he'd fallen for someone else and that Gréta is making a lot of this up for face-saving reasons.'

'She mentioned one of the Semmelweiss daughters on one tape.'

'Who vanished and probably therefore died according to this tape.'

I caught the odd note in his voice and said quickly, 'Don't let's get ahead of ourselves, David. I'll wait till Luke comes.'

'I don't think that's the way forward,' he replied. 'Luke isn't going to speak unless you know your own mind. He might not even speak at all.'

'So...' I stopped. There was no point asking him what I should do next. I could see it was showdown time. 'Magda?' I asked, dread in my heart that loins would have to be girded.

'She may know nothing, she may know a

whole lot more. Whether she'll tell you if so is another matter. It's up to you to make her.'

Thanks, David. I knew he was right, but I wasn't looking forward to this. I'd made an appointment with Magda through Pamela (doing things the formal way so it was down in the diary) and drove down to Edenshaw two days later. I decided I'd take Mum again. After all, it was still July and the gardens would be full of things for her to peer at. Since she knew nothing of what was going on, she'd be a good bulwark, and while she chattered, I could think my own thoughts. Also, I could mentally sob on her shoulder, if everything went pear-shaped. It's a great comfort to know there's someone who still loves you if the world caves in around you. Mothers do what lovers can't: they go on loving you right or wrong, and which I was at the moment I couldn't judge. I left her in the restaurant armed with the *Daily Telegraph* and the *Mail*, and marched into what I hoped was not going to be battle.

'So what's up, Lucia? You sounded agitated according to Pamela.'

Good one, Magda, I thought. Nothing like getting in her first blow quickly. She didn't look prepared for battle though. She looked just as usual – smart casual in clothes and warm casual in expression. Once installed in her office, I told her the truth. 'It's about the last tape, Magda.'

'What about it?'

'Have you listened to it?'

'Yes. I played all of them through.'

'Does it bear out what you've always under-stood to be your grandparents' story?'

'Of course. What else could it do?'

It came out perfectly naturally and I might have been intimidated by her astonishment and left it at that – had it not been for her reaction to my next question.

'Is there any way – other than through Luke perhaps – that we could get corroboration of it?'

'Corroboration?' She stared at me as if I were potty. 'Why do we need it? We have the story.'

'But no supporting evidence for it.'

The beautiful princess began slowly to change into the witch. I was fascinated and terrified at the same time. The soft lines hard-ened, the eyes lost their warmth and the voice dripped ice. 'We've been here before, Lucia. Why should we need corroboration? It's in-sulting to an old lady, to say the least. And for the proof, we have the paintings themselves.'

'Do we? Let's think about this. Where in your grandmother's account is the dark side of the story of their love which is fifty per cent of what *The Happening* represents, or so we agreed earlier?'

She waved this impatiently aside. 'The paintings talk the language of symbolic love, of course my grandparents probably had rows – it's all part of love.'

'*The Happening* reveals more than a slight lovers' tiff, don't you think? What about the monster on top of the hill? Where you assume there is love, there's a monster, at the foot of the hill, hidden away, waiting to be discovered, is the true love.'

'Very poetic,' she sneered crisply. 'Has it occurred to you that the monster, as you call it, is the war that parted them?'

'A minute ago you said the monster was merely a lovers' tiff. Which is it? You're the custodian, Magda. You should have a view.'

She lost it, and hey presto, the wicked witch snarled out. 'And you're the biographer. No theories of your own, Lucia. Stick to the facts.'

'Have I been given them?'

The eyes narrowed. Magda must have realized I wasn't going to give up, for she brought in the big gun for the final round. She laughed, and it wasn't a pleasant laugh. 'You want the truth, Lucia? You really want to know the grimy details of what my grandmother has done so much to cover up all these years, just for the sake of her love for Charles? All right, you can have them, and believe me there's evidence for this story all right.'

'What is it?' I might have been standing my ground, but I was shaken, wondering what the hell was going to come out of this.

'Your precious Charles Carr was no protector of the Jews, Lucia. The great painter, the great recluse. Did you ever stop to wonder

331

why he hid himself away, *why* he was so reticent about the past, *why* he left no written record of his life? No? Well, I'll tell you. He hid himself away, did my beloved grandfather, because he was a marked man by the Jews. They knew where he was here in Kent, but they decided to let him squirm here, where he'd always be scared they'd come after him. He was a betrayer of Jews, not a protector. It shattered my grandmother when she found out. You remember his famous failed mission to Turkey, when he was sent back at the border but not then imprisoned? Why do you think that was? The Nazis needed a stool pigeon, especially one with such a useful link with the Buda Palace. Their eye was on him throughout. His task was to befriend Jews, and the Semmelweiss family was perfect because the father's brother Zoltán was on the Jewish Council, a respected Jewish leader who was privy to the plans and whereabouts of the whole community.'

'I don't believe you.' It sounded weak even to me, but it was coming at me so fast I was having difficulty assimilating her story, comparing it with the one I knew. Or thought I knew.

'I'll tell you more, shall I? Charles chatted up one of the daughters in particular; as she was fair-haired it was easy for her to pretend she wasn't Jewish. He got her false papers and they lived together with Luke in Charles's apartment to gain her trust that he was on their side. My grandmother had rescued

Luke when he was shot down on a mission, as you know, and reluctantly let him go to live with Charles. Maybe she was already having her suspicions. Luke was sucked in too, by Charles's holier-than-thou attitude and actions. It wasn't until the putsch after the so-called armistice in October in which the whole Semmelweiss family disappeared, including the girl that Charles had befriended and whom Luke had fallen for, that Luke realized what he was up against in Charles. Luke toughed it out till the end of the war, but gallant Charles, having made my grandmother pregnant, disappeared at the first whiff that his activities as an informer on the Jews were known. Once that reached Raoul Wallenberg at the Swedish Legation he would have been finished in Budapest, and would stand no chance of saving his own neck. So, he went without a word to my grandmother. It broke her heart.'

'Then why' – my voice didn't sound my own – 'did she protect him with this false story on the tape?'

'Because, dear simple Lucia, she loved him, right or wrong. There are women like that, but thank heaven I'm not one of them. He was a weak man, she said, but he had loved her, truly loved her, and she him, so she wasn't going to betray him then or now. There you are, you know the truth, but it's a story that my grandmother will never put her name to. So what are you going to do, seek out corroborating evidence of the truth? Not with my help.'

'You're forgetting Luke.'

She seemed amused. 'Luke? You think he'd utter a word against Charles? Even if he turns up again and denies the story you can hardly take his word for it. He lived with Charles, he shared the information being passed on by my grandmother, he knew about Charles's activities at the time and probably shared them. Of course he'll deny the whole thing.'

'I've no evidence for either story,' I said as steadily as I could manage. I'd think later about the Luke angle – that was the last prop being tugged from under me. 'But I can try to get some.'

'By all means try,' she answered immediately. 'However, Charles Carr is hardly an Eichmann or a Mengele. Have you any idea just how many informers at Charles's level there were? It was a big trade. I told you my grandfather was left to squirm after the war. Do you think if there were any hard evidence against him they would have done so? Of course not. They had none. My grandmother would say nothing, and the Soviets were more interested in Nazi crimes against them than against the Jews. So, Lucia, let me suggest your only course.'

'I don't like the sound of "only course".' I did my best but I felt I was finished. No fight left in me, even though it did seem to me the goalposts were changing slightly as she talked.

'I should have added: apart from backing

out of the project. Your only course, with that exception, is to use my grandmother's version. Luke can't prove otherwise, nor may he wish to, and nor can you.'

'And if I don't. If I write the story you told me?'

'I don't advise that. Without evidence,' she emphasized, 'the trustees would never pass it, because it would ruin Charles Carr's reputation, and also upset all *your* careful theses as to what *The Happening* is about.'

'So, I publish it on my own.'

'Not a good idea. You'd have to attribute the true story to a source in order for it to be taken seriously. And if you attribute it to me, I'll deny it.'

'I could publish and be damned.'

'You'll be a laughing stock. I'll send out a press release explaining that you are a demented theory-driven writer who's obsessed with destroying me through attacking Charles Carr because you're head over heels in love with my former husband – who incidentally is still in love with me. Good lover, isn't he?'

I don't know quite how I got out of there. Looking back, I think I tried to drag my shattered mind and dignity together with a few words such as I'd come back to her on the matter. I needed David, but with her last zinger still in my mind, I preferred to cope alone. Then I remembered my mother, still, I hoped, sitting in the restaurant waiting my return.

I staggered in, and found her talking to

335

Myrtle. One look at my face, and my mother said quickly, 'Have some soup, darling. It will do you good.'

'Had a set-to with madam, have you?' Myrtle asked matter of-factly, handing me a bowl of this restorative elixir.

'How did you guess?' I tried to laugh, but it didn't work.

'It's not hard. She can be tricky.'

'I'll say.' I was glad of her friendly concern. If a member of Magda's staff thought her tricky, it made me feel I wasn't going off my head.

And then I began to cry. So much for maturity and coping alone. Mum was splendid, and so was Myrtle. The restaurant was empty and so she came out from behind her counter, and helped Mum scoop me up and take me to the table to sit down, soup and all. When I'd finishing sobbing my heart out, they were waiting patiently, all attention.

'That's better,' Myrtle observed. 'I can guess what all this is about.'

'Charles Carr,' I said hollowly.

'I don't know much, as I told you, and this isn't to run my boss down, but Charles never wanted madam to be a trustee.'

'I know, because he didn't want both her and David on the board.'

'That's not the real reason, love. He didn't want her and that's flat. Don't ask me why, he seemed very fond of her when she arrived, but he didn't want her anywhere near his foundation. Mr David was the one and Mr

336

Tony. It's my belief Charles would turn in his grave if he knew that she was CEO. Mind you, she's a good one, I'll grant you that, now she's got her own way.'

I clutched at a forlorn hope. 'I suppose he didn't talk to you about Budapest? You weren't just being discreet?'

'No, he didn't. Nor about his painting of *The Happening*, and I wish I had a pound for every critic and fan who ever asked me that question.' She regarded me thoughtfully, and then said, 'There was one odd thing about *The Happening* I recalled after I talked to you last time. It might just help you.'

'What's that?' I snivelled.

'I met Charles long before I came to work here. I was still married to my first husband Alfred then, and Charles was painting *The Happening*. He came to see us both one day, having seen us in the pub together. He explained about his being a painter, though not the kind that needs models. What he did need, he said, was a lock of fair hair. He couldn't get the light right.

'Being young we thought he was a weirdo but he stood us a grand meal in Tunbridge Wells, and a nice evening we had, all three of us. Alf was a bit suspicious that he was really after me, but I said no, there was nothing like that. You can sense it, can't you, and he always seemed dead that way. All his energy went inward into his painting.'

A lock of fair hair? I suddenly got excited. 'Could you wait here a bit longer?' I said to

Mum. 'I want to go round the garden again, and *The Happening*.'

'Have some quiche first,' she said practically.

'Afterwards,' I flung back over my shoulder as I sped out.

I ran back into the house and as luck would have it Magda was just coming out. 'You're back quickly,' she observed, no trace of the wicked witch in sight.

'Yes,' I replied cheerfully. 'You're quite right, Magda. I'll think it over, and if necessary back out.'

'Good,' she smiled brightly. 'I'm glad you've seen sense.'

I ought to have seen it long ago, I thought viciously, as I worked my way round *The Happening*, and confirmed my memory of the paintings. Like hell, I'd back out! I was going on. Then I went to the garden, this time first to the cottage at the foot of the hill. The swirl of the loving figure, the fair-haired loving figure. Oh yes, I said softly. I see it now.

Then, as I walked back to the fountain, I thought of the painting in the Louvre and the lock of hair, caught in the sunlight, just like the one in *The Happening*. I thought of the butterfly in the painting too, and I thought of the Ilonka legend. Of course Charles had known both versions.

I needed to see the fountain just once more to ensure its message to me was still the same. I knew what I had seen here, but what had Charles seen? I asked myself. He had

338

said to David, 'Mathias was a fool. But so was I.' It was obvious now that the girl on the fountain was not Gréta and not a representation of one of the two sides of love. I had misread the whole of *The Happening*, but this fountain was the key. The blind fool of the king, Charles, the girl who suffered for it, and Gréta who spun him a tale to suit herself, just as she was spinning me one now. This did not tie in with Magda's story of Charles the betrayer. He could not have built this fountain if he were; he could not have painted *The Happening* with such passion. He could not have produced the great art he did by painting a falsehood, or be laughing at the world by pretending that he himself was the chronicler. Art is not built on lies, though it can reveal them, as Charles's had. Charles was recording the truth for posterity, the love affair with Gréta that had gone disastrously wrong and his love for this other girl.

Now I had to ask myself why had the love affair gone so wrong? Was it just the jealousy of a woman spurned by her lover that led to their parting and the monstrosities of *The Happening*, or did I still not yet know the full story?

Two days later I was ready to meet David. It was August and a good day for a picnic. We went to Knole Park in Sevenoaks, took a picnic and sat on a grass hill overlooking the splendours of history. The magnificent house blended into the landscape calmly and serenely, not dominating, but sharing with it all its secrets, all its glories.

'Do you think Charles Carr would have painted *The Happening* to hide the truth, rather than represent it?' I ventured, just to clear my mind.

'Say that again.' David was busy unwrapping pâté and bread.

I did, with further explanation and to this he replied, 'No. I doubt if any true artist could. It has to be the truth, or to be more specific the truth as the artist sees it.'

I took a deep breath and plunged. 'I'm going to have to write this biography as I want, regardless of what happens. Push, as you once put it, has come to shove. But I won't be shoved. Do you mind?'

'You'd better tell me about it,' he said quietly.

'You as David Fraser or you the trustee?'

'They're the same.'

'Even if Magda is involved?'

I saw him hesitate, and my control snapped. 'You have to make a choice, David. Me or her. I've done my best but I'm getting nowhere. How can you say you're able to be objective when you don't see her that way? You're still blinded with love for her...' I was beginning to shout.

'Lucia—'

'You admitted it yourself,' I hurled at him. 'Fine, I thought I could live with that, but I can't, I can't, I *can't*—'

'Lucia—'

I ignored him. 'I thought I could handle it until the biography was finished, because that was the key, but it isn't. The key is you, David, and you're stonewalling. Can't you see she's controlling you, just like Gréta does her? It's a set-up between them, they're both control freaks, dangerous ones. Are you still sleeping with her?'

'*Lucia!*'

This time I stopped, red in the face, appalled at what I'd said. Like all stupid heroines I'd broken the rules of the fairy godmother. Great. Well done.

'Lucia, would you just repeat what you said?'

'No.'

'Did you say I was blinded with love for Magda?'

'Yes, you are. You admitted it. You're still under her spell.'

'Maybe that, but I never said I still loved her, Lucia.'

'Even so, you can't break away – any more than Charles could,' I said despairingly.

'Shut up about Charles for once. This is about us. Lucia, I may be mentally shackled to Magda and not only because of Toby. I admit that—'

'There you are then.' I began to get worked up again.

'Will you be quiet and listen? I don't love her. I *hate* the woman. That can shackle you as much as love.'

I stopped. I was silent, and so was the

341

world. 'Hate?'

He gave a wry smile. 'We have opposite problems, Lucia. You keep running away. I can't run away. What do you think it was like, marrying someone like Magda, having a son you love by her, and then finding out that she married you to get in on the Charles Carr scene? She simply wanted to acquire control through marriage, as Charles wouldn't let her be a trustee. Even she couldn't charm him into that.'

I wasn't yet taking this in. I was still stuck on point number one. The most important.

'You're not in love with her?'

'The opposite. And I'm most certainly not sleeping with her. How could you even think that?' He looked truly appalled.

'Then why...?' I stopped.

'Go on, let's hear it.'

'Make me run after you?' I finished.

He obviously felt guilty because he flushed bright red. 'Magda didn't do much for my self-esteem. I looked at the world in a different way after that episode. I began to look at women in a different way too. I was besotted with her when I married her. I was besotted for the next year or two, and then quite suddenly I saw the mask fall away and she realized that. You want to know how?' He'd read my face correctly. 'We were talking about what to call Toby. I suggested Benjamin and she immediately refused. It was a Jewish name she said, and her tone left me in no doubt that to her Jews were not only different

342

but on a lower level to herself. We had a row about it and she laughed at me, making no bones about her views. Then she went on to explain why she had married me. She's a lady who loves money and power. She saw the way to power through me, then she saw the way to money through Michael. Fortunately she does love Toby, but my great fear is that she will control him as she does Michael. That's why I'm still around here and not doing a Paul Gauguin in Tahiti.'

'Why didn't you tell me, David? We're lovers.' I felt immeasurably hurt.

'I couldn't. The biography, remember? Besides, Magda made me pretty cautious about commitment. Every woman might be another Magda in disguise. I decided I preferred to control myself, stay alone, and keep affairs casual. So then I met you.'

'Are you sorry you did?'

He proceeded to show me in the nicest kissable way that he was not. When I'd recovered enough to return to the fray, I asked, 'I'm being objective, David, so forgive me here, but why would Magda go to all that trouble to marry you for what is a little known museum? Not much power there – though the scholarships come near to it, I suppose.'

He put his arm round me. 'I don't know, Lucia. All I know is that she did. For some reason she wanted control of the Charles Carr Foundation – and that desire, I deduced without great difficulty, goes back to her grandmother.'

'Magda told me that Charles was a traitor to the Jews he befriended, and that he walked out on her grandmother. And that Luke is far from being clear of suspicion himself.'

'Did you believe her?'

'I believe she believes it. Didn't she ever tell you that story?'

'No. She would have loved to have done so,' he said bitterly, 'but she's too clever. She would know I wouldn't believe it for a minute – and anyway as a trustee I'd get her booted out as CEO.'

'So we come back to it again. What does she see in Edenshaw, or perhaps need. Besides the power of being CEO?'

'From what you've told me, Lucia, it could be hate. But not of me.' He hesitated. 'Would you think me crazy if I suggested it was of Charles?'

Sixteen

Evidence. How I began to hate that word. It wrote itself in large letters before my eyes, it was dancing on my computer screen every time I opened up. It was there in the blank page of my notepad. I needed it, regardless of what I had said to Magda, and there was no way I was going to back out of the project now. It would be letting David down, because I realized what had kept us apart. He hadn't wanted to write the book himself, being too tied up with Magda; the foundation would not allow Magda to do it. In addition, I suspected he had feared what he might find, not that his faith in Charles had been undermined, but he too could find no evidence for other than Gréta's version. Or, now, for Magda's. No wonder he had been so off-putting when I brightly put my innocent foot in it and said I'd like to write the book, please.

Did Magda really hate Charles, as David had suggested? I decided to take one step at a time, and leave Magda on one side for the moment. Did I, I asked myself, believe Gréta's story? Answer: no. Why not? There I was stumped. All I had to go on was instinct and one or two slight discrepancies in the tapes – and in a ninety-year-old lady no one could legitimately quibble about that. Nevertheless I decided to write down all the queries that I had accumulated. There were quite a few, and they were the only arrows in my armoury; whether Magda, in the circumstances, would ever allow me to put them to Gréta was another matter, however. I could telephone her without asking Magda, but I knew I should be on safer ground first before I took this option.

One of those queries concerned the photographs: if she had never been to Charles's apartment, how did she come to have the photograph of the Semmelweiss family – and,

it occurred to me, did she have more? She
had made the selection for me, I hadn't been
allowed to see them all. She had told me
Charles had given the photo to her, but that
didn't seem likely. I suppose it was clever of
her to let me see a picture of the Semmelweisses at all – I already seemed to be acting
as counsel for the prosecution. Perhaps I was
being unjust in doubting her story, though
the fact that Magda had given such a devas-
tatingly different one suggested otherwise.
The interesting thing to me was whether
Magda's version of Charles's story was based
on her own deductions or whether it was
sanctioned by Gréta. I suspected the latter –
which did not necessarily affect its truth or
otherwise.

I couldn't believe in Charles the villain any
more than in Charles the romantic spy hero.
My only evidence for either story lay in *The
Happening*. To study this in the light of there
being two women, not one, now made sense.
The fair-haired girl he 'chatted up' in Magda's words could well be the 'other woman' in
the story; and in the light of the golden lock
of hair he needed when he was working on
The Happening, it was a reasonable propo-
sition that she was Gréta's rival not just a
friendly neighbour.

Could *The Happening* be symbolizing his
own self-hate for his betrayal which had
resulted in the disappearance of the Semmelweiss family? If not, I couldn't see how
Magda's story about Charles the villain stood

up. Even if I could somehow tie the paintings in with this theory, it didn't tie up with the fountain. Nor did the Charles the villain thesis fit in with Charles's own words to David that both Mathias and he had been fools. The same arguments applied to the Charles the romantic hero thesis. There was too much anger and frustration in the paintings for Gréta's story to be given validity, and it was a personal anger rather than an anger directed at war itself.

So if I ruled both these theories out, I was left with the bleak fact that I hadn't a clue what had really happened to Charles Carr in Budapest. It was not a happy situation with half my book completed. I had barely been managing to keep up with my children's writing and I was not the most popular client on Agent Sue's books. It would be good news for her if I chucked the whole biography idea on the scrapheap. But how could I? There was David to consider. What would he think of me if I chickened out now?

I made a list of the pointers I had. Firstly it was fairly safe to assume that Charles had indeed left Budapest about the time of the putsch in October 1944. Gréta's facts were correct there, I'd looked them up. The fair-haired girl was also a fact, and could provisionally be linked to Myrtle's lock of hair story. The more I studied my photographs of *The Happening* the more certain I became that she was Jewish, and a Semmelweiss. That the family, together with Elisabeth, had vanished or perished in the putsch or shortly afterwards also seemed certain. The story I had yet to verify was what part Gréta, Charles, and possibly Luke, played in that last terrible drama. I studied *The Happening*, both house and garden, but there was nothing further to learn. In recording the emotion, the inner meaning of the events, Charles had deliberately omitted the facts.

How could I hope to reach them?

October 1944

Budapest was torn open in a day. The city's fair face was being ripped from it and leaving only chaos, the threat of nightmare ahead and the menace of darkness beneath. The wounds were not yet physical, but no one had any doubt that the city's population was swallowed up by the machine of war. Ever since the regent's announcement that morning, Charles had been alert for trouble. When by early afternoon there was no signs of a rejoicing Hungarian army on the streets outside, he and Luke had decided to leave the apartment. He told Elisabeth on no account to try to visit her family today; she must stay in in case of trouble. She had been mutinous but reluctantly agreed to stay until one of them came back with news.

Although it was Sunday, Charles knew that Raoul Wallenberg would be in the office at the Swedish Legation, for he too would be prepared for trouble and Charles was in no doubt that they should join him. The radio broadcast had announced the coming of peace, but where were the signs of the SS retreating? Where, come to that, were the sounds of rejoicing citizens flocking in the streets to celebrate? There was only a deathly quiet.

Then, as they made their way across the river, they began to hear rumours, the regent's son had been kidnapped by the SS, then worse that the regent had surrendered and disappeared. There were no signs of the Hungarian army, nor of the Soviet army said to be so close to Budapest. Leaving Luke at the Swedish Legation, where queues of anxious Jews had already begun to gather, Charles decided to make for the Swiss Legation, which might have further news. In July, the so-called 'Palestine Office' in the legation had been overwhelmed by applicants for *Schutzpassen* to avoid the threatened mass deportation. That had never taken place, but no one doubted that one day it would happen. The day was now upon them and the legation in Vadász utca would once more be besieged by terrified people. Which was the city to fear more, the Russians or the Nazis? For the Jews there could be little doubt: the Nazis; even the Russian army offered some kind of hope.

For once Charles longed to meet Gréta again. She of all people would know what was happening at the Buda Palace. A terrible thought came to him. She and Miklós were close to the regent. If there was anything in this rumour, then they too might be under arrest. Charles tried to stop himself from thinking ahead to a nightmare that couldn't yet be assessed. The sky was so calm, so peaceful, as he walked through the streets; the sun even shone from time to time. If he painted it now, what would his painter's all-seeing eye record: the calmness of good, the surety that God was in control, not man? Or would it see a menace in the still white clouds, a warning that when they overtook the sun they would gather darkness and rain their fury down upon the city? There were few strolling the streets as would be usual on a Sunday afternoon, but the cafés were full, spreading the rumours of frightened men.

When he arrived at the Swiss Legation it was to the worst possible news. The Arrow Cross, the fanatically Nazi Hungarian Green-shirt party, had seized power. There was already a long queue for the 'Palestine Office', as he had guessed. Jews were clamouring for protective passports and Charles was kept busy, unable to return home. The telephone links were down, and he had no way of knowing whether Luke was still at the Swedish Legation, or if he had managed to get home to Pest from the Gellért Hill in Buda. The great fear of Budapest was that retreating armies or occupying armies would blow the bridges, dividing the two cities, and there was already a rumour that the bridges had been mined. He knew Luke could be trusted to think of the dangers and return to Pest as soon as he could, and he himself had to leave very soon, for the light was going fast.

Under the cover of the blackout he would get the Semmelweiss family to safety in his apartment, if indeed they had not already fled there. The blackout provided opportunities for gangs of Nazi thugs to roam the streets seeking for yellow-starred victims and homes. Charles seized his coat and hat, feeling suddenly claustrophobic within four safe walls when the nightmare might be beginning outside. His place was with Elisabeth, not here. He had done what he could. The queue was restless now, for the dangers of waiting in the dark were greater. Parked outside the legation was a luxurious motor car – surely an anomaly in a world gone mad, he thought – and then he realized that he recognized it. It was Gréta's and she herself was stepping out.

Gréta? Was she mad, coming here in a car like that? On today of all days?

'Charles, thank heavens, I have caught you. You must not go home. I have come to warn you.'

Even in the midst of this craziness, her beauty as she ran to him made him feel he was playing a part in a movie, even though she was untidy and anxious, with a headscarf over her shining black hair.

'The gangs of the new government are out looting yellow-star houses,' she continued.

'They are crazed with power and drink, it does not look good. You must come with me.' She grabbed his arm urging him to get into the car quickly. He tried to pull back, but she would not let him.

Dear God. 'Papa Jákob, the family—' he began, still resisting.

'Do not worry, Charles. I have just seen Luke. I thought you might both be at the Swedish Legation, so I went there first and found him. He is taking the Semmelweiss family to my home.'

Elisabeth was Charles's immediate fear. She would be at his apartment in Mozsár utca, not her family home. Suppose the Arrow Cross knew about her? Suppose the janitor informed on her?

She seemed to read his mind. 'Luke told me about your friend. She too comes with them. It is not safe for her either, even though you have no star on the door. He says it is well known in your block that she is a Jewess, so he will collect her as well.'

Charles's mind was alert now, thinking this through.

'It is not safe for you to have them at the Öszödy palace,' he said. 'We must get them to safety elsewhere.'

'Tomorrow,' she said impatiently. 'Tonight only safety counts, and then tomorrow we think what to do. Come, we must go.'

The crowds were gathering, and Charles quickly realized she was right. A car meant escape from the city, and at any moment they could be attacked.

The twilight added a menace to the un-naturally quiet streets. The driver, István, was long known to Charles and were it not for the eerie silence everywhere the drive could have had the comfort of familiarity. Not tonight. Tension knotted his stomach, and as they arrived at the Öszödy palace he had to work hard to control his fear. Gréta took his hand.

'Come, Charles, and then I will find out whether your friends have yet arrived. I think it will be too soon yet.' She took him into the drawing room. It was strange to be back here, the fire glowing and servants about their work as though nothing unusual were happening outside.

'I will go now, Charles.' Gréta threw her hat and coat on a chair.

'Let me come.' He needed to see them with his own eyes.

'That will arouse suspicion,' she said sharply, and knowing she was right Charles yielded. He paced restlessly round the room. There was the first portrait he had painted of Gréta. He remembered it so clearly. For the first time for many months, even years, it seemed that the Gréta he had first loved was back. Her beauty was warm and alive again for him. He had misjudged her, he realized, overwhelmingly grateful to her as he began to relax. She was not the luxury-loving countess but the vulnerable loveable woman he'd first met.

When she returned, she came right to him

and took his hand. 'As I thought, they have not yet arrived, Charles.'

Terror gripped him, even as she continued, 'Do not worry so, Charles. It is too soon. Luke sent a message, I am told, that he has them all safely at your apartment and is leaving now with them.'

'But it is dark.' Relief was immediately replaced with a new fear. 'I'll go—'

'Do not worry. Luke knows the hidden ways. There is more danger in larger groups. I have given instructions they are to be taken to the garages when they arrive.'

'Why not here? I must see them—'

'Darling Charles, we can trust no one. They will be safer there than in this house. I do not want our servants to see them. You under-stand? There is an upstairs room in the garages not visible from the outside. They will be safe there for the night. Any of the servants might betray them, and, my darling, us. If we are seen to harbour Jews – who knows?'

Charles was full of remorse. She was right. She was taking a risk for him, and he must co-operate. 'Can I see them?'

'When it is safe and everyone is asleep.' She looked at him gravely. 'You trust Luke, do you not?'

Trust Luke? Her words didn't make sense. 'Of course.'

'Then leave it to him. He is a resourceful young man. He will get your Elisabeth and her family to safety with our instructions. And, Charles my darling, just to set your mind at rest, I have told István to remain in the garages until they have arrived, and then to tell me immediately.'

Two hours passed slowly. He could not eat, he could not drink, or relax. At last he could bear it no longer.

'I'll go the garages myself and wait,' he told her gently.

'And jeopardize our safety? If István is there, no one thinks it strange. If you are, they will know there is a prize there.'

He slumped back in his chair, grateful that at least one of them had a clear mind, and he told her so. A further half-hour passed until Gréta was summoned from the room. Minutes ticked by like hours though it could only have been ten minutes or so before she returned smiling. 'They are here and Luke too. They are safe, and István is taking them food and drink. In the middle of the night we shall go to see them, yes?'

A tide of relief consumed him, sweeping him along, and he began to realize how tired he was in body and mind. Tonight at least they were safe, and he would see them soon. With the coming of the morning he could work out some plan, with Gréta's help, for by then they would know the political situation. She came to sit next to him, taking his hand.

'Poor Charles, I am glad I have made you happy again. We had such good times together, did we not?'

He held her close to him and felt her warmth with gratitude and desire.

'We should go to bed, Charles,' she whispered. 'Come, sleep with me, please.'

'I can't, Gréta. Not tonight. Not now.'

'My love, please. I need you. There is something I have not yet told you. The Arrow Cross have forbidden the crossing of the Danube. Miklós was in the Buda Palace and is trapped there. Even worse, he might now be in the Margit prison. I do not know, and I fear for him so much. I need you, Charles. I have made you happy. Is it so much that you should make me happy once again?'

Compassion, horror at his selfishness, desire for love – he did not know which of these reasons, but perhaps all of them, made him take her into his embrace. He owed her a great debt for Elisabeth, tiredness took over his body together with an overwhelming love and gratitude for the past. Somehow he found himself in the familiar bedroom and between the cool blue silk sheets, and Gréta was in his arms.

He awoke to see her swathed in a house-coat standing by the window. It was still dark outside, and with sudden clarity he remembered every detail of what was happening.

'Is it time?' he asked.

'Yes, it is time, my darling. Come here. Do you wish to see where your friends are?'

There was a curious note in her voice, but he came to the window as she drew back the blackout curtains, and he looked out into the dark, lit fitfully by the moon as clouds crossed it. Moonlight falling on her face, on the blue gown, and the blue sheets, with the dark blue and the pearl moonlight outside. That's how he remembered her later, pale, emotionless.

He came to kiss her hands. 'My lovely Gréta.'

'Look, Charles. There is the garage I told you of.'

He could see it, stark and functional, but a place of salvation for him. 'All you have done. All that for me.' He kissed her again, but she did not respond.

'Let's go,' he urged. 'You must meet them.'

'I shall not have that privilege, Charles.'

Her voice was brittle and he looked at her in surprise. She laughed, a shrill sound that pierced through him. 'They are all dead. That's what István came to tell me.'

'Dead?' The word didn't seem to make sense.

'Poor stupid Charles. Luke is down there in the garage, as stupid as you are. Your beloved Semmelweiss family is in your apartment – all four corpses. As they should be, vermin. I only hope they gave the women a good time before they shot them.'

Her face was slowly changing before his eyes. The Gréta he had known for over three years had dissolved into a devil dancing in Elisabeth's blood. The moonlight shot shafts of blue ice across her face, across the bed, across his life.

'You really thought I would save them?' he heard her say. 'They're Jews, Charles. *Only Jews.* I was so mistaken in you. You had me,

357

and you left me for a Jew.'

They are dead, he told himself. Papa Jákob is dead, Mama Márta, Katie – and Elisabeth. He fastened on fact, for of that he had no doubt. Gréta would not make this up, not joke about it. This was her moment. It had been coming for so many months and now it was here. Fool that he was. Blind, and mocked.

'I told Luke to take them to your apartment where they would be safe with your little blonde Jewess. I told him he should then come here, so we could all discuss in the morning what best to do. So simple.'

'But there's no yellow star on my door.' He had no hope, but while he spoke the pain would not strike.

'And then, darling Charles, I told our efficient new government where they would find them. Of course I knew where you lived. So easy, Charles. I even stole a photograph from your wallet while you slept once so that I could use it if I had the chance. I did, to reveal to the Greenshirts that a blonde can be a Jewess.'

'You betrayed them.' The words came out like bullets, so straightforward, so outrageous in their meaning.

She was laughing now, and he wondered however he could have thought her beautiful. Beauty is born inside.

'Betrayal depends which side you are on. I have always been on the Nazi side for they will win this war. Oh, you need not worry.

358

The information I gave you was true enough. I did love you, Charles, until you betrayed me.'

'And Miklós?'

'He's stupid, like you, Charles. He was true to the regent, but of course he loved me, so often we talked. He even told me about Horthy's mission to Russia. So foolish of him.'

Charles stared at her, and then the truth dawned. She would never have betrayed her husband too. This was her macabre joke. 'They're not dead, are they? You're taunting me. This is your revenge. You would never have gone so far.'

'Oh yes, Charles. I thought you might not believe it, but they are most certainly dead. It is always hard to acknowledge one has been a fool, so I am not surprised you doubt it. To convince you I asked István to go to the apartment and cut a lock of the girl's hair. There's some blood on it, I'm afraid, but you should recognize it. Look...'

Charles spun round to where she was pointing before he could stop himself. It lay on her dressing table, the hair he had caressed and loved. There was no sunlight on it now, only the dark red stain of blood. The sound from his mouth began as a moan and then grew louder.

'Please don't shout,' she said icily. 'If you should be so foolish as to attack me, István is now outside the door and would not hesitate to kill you – or perhaps to give you over to the

359

Gestapo or Greenshirts who have more interesting ways of doing that.'

'Let them.' He had nothing to live for now.

'No,' Gréta said thoughtfully. 'I've a much better idea. You can live with the knowledge that while Elisabeth was dying you were making love to me.' She began to shriek with a monstrous, demoniacal laughter, her gaping mouth turning her into a hideous parody of a woman.

He felt himself heave, then retch and vomit, but detached as though somewhere, somehow, he was still with Elisabeth.

'Get out,' she yelled in disgust, 'and take your imbecile cousin with you. Be grateful I don't inform on both of you. He's in the garage.'

Somehow Charles managed to find his way down the stairs and out into the cool night air. He breathed it in, swaying slightly. Then he set his mind on Luke, fearing that he too might be dead. But he was not. He came rushing down the steps from the upper room of the garage when he heard Charles enter.

'Is it true?' Charles croaked.

Luke caught him as he half stumbled, half fell against him.

'Is what true?'

Somehow Charles managed to tell him. Even then hope flickered, despite the mounting horror in Luke's face. 'Perhaps—'

But Luke cut in sharply. 'She'll have done it. She's made fools of us both, Charles.' His voice rasped out of the near dark.

Walking with only the help of the fitful moon to guide them through the blacked-out lanes and alleyways, they reached the apartment an hour later. There were still gangs wandering on the streets, which forced them to shelter in the dark until they had passed. They had long had an illicit key to the back of the building, and made their way up the dark stairs. The door to their apartment was open, and even from the stairs they could see lit by a shaft of moonlight what lay within.

It took three days for them to deal with what had to be done, three days in which the agony of grief played no part. If Gréta still represented a threat to them, neither of them thought of it. After those three days Charles sent Luke back to help at the Swedish Legation, and he shut himself up in the apartment for a further few days alone. At the end he told Luke he was going to leave Budapest. The Russians were on the southern outskirts of Pest, and the Margit Bridge had been blown up, albeit by accident. The others could follow suit at any moment since they had been mined by retreating Germans as the Russians advanced, so that if Pest fell, Buda would still be secure. Charles had not decided whether to flee into the countryside or to take a risk with one of the protective passports. The Greenshirts were still recognizing them as valid, but at any moment that might cease to be the case. If he could get to Switzerland, he could get somehow back to the US. There he would find László and somehow atone for his responsibility for Katie's death. Charles felt quite calm now for his heart and his emotions were dead.

'What will you do, Luke? Come with me?'

Luke hesitated. 'Nope. I guess I'll stay and take my chances at the legation. Wallenberg's people are disappearing like fleas in a soap spray.' He looked at though he wanted to say more, but Charles did not encourage it.

'In that case, I'll give you this. I've finished with it. Keep it or throw it away, as you like.'

Luke opened the loose-leafed book, and looked through it. 'Oh my dear Lord,' he whispered. 'Are you sure?'

Charles nodded. They understood each other.

★　　★　　★

I finally decided what I was going to do. I would write and be damned. I'd write both stories, and intimate that there were no grounds for believing either of them, and that I thought the real story remained to be told. If Magda didn't like it, it could go before the board. If it was vetoed – which I doubted – then I'd discuss it with the publishers. I would have some arrows in my bow. I couldn't use the tapes as evidence or the photographs because they would all be in Gréta's or the foundation's copyright. What I could use – though it might be a sticky point – were the interview notes I had taken. They would be my copyright although Gréta might hold the high moral ground on the issue. I could suggest to a TV producer or World War II historian that here was a pretty good story to investigate, but I didn't fancy this option. I wanted *my* truth to be registered. I had a stake in this and it wasn't just David. I felt responsible myself.

'I'm ready for D Day,' I told David more cheerfully than I felt. 'I'm going to see Magda.'

'Ah. Want to come to stay here?'

I considered this. Yes, I most certainly did fancy that, but I wouldn't accept. 'I'd love to come, but maybe not stay overnight with you – yet?' I told him virtuously.

'To hell with that. I don't give a damn whether the trustees think I'm prejudiced or not.'

'I do, though.'

A silence. 'OK.'

My usual B and B was full, so I found a room at the pub. It wasn't so quiet which didn't help my preparation.

This time I both made an appointment and brought a tape recorder with me. David had wanted to come with me to see Magda but I thought the tape might prove a better witness than he.

'That looks ominous,' Magda said. She was back in light-hearted mode now, as if we'd never clashed.

'Not necessarily, but I thought it would be wise,' I rejoined. 'Then we're in no doubt

363

what we both talked about if it has to go to the trustees.'

'Very ominous.'

I then told her what I intended to write in the biography about the war years. She thought this over, her face unreadable, and at last she said, 'I can't say I'm surprised in view of your outburst last time. I'll warn the publishers we may be late.'

'There's no need for that yet,' I replied steadily. 'I'm due to deliver to them anyway, not you.'

'But they won't get any illustrations from me if I don't like it.'

'You or the foundation?'

'I'm sorry. Slip of the tongue. I get used to making them since I do all the work round here.'

Oh good one, Magda: the silver tongue that licks the golden spoon.

'All the same.' She frowned. 'I think I ought to raise it with the board. Do you want to finish the book or have it discussed in principle?'

My, we were being restrained today, I thought. I wondered why. 'In principle will do,' I answered her. 'I've brought a broad statement of intent with me – just a few paragraphs. You can show it to all five members at the meeting.' No way was I going to let her put my argument in her own words.

'Very wise. And what,' she asked, 'do I tell my grandmother?'

'The truth,' I answered as if surprised that it

364

was under question. 'I'm sure you can put it to her so that it doesn't sound outrageous. After all, she gave me one story and you've now given me quite another. She might not want yours published.'

'I told you that in confidence.'

'I don't recall that. How could you expect me or any biographer to record one story, knowing it is a false one – as you claim Gréta's is?'

'It happens all the time.'

'Not in my book.'

I think Magda now perceived she might have made a mistake in her earlier spat with me, but she fought her corner valiantly. 'I'll let my grandmother know. It may be that she doesn't mind the truth coming out.'

'Which truth?' I asked sweetly. 'Hers, yours, or another one? You'll see I've worded the statement accordingly. There's a third option. A truth I intend to track down.'

She read it without saying a word, and then looked at me. I saw real enmity in her eyes. 'Then I shall add my views in a statement of my own.'

'In that case I'd like to be present to listen to it.'

'I can't agree to that,' she snapped, taken by surprise.

'Perhaps, Magda, it isn't up to you to decide the matter.'

Fortunately the trustees saw it my way – at least, three of them did. The meeting was held in Edenshaw House itself, on neutral ground. It was apparently usually held at Magda's home on the pretext that it was easier for childminding. (Thanks, David, for arranging this, I thought gratefully.)

It was a much livelier and more tense event than I had expected, mainly, I admit, because the discussion wasn't going all my way. My statement was read, so was Magda's, and then the discussion focused on an angle I hadn't considered. I had been so set on my path to truth, that I had skated over the fact that hand in hand with that went the reputation of Charles Carr and Edenshaw House. There was no doubt that its reputation – even under my choice of what was effectively a not-proven verdict – could be affected. Faced with the choice of a perfect love story or an out-and-out traitor, and despite all the assurances that a biographer gave that there was no real evidence either way – the press would undoubtedly publicize the out-and-out traitor. And what would that do to Edenshaw? I had given little thought to this aspect, and nor, I suspect, had David. Forced to consider it now, I could see the board had a real dilemma. So did I.

'How about a compromise?' Sir Rupert Packard asked hopefully. 'Suppose Lucia goes ahead with the biography as she wishes but the foundation doesn't support it except with illustrations. We don't have our name on it, and we can sell copies if we choose to.'

'I don't think,' Magda said smugly, 'that the publishers would like that very much. They want a commitment now of how many copies we want so they know how many to print.'

'Would you be happy with it, Lucia?'

It was crunch time. They all looked at me. By the expression on Magda's face she thought she had already won. She knew there was no way the publishers would risk not having support from the foundation, and so did I.

And then the deus ex machina strolled in – just in time to save the heroine (me, a heroine? Hardly, but the word will have to do) from the horrible fate of having to make up her own mind.

'Hi there, folks.'

It was, of course, Luke ambling in. Now wasn't the time to go into whether this was coincidence or not. I was just so glad to see him I could have thrown my arms round his mucky old anorak and kissed his stubbly cheeks. In fact I did.

'Luke, what in hell's name are you doing here?' Magda was furious. 'This is a board meeting.'

'Then why's the Duchess here?'

'Who – oh you mean Lucia.'

'Yup. I guess she's here on Charles's business. Me too. Seems it's time I spoke out – someone needs to represent the old guy himself.'

There was a hasty vote among the five trustees, and since all of them voted for his staying, Magda had no choice in the matter. She was livid though, and sat very silently, very pale, and forgetting all about the fact that to remain a beautiful icon one has to keep a lovely expression on one's face.

'You should read my statement,' she said swiftly to Luke, after he'd slowly divested himself of moth-eaten old scarf, anorak, gloves, and baseball hat.

'And mine, Magda,' I added, handing it to him.

'Now why don't you get one of your ladies to fetch me a nice cup of coffee while I'm reading this stuff?'

I giggled, and since Magda made no move to comply with this non-politically correct request, I told Myrtle to sit down again, I would do it. I performed a little jig of joy in the kitchen to Pamela's surprise, as I boiled up the water for the instant, and tore into the last packet of shortbread. I'd stand them some more, I vowed. I'd stand anyone anything at this point. I negotiated the tray with eight cups on it, plus shortbread, and walked back into the lions' den.

Luke had finished reading the statements and there was already a buzz of discussion going on – not from Luke, though. I had to remind myself that I still had to be careful about this. Firstly, he might have something to say that I didn't want to hear, i.e. that Gréta was St Joan and Mother Teresa all in one. Secondly, that Gréta was right and Charles was the villain Magda claimed.

'You know, Duchess,' Luke said to me, 'I admire your spirit. If I hadn't read this, I'd

368

have gone right back home and kept my mouth shut.'

'Why?' David asked curiously.

'You've got two stories, eh? Now most writers would have gone for one of them, but you say here, Lucia, you're going for gold, right? The truth?'

'Yes.'

'Then here it is, folks. Version Number Three of Charles Carr's life in Budapest.'

Accompanied by loud slurps followed by belches, and a shower of shortbread crumbs, Luke told us of the conditions in Budapest during the last part of the war, of the work he and Charles did at the legations, of his own failed mission, his own life first at the Öszödy palace and then at Charles's apartment with him and the fair-haired girl.

'She was really something that girl,' he told us. 'She was called Elisabeth. The loveliest little thing. Real beauty that went down deep inside and a heart to match. Charles was a different man to the one I'd known. I'd always liked Cousin Charles, though he was a dreamer, and so serious. I guessed when he fell for someone he'd fall hard—'

'He did. For my grandmother,' Magda said in a hard voice.

'Quiet, sweetheart, I'm getting to that. He loved Gréta, sure, who wouldn't? Hungarian countess connected to the Buda Palace? Charles's head, heart and John Thomas were up-turned all right.'

'He loved her for over three years. Is it likely

that would change?' she challenged him.

'Magda, be quiet and listen,' David snapped. 'You've all the time in the world to talk to Luke after he's finished.'

'Thanks, son. Sure, he loved Gréta. Most of us take love hard and then realize that's all over when we meet someone else. Why should Charles be any different? When he met Elisabeth, it was something different. He loved her, he told me, from the inside out, he'd loved Gréta from the outside in, influenced by the first to see the second. It was different altogether with Elisabeth. I've never seen a man so happy. They had barely six weeks together.'

And then Luke told us what had happened on the night of the putsch. How Gréta had come to him at the Swedish Legation and told him to collect the Semmelweisses and take them to the apartment. Then he himself was to leave them with Elisabeth and come alone to the garage at the Öszödy palace where he could sleep until morning and they could best discuss what to do next.

'It was crazy to fall for it, I guess, but we did. You know, you get caught in a trap, seeing no way out, so that when someone shouts "Follow me", you're mighty tempted to do it.

'So I obeyed her, fool that I was, and when I got to the garage everything seemed fine. Someone checked I'd arrived and told me Charles would come to see me in the middle of the night. Well, my Lord, he did that all right. I've never seen any man look like that.

Sort of torn apart. What the hell's wrong? I asked him. They're dead, he told me. All of them.

'I couldn't believe it at first, then I realized it had been a set-up. She'd told Charles we were all coming but had told me to come alone. I wanted to tear that bitch apart, I was more of a madman than Charles. He told me we had to leave, right now, and go back to the apartment. They were dead all right. Dead, all of them.'

He stopped for a minute or two while we all – even Magda – stayed silent. 'Well, I guess that wraps it up,' Luke said. 'Charles decided to get the hell out of Budapest while he could. I decided to stay on. I had a reckoning with Gréta, and anyway there was work to be done at the legation. Things got worse in Budapest. You've heard of the death marches?'

We shook our heads.

'November that was. Able-bodied Jewish men from sixteen to sixty were rounded up for labour camps; women and children marched out of Budapest on foot to starve to death if they didn't make it to Auschwitz. When the Russians finally broke the siege in the middle of January '45 that stopped of course, but Budapest was in ruins by that time, so conditions weren't too hot. Wallenberg simply disappeared – we presumed he was dead – oh heck, read about it in the history books. It was a mess. War always is.

'I'm going to tell you what Charles told me

about his last meeting with Gréta. Believe it if you want to. I did. And I believe it to this day.'

He soberly recounted it, and the images of *The Happening*, the terrible monsters, appeared before my eyes. The blues and whites of that last meeting.

His final word was for me. 'Now Duchess, what do you think? Are you going to put this in as the truth or as Story Number Three?'

Magda leapt in before I could answer. 'Without any evidence?' she sneered. 'My grandmother's story is apparently not acceptable without evidence. She is alive. Is it acceptable that Luke's story should be acceptable without evidence?'

'I didn't say I had no evidence, sweetheart,' Luke said matter-of-factly. 'Of course I got evidence. I got it right here.'

I held my breath, at this wonderful turn of events. Please, please, let it be real proof. I prayed fervently.

'What possible evidence can you have?' Magda demanded. 'There is none. My grandmother...' She stopped.

'You just wait now, Magda, I know you're enthusiastic but I'm an old man now. Fingers don't work so well.' Luke was fumbling in his dilapidated travelling bag; then he took a fair sized package out and laid it on the table before us.

'Charles shut himself up in the apartment and wouldn't let me come near him for several days after we'd cleared the bodies and buried them as decently as we could. Zoltán took care of that. Charles gave this to me when he left. He didn't care what I did with it.'

'What is it?' I asked.

'I guess it's what you'd call the truth, Duchess. You may need it sometime or other.'

'Why not you?' I asked.

'It's finished. If I come back to it, it won't be for many years.'

We watched as Luke carefully unwrapped the ancient brown paper and took out the looseleaf book. Gently he turned the pages. There before our eyes was the story Luke had told us, retold in paint. There was Elisabeth, cooking supper, caught turning to smile at the artist, her fair hair catching the sunlight streaming through the window. There was one of two dumplings, a still life so vivid you'd think they were making love. There was Gréta stretching a hand towards the artist, enticing him; Gréta in the moonlight, a study in icy blue and streaks of moonlight like daggers shooting across the page. There were about twenty paintings in all, the most beautiful a portrait of Elisabeth herself, just her face out of which shone Charles Carr's love, and the last – the most terrible – an open door through which four dead bodies could be seen, stripped, bloodied and mutilated.

'I guess that's evidence.' Luke spoke for all of us – perhaps even Magda.

She made a half-hearted attempt at protest. 'My grandmother told me – Lucia will verify this – that Charles Carr was a traitor. He betrayed the family himself.'

But no one commented. We could all see the message of those paintings, and we all believed them.

'What now?' I asked David that evening. Luke took over my room at the pub so that I could stay with David. He liked pubs, he said. Certainly the pub seemed to like him; whenever we called in for him over the next week or so he was a central figure, surrounded by an admiring audience, recounting stories – true or false – about his travels.

'The trustees have to talk the matter over. At the very least there's the question of libel.'

'There's no libel if it's true.'

'Correction. If you can *prove* it's true. Maybe we can, maybe not, but this is the road we should go down. We need to sleep on it. All of us.'

So we slept – and I mean that. We were too tired to think of ourselves; it was enough to be together, to hold each other and feel each other's warmth. There was all the time in the world now. We were nearly there, and the past was almost at an end.

Almost, but not quite. There was still the problem of Magda.

I spent the next day with Luke, wearing my biographer's hat in earnest now. He talked and I listened – and recorded. As he talked I got at last a picture of Charles Carr himself, which I had grasped at in vain for so many months. True, it was only one person's picture of Charles, but coupled with David's and Tony's recollections (which they now gave freely) they added up to a living person – if only in my mind. No matter how great the trauma he had endured, no matter how much Charles had spent the rest of his life working through it for himself and posterity, sometimes he had still joked, he had laughed, drunk a brandy at home, watched TV and read novels. What had happened to him gave me the story, but in order to convey that, I had needed to 'know' Charles – and this is what, in the next few days, I came to do.

But there was still Magda. David and I were united in thinking that Magda had been so conditioned into hate for Charles Carr by Gréta that the true story was, or had been, as much as a shock to her as to us. He told me, though it was only his guess, that it was the Louvre painting that had first made Magda aware of the true extent of Gréta's hatred for Charles, and that was why she had wanted it destroyed. She had, David knew, taken a photograph of it to show Gréta after their marriage, and he could recall that it was after that that her hatred of the painting became evident. It was even possible that Gréta told her of her own true part in the story, something so terrible that Magda had half blocked it out.

It had, we guessed, been Gréta's plan that if she had been supplanted by Elisabeth in Charles's affections when he was alive, now

375

he was dead, she would take her rightful place at his side, and she'd intended to do this through Magda.

The Happening could be interpreted several ways, though once one knew the true story it was impossible to see how one could ever have mistaken the correct interpretation. Two women, two sides of love, love and war. But for Charles Carr there had only been the first: two women. Had *The Happening* failed then? No. David inclined to the view that all interpretations were valid, and I saw his point.

We decided between ourselves that the best route for the biography was to tell the true story but to base it on *The Happening,* and Luke's pictures, with the Charles and Elisabeth story central and an anonymous betrayer. It was compromise, but a reasonable one given that the object of the biography was to explain *The Happening.*

David returned from the trustees' meeting with a face like thunder. The problem was now that Magda wasn't going to give up.

'What's up?' Luke enquired.

'Magda won't resign as CEO.' Given her attitude to Charles Carr, all trustees had been resolved that this was the best course.

My heart sank. To dismiss her would lead to litigation and the foundation could not afford the time or the cost. In all good fairy stories the wicked witches collapse into ashes or disappear on a scream of rage at being defeated. It seemed Magda was going for the second option, though determined not to do the disappearing bit.

'She says she has done her job well as CEO and sees no reason at all that she should leave. She's Charles Carr's granddaughter and that's that. He would want her to stay on, for she can't be blamed for what her grand-mother might or might not have done.'

Silence. 'She has a point,' I tried valiantly, wondering how I could cope, thinking of the innumerable pinpricks that would be put in the way of my biography.

'Oh heck.' Luke's reaction was a simple one but said so strangely that both David and I stared at him.

'I know you like her, Luke, despite all that's happened, but I have to say, I think she's a first-class bitch.' It gave me some pleasure to put this into words, and David didn't seem about to faint with shock.

'That's it, Duchess,' Luke grinned. 'The first class I like. The rest I can deal with. You just leave the bitch part to me.'

Without much hope, we did so – and twenty-four hours later, Magda's resignation had been given to the trustees to take effect immediately. Pamela was promoted to acting CEO, and later unanimously approved as permanent CEO. But a lot of water had flown under the bridge by then.

'Can we ask how you did it, Luke?' David asked over dinner at the pub.

'I guess you can at that. It's not something I'm proud of.' Luke shrugged. 'I hadn't plan-ned on telling no one. But I reckoned I owed it to Charles. Now I told you everything I knew about old Charles in Budapest, and every word was true. Anything strike you that I left out though?'

David and I looked at each other, puzzled.

'Me,' Luke answered modestly for himself. 'You never asked what I was thinking and doing. I was a nineteen-year-old kid who'd never been out of the US before, and dropped into the middle of a country I didn't know existed swarming with Gestapo and SS. Not a word of Hungarian could I speak, and only please and thank you in German. How do you think I then felt to be scooped up by the aristocracy and bedded down in the Öszödy palace, with a beautiful Hungarian countess, and then told my cousin was going to drop by to see me?

'Well, I see now Gréta used me as a tool to get at Charles, and I was a sap not to realize it. Gréta's one of those women who likes to play safe by keeping in with both sides; I reckon that's why she took up with Charles in the first place. Nice bit of ass, painter into the bargain and a useful contact with the US if they came into the war. She's a power freak, and when she saw Charles was getting out of her clutches, she used me. She needed a stooge. She was too clever to say outright that Charles was a skunk but she intimated she needed comfort now he'd found Elisabeth. I served my term – like poor old Miklós.'

'Are you saying you slept with Gréta too?' David demanded incredulously.

'Sure I did. I'd been sleeping with her for two months before that last night Charles had with her. That tell you anything?'

I was really dim. 'No.'

David wasn't dim at all. 'Surely you don't mean—'

'Yup. Magda's *my* granddaughter, not Charles's.'

Magda demanded evidence of this of course, once she got over the demeaning shock that an American hobo was her grandfather, not a relatively famous artist. Luke showed her the birth certificate for April 1945, but since, of course, Miklós was named as the father she said that didn't mean a maybug in Maytime, as Luke put it when he told us about it. So he offered her a DNA test. Charles and he would certainly share some of the same genes, but Magda would have been hard put to it to get round the fact she shared some of the same genes as Luke's father.

Then there was Robin. Somehow I had to break the news to him that all was not happy in the Edenshaw nest, and that he would have to choose between his commission for the book or his lady love.

He stood, with his back to me, in my flat, staring out of the window. My heart bled for him, even if he'd been a fool so far as Magda was concerned.

'In the best traditions of the legend, Robin,' I said brightly, 'we've all been fools. Mathias,

Charles, David, me, you.'

'Even,' he added, 'Magda.'

'No,' I said sharply. 'She knew the story behind the choices.'

'Now I've got the choices. Is that it?'

'Yes.'

I watched him. I could do nothing for him now. He had to make his own way.

'All right.' He turned round and glared at me. 'I'll choose the bloody book.'

'Give up Magda?'

'Actually,' he admitted, 'she probably would not want me without the book. She engineered it, you know. Checked out your background with Tony and hauled me in as a distraction from David for you.'

I saw red. Wait till I saw Tony Loring again. And then I calmed down. After all, Tony's cauldron had led me to my true love.

'I'm sorry, Robin.'

'What for?'

'Your losing Magda.'

'Actually,' he said carefully, 'even the oaf in this fairy story might do well in the end. I met a rather nice blonde at your new publishers.'

Closure.

And new beginnings.

'Magda and Michael are planning to move to France,' David said tentatively one evening to me.

I was aghast. 'What about Toby?' I had visions of David going to up stumps and

380

moving to France to be near him.

My last lesson. In fairy tales it's important to keep looking upwards all the time – otherwise you might miss the wicked witch's last trick.

David read my fear correctly. 'No, I'm not going.' He put his arm round me. 'I'm staying here. Where would you like to live, Kent or London?'

I was too busy grappling with fall-out to take this in. 'But Toby—'

'He's staying too. With me.'

Even more fall-out to grapple with. Pleasure, worry – could I cope with being a stepmother? They were always fairly rum characters in fairy tales.

He saw the doubt and misconstrued it. 'Are you,' he looked at me seriously, 'going to do a runner, Lucia?'

Just for a moment I could hear the wicked witch cackling like crazy. I saw Magda with 'I told you so' written all over her face, I saw Robin laughing his socks off, I saw my mother's despairing face, I saw myself galloping for the open horizons. Only for a moment. And then I looked at David and stepped daintily over the threshold of my castle of happiness.

'Yes,' I said firmly. 'But my runner is straight at you and I'm staying put.'

I heard a faint cry somewhere. Witches never vanish of course. Nor would Magda. She would whenever possible haunt the lands round our castle, trying to make mischief.

That's what witches do. So what? David, Toby and I would be safe inside, the draw-bridge up, boiling oil at the ready.

For our castle is called Love.